TRENT INTERVENES

TRENT INTERVENES

by

E. C. BENTLEY

DOVER PUBLICATIONS, INC.
NEW YORK

This Dover edition, first published in 1981, is an unabridged republication of the work as published by T. Nelson & Sons, Ltd., London, in 1938.

International Standard Book Number: 0-486-24098-3
Library of Congress Catalog Card Number: 80-69482

Manufactured in the United States of America
Dover Publications, Inc.
180 Varick Street
New York, N.Y. 10014

CONTENTS

TRENT INTERVENES

[1]

THE GENUINE TABARD

IT WAS quite by chance, at a dinner-party given by the American Naval Attaché, that Philip Trent met the Langleys, who were visiting Europe for the first time. During the cocktail-time before dinner was served, he had gravitated towards George D. Langley, because he was the finest-looking man in the room—tall, strongly-built, carrying his years lightly, pink of face, with vigorous, massive features and thick grey hair.

They had talked about the Tower of London, the Cheshire Cheese, and the Zoo, all of which the Langleys had visited that day. Langley, so the Attaché had told Trent, was a distant relative of his own; he had made a large fortune manufacturing engineers' drawing-office equipment, was a prominent citizen of Cordova, Ohio, the headquarters of his business, and had married a Schuyler. Trent, though not sure what a Schuyler was, gathered that it was an excellent thing to marry, and this impression was confirmed when he found himself placed next to Mrs. Langley at dinner.

Mrs. Langley always went on the assumption that her own affairs were the most interesting subject of conversation; and as she was a vivacious and humorous talker and a very handsome and good-hearted woman, she usually turned out to be right. She informed Trent that she was crazy about old churches, of which she had seen and photographed she did not know how many in France, Germany, and England. Trent, who loved thirteenth-century stained glass, mentioned Chartres, which Mrs. Langley said, truly enough, was too perfect for words. He asked if she had been to Fairford in Gloucestershire. She had; and that was, she declared with emphasis, the greatest day of all their time in Europe; not because of the church, though that was certainly lovely, but because of the treasure they had found that afternoon.

Trent asked to be told about this; and Mrs. Langley said that it was quite a story. Mr. Gifford had driven them down to Fairford in his car. Did Trent know Mr. Gifford —W. N. Gifford, who lived at the Suffolk Hotel? He was visiting Paris just now. Trent ought to meet him, because Mr. Gifford knew everything there was to know about stained glass, and church ornaments, and brasses, and antiques in general. They had met him when he was sketching some traceries in Westminster Abbey, and they had become great friends. He had driven them about to quite a few places within reach of London. He knew all about Fairford, of course, and they had a lovely time there.

On the way back to London, after passing through Abingdon, Mr. Gifford had said it was time for a cup of coffee, as he always did around five o'clock; he made his own coffee, which was excellent, and carried it in a thermos. They slowed down, looking for a good place to stop, and Mrs. Langley's eye was caught by a strange name on a signpost at a turning off the road—something Episcopi.

She knew that meant Bishops, which was interesting; so she asked Mr. Gifford to halt the car while she made out the weather-beaten lettering. The sign said "Silcote Episcopi ½ mile."

Had Trent heard of the place? Neither had Mr. Gifford. But that lovely name, Mrs. Langley said, was enough for her. There must be a church, and an old one; and anyway she would love to have Silcote Episcopi in her collection. As it was so near, she asked Mr. Gifford if they could go there so she could take a few snaps while the light was good, and perhaps have coffee there.

They found the church, with the parsonage near by, and a village in sight some way beyond. The church stood back from the churchyard, and as they were going along the footpath they noticed a grave with tall railings round it; not a standing-up stone but a flat one, raised on a little foundation. They noticed it because, though it was an old stone, it had not been just left to fall into decay, but had been kept clean of moss and dirt, so you could make out the inscription, and the grass around it was trim and tidy. They read Sir Rowland Verey's epitaph; and Mrs. Langley—so she assured Trent—screamed with joy.

There was a man trimming the churchyard boundary hedge with shears, who looked at them, she thought, suspiciously when she screamed. She thought he was probably the sexton; so she assumed a winning manner, and asked him if there was any objection to her taking a photograph of the inscription on the stone. The man said that he didn't know as there was; but maybe she ought to ask vicar, because it was his grave, in a manner of speaking. It was vicar's great-grandfather's grave, that was; and he always had it kep' in good order. He would be in the church now, very like, if they had a mind to see him.

Mr. Gifford said that in any case they might have a look at the church, which he thought might be worth the trouble. He observed that it was not very old—about mid-seventeenth century, he would say—a poor little kid church, Mrs. Langley commented with gay sarcasm. In a place so named, Mr. Gifford said, there had probably been a church for centuries farther back; but it might have been burnt down, or fallen into ruin, and replaced by this building. So they went into the church; and at once Mr. Gifford had been delighted with it. He pointed out how the pulpit, the screen, the pews, the glass, the organ-case in the west gallery, were all of the same period. Mrs. Langley was busy with her camera when a pleasant-faced man of middle age, in clerical attire, emerged from the vestry with a large book under his arm.

Mr. Gifford introduced himself and his friends as a party of chance visitors who had been struck by the beauty of the church and had ventured to explore its interior. Could the vicar tell them anything about the armorial glass in the nave windows? The vicar could and did; but Mrs. Langley was not just then interested in any family history but the vicar's own, and soon she broached the subject of his great-grandfather's gravestone.

The vicar, smiling, said that he bore Sir Rowland's name, and had felt it a duty to look after the grave properly, as this was the only Verey to be buried in that place. He added that the living was in the gift of the head of the family, and that he was the third Verey to be vicar of Silcote Episcopi in the course of two hundred years. He said that Mrs. Langley was most welcome to take a photograph of the stone, but he doubted if it could be done successfully with a hand-camera from over the railings—and of course, said Mrs. Langley, he was perfectly right. Then the vicar asked if she would like to have a copy of the epitaph, which he could write for her if they would all come over to his house, and his wife would give them some tea; and at this, as Trent could imagine, they were just tickled to death.

"But what was it, Mrs. Langley, that delighted you so much about the epitaph?" Trent asked. "It seems to have been about a Sir Rowland Verey—that's all I have been told so far."

"I was going to show it to you," Mrs. Langley said, opening her hand-bag. "Maybe you will not think it so precious as we do. I have had a lot of copies made, to send to friends at home." She unfolded a small typed sheet, on which Trent read what follows:

Within this Vault are interred
the Remains of
Lt.-Gen. Sir Rowland Edmund Verey,
Garter Principal King of Arms,
Gentleman Usher of the Black Rod
and
Clerk of the Hanaper,
who departed this Life
on the 2nd May 1795
in the 73rd Year of his Age
calmly relying
on the Merits of the Redeemer
for the Salvation of
his Soul.
Also of Lavinia Prudence,

Wife of the Above,
who entered into Rest
on the 12th March 1799
in the 68th Year of her Age.
She was a Woman of fine Sense
genteel Behaviour,
prudent Oeconomy
and
great Integrity.
"This is the Gate of the Lord:
The Righteous shall enter into it."

"You have certainly got a fine specimen of that style," Trent observed. "Nowadays we don't run to much more, as a rule, than 'in loving memory,' followed by the essential facts. As for the titles, I don't wonder at your admiring them; they are like the sound of trumpets. There is also a faint jingle of money, I think. In Sir Rowland's time, Black Rod's was probably a job worth having; and though I don't know what a Hanaper is, I do remember that its Clerkship was one of the fat sinecures that made it well worth while being a courtier."

Mrs. Langley put away her treasure, patting the bag with affection. "Mr. Gifford said the Clerk had to collect some sort of legal fees for the Crown, and that he would draw maybe seven or eight thousand pounds a year for it, paying another man two or three hundred for doing the actual work. Well, we found the vicarage just perfect—an old house with everything beautifully mellow and personal about it. There was a long oar hanging on the wall in the hall, and when I asked about it the vicar said he had rowed for All Souls College when he was at Oxford. His wife was charming, too. And now listen! While she was giving us tea, and her husband was making a copy of the epitaph for me, he was talking about his ancestor, and he said the first duty that Sir Rowland had to perform after his appointment as King of Arms was to proclaim the Peace of Versailles from the steps of the Palace of St. James's. Imagine that, Mr. Trent!"

Trent looked at her uncertainly. "So they had a Peace of Versailles all that time ago."

"Yes, they did," Mrs. Langley said, a little tartly. "And quite an important Peace, at that. We remember it in America, if you don't. It was the first treaty to be signed by the United States, and in that treaty the British Government took a licking, called off the war, and recognized our independence. Now when the vicar said that about his ancestor having proclaimed peace with the United States, I saw George Langley prick up his ears; and I knew why.

"You see, George is a collector of Revolution pieces, and he has some pretty nice things, if I do say it. He began asking questions; and the first thing anybody knew, the vicaress had brought down the old King of Arm's tabard and was showing it off. You know what a tabard is, Mr. Trent, of course. Such a lovely garment! I fell for it on the spot, and as for George, his eyes stuck out like a crab's. That wonderful shade of red satin, and the Royal Arms embroidered in those stunning colours, red and gold and blue and silver, as you don't often see them.

"Presently George got talking to Mr. Gifford in a corner, and I could see Mr. Gifford screwing up his mouth and shaking his head; but George only stuck out his chin, and soon after, when the vicaress was showing off the garden, he got the vicar by himself and talked turkey.

"Mr. Verey didn't like it at all, George told me; but George can be a very smooth worker when he likes, and at last the vicar had to allow that he was tempted, what with having his sons to start in the world, and the income tax being higher than a cat's back, and the death duties and all. And finally he said yes. I won't tell you or anybody what George offered him, Mr. Trent, because George swore me to secrecy; but, as he says, it was no good acting like a piker in this kind of a deal, and he could sense that the vicar wouldn't stand for any bargaining back and forth. And anyway, it was worth every cent of it to George, to have something that no other curio-hunter possessed. He said he would come for the tabard next day and bring the money in notes, and the vicar said very well, then we must all three come to lunch, and he would have a paper ready giving the history of the tabard over his signature. So that was what we did; and the tabard is in our suite at the Greville, locked in a wardrobe, and George has it out and gloats over it first thing in the morning and last thing at night."

Trent said with sincerity that no story of real life had ever interested him more. "I wonder," he said, "if your husband would let me have a look at his prize. I'm not much of an antiquary, but I am interested in heraldry, and the only tabards I have ever seen were quite modern ones."

"Why, of course," Mrs. Langley said. "You make a date with him after dinner. He will be delighted. He has no idea of hiding it under a bushel, believe me!"

The following afternoon, in the Langley's sitting-room at the Greville, the tabard was displayed on a coat-hanger before the thoughtful gaze of Trent, while its new owner looked on with a pride not untouched with anxiety.

"Well, Mr. Trent," he said. "How do you like it? You don't doubt this is a genuine tabard, I suppose?"

Trent rubbed his chin. "Oh yes; it's a tabard. I have seen a few before, and I have painted one, with a man inside it, when Richmond Herald wanted his portrait done in the complete get-up. Everything about it is right. Such things are hard to come by. Until recent times, I believe, a herald's tabard remained his property, and stayed in the family, and if they got hard up they might perhaps sell it privately, as this was sold to you. It's different now—so Richmond Herald told me. When a herald dies, his tabard goes back to the College of Arms, where he got it from."

Langley drew a breath of relief. "I'm glad to hear you say my tabard is genuine. When you asked me if you could see it, I got the impression you thought there might be something phoney about it."

Mrs. Langley, her keen eyes on Trent's face, shook her head. "He thinks so still, George, I believe. Isn't that so, Mr. Trent?"

"Yes, I am sorry to say it is. You see, this was sold to you as a particular tabard, with an interesting history of its own; and when Mrs. Langley described it to me, I felt pretty sure that you had been swindled. You see, she had noticed nothing odd about the Royal Arms. I wanted to see it just to make sure. It certainly did not belong to Garter King of Arms in the year 1783."

A very ugly look wiped all the benevolence from Langley's face, and it grew several shades more pink. "If what you say is true, Mr. Trent, and if that old fraud was playing me for a sucker, I will get him jailed if it's my last act. But it certainly is hard to believe—a preacher—and belonging to one of your best families—settled in that lovely, peaceful old place, with his flock to look after and everything. Are you really sure of what you say?"

"What I know is that the Royal Arms on this tabard are all wrong."

An exclamation came from the lady. "Why, Mr. Trent, how you talk! We have seen the Royal Arms quite a few times, and they are just the same as this—and you have told us it is a genuine tabard, anyway. I don't get this at all."

"I must apologise," Trent said unhappily, "for the Royal Arms. You see, they have a past. In the fourteenth century Edward III. laid claim to the Kingdom of France, and it took a hundred years of war to convince his descendants that that claim wasn't practical politics. All the same, they went on including the lilies of France in the Royal Arms, and they never dropped them until the beginning of the ninteenth century."

"Mercy!" Mrs. Langley's voice was faint.

"Besides that, the first four Georges and the fourth William were Kings of Hanover; so until Queen Victoria came along, and could not inherit Hanover because she was a female, the Arms of the House of Brunswick were jammed in along with our own. In fact, the tabard of the Garter King of Arms in the year when he proclaimed the peace with the United States of America was a horrible mess of the leopards of England, the lion of Scotland, the harp of Ireland, the lilies of France, together with a few more lions, and a white horse, and some hearts, as worn in Hanover. It was a fairly tight fit for one shield, but they managed it somehow—and you can see that the Arms on this tabard of yours are not nearly such a bad dream as that. It is a Victorian tabard—a nice, gentlemanly coat, such as no well-dressed herald should be without."

Langley thumped the table. "Well, I intend to be without it, anyway, if I can get my money back."

"We can but try," Trent said. "It may be possible. But the reason why I asked to be allowed to see this thing, Mr. Langley, was that I thought I might be able to save you some unpleasantness. You see, if you went home with your treasure, and showed it to people, and talked about its history, and it was mentioned in the newspapers, and then somebody got inquiring into its authenticity, and found out what I have been telling you, and made it public—well, it wouldn't be very nice for you."

Langley flushed again, and a significant glance passed between him and his wife.

"You're damn right, it wouldn't," he said. "And I know the name of the buzzard who would do that to me, too, as soon as I had gone the limit in making a monkey of myself. Why, I would lose the money twenty times over, and then a bundle rather than have that happen to me. I am grateful to you, Mr. Trent—I am indeed. I'll say frankly that at home we aim to be looked up to socially, and we judged that we could certainly figure if we brought this doggoned thing back and had it talked about. Gosh! When I think—but never mind that now. The thing is to go right back to that old crook and make him squeal. I'll have my money out of him, if I have to use a can-opener."

Trent shook his head. "I don't feel very sanguine about

that, Mr. Langley. But how would you like to run down to his place to-morrow with me and a friend of mine, who takes an interest in affairs of this kind, and who would be able to help you if anyone can?"

Langley said, with emphasis, that that suited him.

The car which called for Langley next morning did not look as if it belonged, but did belong, to Scotland Yard; and the same could be said of its dapper chauffeur. Inside was Trent, with a black-haired, round-faced man whom he introduced as Superintendent Owen. It was at his request that Langley, during the journey, told with as much detail as he could recall the story of his acquisition of the tabard, which he had hopefully brought with him in a suitcase.

A few miles short of Abingdon the chauffeur was told to go slow. "You tell me it was not very far this side of Abingdon, Mr. Langley, that you turned off the main road," the superintendent said. "If you will keep a lookout now, you might be able to point out the spot."

Langley stared at him. "Why, doesn't your man have a map?"

"Yes; but there isn't any place called Silcote Episcopi on his map."

"Nor," Trent added, "on any other map. No, I am not suggesting that you dreamed it all; but the fact is so."

Langley, remarking shortly that this beat him, glared out of the window eagerly; and soon he gave the word to stop. "I am pretty sure this is the turning," he said. "I recognize it by these two haystacks in the meadow, and the pond with osiers over it. But there certainly was a signpost there, and now there isn't one. If I was not dreaming then, I guess I must be now." And as the car ran swiftly down the side-road he went on, "Yes; that certainly is the church on ahead—and the covered gate, and the graveyard—and there is the vicarage, with the yew trees and the garden and everything. Well, gentlemen, right now is when he gets what is coming to him. I don't care what the name of the darn place is."

"The name of the darn place on the map," Trent said, "is Oakhanger."

The three men got out and passed through the lych-gate.

"Where is the gravestone?" Trent asked.

Langley pointed. "Right there." They went across to the railed-in grave, and the American put a hand to his head. "I must be nuts!" he groaned. "I *know* this is the grave—but it says that here is laid to rest the body of James Roderick Stevens, of this parish."

"Who seems to have died about thirty years after Sir Rowland Verey," Trent remarked, studying the inscription; while the superintendent gently smote his thigh in an ecstasy of silent admiration. "And now let us see if the vicar can throw any light on the subject."

They went on to the parsonage; and a dark-haired, bright-faced girl, opening the door at Mr. Owen's ring, smiled recognizingly at Langley. "Well, you're genuine, anyway!" he exclaimed. "Ellen is what they call you, isn't it? And you remember me, I see. Now I feel better. We would like to see the vicar. Is he at home?"

"The canon came home two days ago, sir," the girl said, with a perceptible stress on the term of rank. "He is down in the village now; but he may be back any minute. Would you like to wait for him?"

"We surely would," Langley declared positively; and they were shown into the large room where the tabard had changed hands.

"So he has been away from home?" Trent asked. "And he is a canon, you say?"

"Canon Maberley, sir; yes, sir, he was in Italy for a month. The lady and gentleman who were here till last week had taken the house furnished while he was away. Me and cook stayed on to do for them."

"And did that gentleman—Mr. Verey—do the canon's duty during his absence?" Trent inquired with a ghost of a smile.

"No, sir; the canon had an arrangement with Mr. Giles, the vicar of Cotmore, about that. The canon never knew that Mr. Verey was a clergyman. He never saw him. You see, it was Mrs. Verey who came to see over the place and settled everything; and it seems she never mentioned it. When we told the canon, after they had gone, he was quite took aback. 'I can't make it out at all,' he says. 'Why should he conceal it?' he says. 'Well, sir,' I says, 'they was very nice people, anyhow, and the friends they had to see them here was very nice, and their chauffeur was a perfectly respectable man,' I says."

Trent nodded. "Ah! They had friends to see them."

The girl was thoroughly enjoying this gossip. "Oh yes, sir. The gentleman as brought you down, sir"—she turned to Langley—"he brought down several others before that. They was Americans too, I think."

"You mean they didn't have an English accent, I suppose," Langley suggested drily.

"Yes, sir; and they had such nice manners, like yourself," the girl said, quite unconscious of Langley's confusion, and of the grins covertly exchanged between Trent and the superintendent, who now took up the running.

"This respectable chauffeur of theirs—was he a small, thin man with a long nose, partly bald, always smoking cigarettes?"

"Oh yes, sir; just like that. You must know him."

"I do," Superintendent Owen said grimly.

"So do I!" Langley exclaimed. "He was the man we spoke to in the churchyard."

"Did Mr. and Mrs. Verey have any—er—ornaments of their own with them?" the superintendent asked.

Ellen's eyes rounded with enthusiasm. "Oh yes, sir—some lovely things they had. But they was only put out when they had friends coming. Other times they was kept somewhere in Mr. Verey's bedroom, I think. Cook and me thought perhaps they was afraid of burglars."

The superintendent pressed a hand over his stubby moustache. "Yes, I expect that was it," he said gravely. "But what kind of lovely things do you mean? Silver—china—that sort of thing?"

"No, sir; nothing ordinary, as you might say. One day they had out a beautiful goblet, like, all gold, with little figures and patterns worked on it in colours, and precious stones, blue and green and white, stuck all round it—regular dazzled me to look at, it did."

"The Debenham Chalice!" exclaimed the superintendent.

"Is it a well-known thing, then, sir?" the girl asked.

"No, not at all," Mr. Owen said. "It is an heirloom—a private family possession. Only we happen to have heard of it."

"Fancy taking such things about with them," Ellen remarked. "Then there was a big book they had out once, lying open on that table in the window. It was all done in funny gold letters on yellow paper, with lovely little pictures all round the edges, gold and silver and all colours."

"The Murrane Psalter!" said Mr. Owen. "Come, we're getting on."

"And," the girl pursued, addressing herself to Langley, "there was that beautiful red coat with the arms on it, like you see on a half-crown. You remember they got it out for you to look at, sir; and when I brought in the tea it was hanging up in front of the tallboy."

Langley grimaced. "I believe I do remember it," he said, "now you remind me."

"There is the canon coming up the path now," Ellen said, with a glance through the window. "I will tell him you gentlemen are here."

She hurried from the room, and soon there entered a tall, stooping old man with a gentle face and the indescribable air of a scholar.

The superintendent went to meet him.

"I am a police officer, Canon Maberley," he said. "I and my friends have called to see you in pursuit of an official inquiry in connection with the people to whom your house was let last month. I do not think I shall have to trouble you much, though, because your parlour-maid has given us already most of the information we are likely to get, I suspect."

"Ah! That girl," the canon said vaguely. "She has been talking to you, has she? She will go on talking for ever, if you let her. Please sit down, gentlemen. About the Vereys—ah yes! But surely there was nothing wrong about the Vereys? Mrs. Verey was quite a nice, well-bred person, and they left the place in perfectly good order. They paid me in advance, too, because they live in New Zealand, as she explained, and know nobody in London. They were on a visit to England, and they wanted a temporary home in the heart of the country, because that is the real England, as she said. That was so sensible of them, I thought—instead of flying to the grime and turmoil of London, as most of our friends from over-seas do. In a way, I was quite touched by it, and I was glad to let them have the vicarage."

The superintendent shook his head. "People as clever as they are make things very difficult for us, sir. And the lady never mentioned that her husband was a clergyman, I understand."

"No, and that puzzled me when I heard of it," the canon said. "But it didn't matter, and no doubt there was a reason."

"The reason was, I think," Mr. Owen said, "that if she had mentioned it, you might have been too much interested, and asked questions which would have been all right for a genuine parson's wife, but which she couldn't answer without putting her foot in it. Her husband could do a vicar well enough to pass with laymen, especially if they were not English laymen. I am sorry to say, canon, that your tenants were impostors. Their name was certainly not Verey, to begin with. I don't know who they are—I wish I did—they are new to us and they have invented a new method. But I can tell you what they are. They are thieves and swindlers."

The canon fell back in his chair. "Thieves and swindlers!" he gasped.

"And very talented performers too," Trent assured him. "Why, they have had in this house of yours part of the loot of several country-house burglaries which took place last year, and which puzzled the police because it seemed impossible that some of the things taken could ever be turned into cash. One of them was a herald's tabard, which Superintendent Owen tells me had been worn by the father of Sir Andrew Ritchie. He was Maltravers Herald in his day. It was taken when Sir Andrew's place in Lincolnshire was broken into, and a lot of very valuable jewellery was stolen. It was dangerous to try to sell the tabard in the open market, and it was worth little, anyhow, apart from any associations it might have. What they did was to fake up a story about the tabard which might appeal to an American purchaser, and, having found a victim, to induce him to buy it. I believe he parted with quite a large sum."

"The poor simp!" growled Langley.

Canon Maberley held up a shaking hand. "I fear I do not understand," he said. "What had their taking my house to do with all this?"

"It was a vital part of the plan. We know exactly how they went to work about the tabard; and no doubt the other things were got rid of in very much the same way. There were four of them in the gang. Besides your tenants, there was an agreeable and cultured person—I should think a man with real knowledge of antiquities and objects of art—whose job was to make the acquaintance of wealthy people visiting London, gain their confidence, take them about to places of interest, exchange hospitality with them, and finally get them down to this vicarage. In this case it was made to appear as if the proposal to look over your church came from the visitors themselves. They could not suspect anything. They were attracted by the romantic name of the place on a signpost up there at the corner of the main road."

The canon shook his head helplessly. "But there is no signpost at that corner."

"No, but there was one at the time when they were due to be passing that corner in the confederate's car. It was a false signpost, you see, with a false name on it—so that if anything went wrong, the place where the swindle was worked would be difficult to trace. Then, when they entered the churchyard their attention was attracted by a certain gravestone with an inscription that interested them. I won't waste your time by giving the whole story—the point is that the gravestone, or rather the top layer which had been fitted on to it, was false too. The sham inscription on it was meant to lead up to the swindle, and so it did."

The canon drew himself up in his chair. "It was an abominable act of sacrilege!" he exclaimed. "The man calling himself Verey—"

"I don't think," Trent said, "it was the man calling himself Verey who actually did the abominable act. We believe it was the fourth member of the gang, who masqueraded as the Verey's chauffeur—a very interesting character. Superintendent Owen can tell you about him."

Mr. Owen twisted his moustache thoughtfully. "Yes; he is the only one of them that we can place. Alfred Coveney, his name is; a man of some education and any amount of talent. He used to be a stage-carpenter and property-maker—a regular artist, he was. Give him a tub of papier-mâche, and there was nothing he couldn't model and colour to look exactly like the real thing. That was how the false top to the gravestone was made, I've no doubt. It may have been made to fit on like a lid, to be slipped on and off as required. The inscription was a bit above Alf, though—I expect it was Gifford who drafted that for him, and he copied the lettering from other old stones in the churchyard. Of course the fake signpost was Alf's work too—stuck up when required, and taken down when the show was over.

"Well, Alf got into bad company. They found how clever he was with his hands, and he became an expert burglar. He has served two terms of imprisonment. He is one of a few who have always been under suspicion for the job at Sir Andrew Ritchie's place, and the other two when the chalice was lifted from Eynsham Park and the Psalter from Lord Swanbourne's house. With what they collected in this house and the jewellery that was taken in all three burglaries, they must have done very well indeed for themselves; and by this time they are going to be hard to catch."

Canon Maberley, who had now recovered himself somewhat, looked at the others with the beginnings of a smile. "It is a new experience for me," he said, "to be made use of by a gang of criminals. But it is highly interesting. I suppose that when these confiding strangers had been got down here, my tenant appeared in the character of the parson, and invited them into the house, where you tell me they were induced to make a purchase of stolen property. I do not see, I must confess, how anything could have been better designed to present any possibility of suspicion arising. The vicar of a parish, at home in his own vicarage! Who could imagine anything being wrong? I only hope, for the credit of my cloth, that the deception was well carried out."

"As far as I know," Trent said, "he made only one mistake. It was a small one; but the moment I heard of it I knew that he must have been a fraud. You see, he was asked about the oar you have hanging up in the hall. I didn't go to Oxford myself, but I believe when a man is given his oar it means that he rowed in an eight that did something unusually good."

A light came into the canon's spectacled eyes. "In the year I got my colours the Wadham boat went up five places on the river. It was the happiest week of my life."

"Yet you had other triumphs," Trent suggested. "For instance, didn't you get a Fellowship at All Souls, after leaving Wadham?"

"Yes, and that did please me, naturally," the canon said. "But that is a different sort of happiness, my dear sir, and, believe me, nothing like so keen. And by the way, how did you know about that?"

"I thought it might be so, because of the little mistake your tenant made. When he was asked about the oar, he said he had rowed for All Souls."

Canon Maberley burst out laughing, while Langley and the superintendent stared at him blankly.

"I think I see what happened," he said. "The rascal must have been browsing about in my library, in search of ideas for the part he was to play. I was a resident Fellow for five years, and a number of my books have a bookplate with my name and the name and arms of

All Souls. His mistake was natural." And again the old gentleman laughed delightedly.

Langley exploded. "I like a joke myself," he said, "but I'll be skinned alive if I can see the point of this one."

"Why, the point is," Trent told him, "that nobody ever rowed for All Souls. There never were more than four undergraduates there at one time, all the other members being Fellows."

2

THE SWEET SHOT

"No; I HAPPENED to be abroad at the time," Philip Trent said. "I wasn't in the way of seeing the English papers, so until I came here this week I never heard anything about your mystery."

Captain Royden, a small, spare, brown-faced man, was engaged in the delicate—and forbidden—task of taking his automatic telephone instrument to pieces. He now suspended his labours and reached for the tobacco-jar. The large window of his office in the Kempshill clubhouse looked down upon the eighteenth green of that delectable golf course, and his eye roved over the whin-clad slopes beyond as he called on his recollection.

"Well, if you call it a mystery," he said as he filled a pipe. "Some people do, because they like mysteries, I suppose. For instance, Colin Hunt, the man you're staying with, calls it that. Others won't have it, and say there was a perfectly natural explanation. I could tell you as much as anybody could about it, I dare say."

"As being secretary here, you mean?"

"Not only that. I was one of the two people who were in at the death, so to speak—or next door to it," Captain Royden said. He limped to the mantelshelf and took down a silver box embossed on the lid with the crest and mottoes of the Corps of Royal Engineers. "Try one of these cigarettes, Mr. Trent. If you'd like to hear the yarn, I'll give it you. You have heard something about Arthur Freer, I suppose?"

"Hardly anything," Trent said. "I just gathered that he wasn't a very popular character."

"No," Captain Royden said with reserve. "Did they tell you he was my brother-in-law? No? Well, now, it happened about four months ago, on a Monday—let me see—yes, the second Monday in May. Freer had a habit of playing nine holes before breakfast. Barring Sundays—he was strict about Sunday—he did it most days, even in the beastliest weather, going round all alone usually, carrying his own clubs, studying every shot as if his life depended on it. That helped to make him the very good player he was. His handicap here was two, and at Undershaw he used to be scratch, I believe.

"At a quarter to eight he'd be on the first tee, and by nine he'd be back at his house—it's only a few minutes from here. That Monday morning he started off as usual—"

"And at the usual time?"

"Just about. He had spent a few minutes in the clubhouse blowing up the steward about some trifle. And that was the last time he was seen alive by anybody—near enough to speak to, that is. No one else went off the first tee until a little after nine, when I started round with Browson—he's our local padre; I had been having breakfast with him at the Vicarage. He's got a game leg, like me, so we often play together when he can fit it in.

"We had holed out on the first green, and were walking on to the next tee, when Browson said, 'Great Scot! Look there. Something's happened.' He pointed down the fairway of the second hole; and there we could see a man lying sprawled on the turf, face down and motionless. Now there is this point about the second hole—the first half of it is in a dip in the land, just deep enough to be out of sight from any other point on the course, unless you're standing right above it—you'll see when you go round yourself. Well, on the tee, you *are* right above it; and we saw this man lying. We ran to the spot.

"It was Freer, as I had known it must be at that hour. He was dead, lying in a disjointed sort of way no live man could have lain in. His clothing was torn to ribbons, and it was singed too. So was his hair—he used to play bareheaded—and his face and hands. His bag of clubs was lying a few yards away, and the brassie, which he had just been using, was close by the body.

"There wasn't any wound showing, and I had seen far worse things often enough, but the padre was looking sickish, so I asked him to go back to the clubhouse and send for a doctor and the police while I mounted guard. They weren't long coming, and after they had done their job the body was taken away in an ambulance. Well, that's about all I can tell you at first hand, Mr. Trent. If you are staying with Hunt, you'll have heard about the inquest and all that, probably."

Trent shook his head. "No," he said. "Colin was just beginning to tell me, after breakfast this morning, about Freer having been killed on the course in some incomprehensible way, when a man came to see him about something. So, as I was going to apply for a fortnight's run of the course, I thought I would ask you about the affair."

"All right," Captain Royden said. "I can tell you about the inquest anyhow—had to be there to speak my own little piece, about finding the body. As for what had happened to Freer, the medical evidence was rather confusing. It was agreed that he had been killed by some tremendous shock, which had jolted his whole system to pieces and dislocated several joints, but had been not quite violent enough to cause any visible wound. Apart from that, there was a disagreement. Freer's own doctor, who saw the body first, declared he must have been struck by lightning. He said it was true there hadn't been a thunder storm, but that there had been thunder about all that week-end, and that sometimes lightning did act in that way. But the police surgeon, Collins, said there would be no such displacement of the organs from a lightning stroke, even if it did ever happen that way in our climate, which he doubted. And he said that if it had been lightning, it would have struck the steel-headed clubs; but the clubs lay there in their bag quite undamaged. Collins thought there must have been some kind of explosion, though he couldn't suggest what kind."

Trent shook his head. "I don't suppose that impressed the court," he said. "All the same, it may have been all the honest opinion he could give." He smoked in silence a few moments, while Captain Royden attended to the troubles of his telephone instrument with a camel-hair brush. "But surely," Trent said at length, "if there had been such an explosion as that, somebody would have heard the sound of it."

"Lots of people would have heard it," Captain Royden answered. "But there you are, you see—nobody notices the sound of explosions just about here. There's the quarry on the other side of the road there, and any time after seven a.m. there's liable to be a noise of blasting."

"A dull, sickening thud?"

"Jolly sickening," Captain Royden said, "for all of us living near by. And so that point wasn't raised. Well, Collins is a very sound man; but as you say, his evidence didn't really explain the thing, and the other fellow's did, whether it was right or wrong. Besides, the coroner and the jury had heard about a bolt from a clear sky, and the notion appealed to them. Anyhow, they brought it in death from misadventure."

"Which nobody could deny, as the song says," Trent remarked. "And was there no other evidence?"

"Yes; some. But Hunt can tell you about it as well as I can; he was there. I shall have to ask you to excuse me now," Captain Royden said. "I have an appointment in the town. The steward will sign you on for a fortnight, and probably get you a game too, if you want one to-day."

Colin Hunt and his wife, when Trent returned to their house for luncheon, were very willing to complete the tale. The verdict, they declared, was tripe. Dr. Collins knew his job, whereas Dr. Hoyle was an old footler, and Freer's death had never been reasonably explained.

As for the other evidence, it had, they agreed, been interesting, though it didn't help at all. Freer had been seen after he had played his tee-shot at the second hole, when he was walking down to the bottom of the dip towards the spot where he met his death.

"But according to Royden," Trent said, "that was a place where he couldn't be seen, unless one was right above him."

"Well, this witness *was* right above him," Hunt rejoined. "Over one thousand feet above him, so he said. He was an R.A.F. man, piloting a bomber from Bexford Camp, not far from here. He was up doing some sort of exercise, and passed over the course just at that time. He didn't know Freer, but he spotted a man walking down from the second tee, because he was the only living soul visible on the course. Gossett, the other man in the 'plane, is a temporary member here, and he did know Freer quite well—or as well as anybody cared to know him—but he never saw him. However, the pilot was quite clear that he saw a man just at the time in question, and they took his evidence so as to prove that Freer was absolutely alone just before his death. The only other person who saw Freer was another man who knew him well; used to be a caddy here, and then got a job at the quarry. He was at work on the hillside, and he watched Freer play the first hole and go on to the second—nobody with him, of course."

"Well, that was pretty well established then," Trent remarked. "He was about as alone as he could be, it seems. Yet something happened somehow."

Mrs. Hunt sniffed sceptically, and lighted a cigarette. "Yes, it did," she said. "However, I didn't worry much about it, for one. Edith—Mrs. Freer, that is: Royden's sister—must have had a terrible life of it with a man like that. Not that she ever said anything—she wouldn't. She is not that sort."

"She is a jolly good sort, anyhow," Hunt declared.

"Yes, she is; too good for most men. I can tell you," Mrs. Hunt added for the benefit of Trent, "if Colin ever took to cursing me and knocking me about, my well-known loyalty wouldn't stand the strain for very long."

"That's why I don't do it. It's the fear of exposure that makes me the perfect husband, Phil. She would tie a can to me before I knew what was happening. As for Edith, it's true she never said anything, but the change in her since it happened tells the story well enough. Since she's been living with her brother she has been looking far better and happier than she ever succeeded in doing while Freer was alive."

"She won't be living with him for very long, I dare say," Mrs. Hunt intimated darkly.

"No. I'd marry her myself if I had the chance," Hunt agreed cordially.

"Pooh! You wouldn't be in the first six," his wife said. "It will be Rennie, or Gossett, or possibly Sandy Butler—you'll see. But perhaps you've had enough of the local tittle-tattle, Phil. Did you fix up a game for this afternoon?"

"Yes; with the Jarman Professor of Chemistry in the University of Cambridge," Trent said. "He looked at me as if he thought a bath of vitriol would do me good, but he agreed to play me."

"You've got a tough job," Hunt observed. "I believe he is almost as old as he looks, but he is a devil at the short game, and he knows the course blindfold, which you don't. And he isn't so cantankerous as he pretends to be. By the way, he was the man who saw the finish of the last shot Freer ever played—a sweet shot if ever there was one. Get him to tell you."

"I shall try to," Trent said. "The steward told me about that, and that was why I asked the Professor for a game."

Colin Hunt's prediction was fulfilled that afternoon. Professor Hyde, receiving five strokes, was one up at the seventeenth, and at the last hole sent down a four-foot putt to win the match. As they left the green he remarked, as if in answer to something Trent had that moment said, "Yes; I can tell you a curious circumstance about Freer's death."

Trent's eye brightened; for the Professor had not said a dozen words during their game, and Trent's tentative allusion to the subject after the second hole had been met merely by an intimidating grunt.

"I saw the finish of the last shot he played," the old gentleman went on, "without seeing the man himself at all. A lovely brassie it was, too—though lucky. Rolled to within two feet of the pin."

Trent considered. "I see," he said, "what you mean. You were near the second green, and the ball came over the ridge and ran down to the hole."

"Just so," Professor Hyde said. "That's how you play it—if you can. You might have done it yourself to-day, if your second shot had been thirty yards longer. I've never done it; but Freer often did. After a really good drive, you play a long second, blind, over the ridge; and with a perfect shot, you may get the green. Well, my house is quite near that green. I was pottering about in the garden before breakfast, and just as I happened to be looking towards the green a ball came hopping down the slope and trickled right across to the hole. Of course, I knew whose it must be—Freer always came along about that time. If it had been any one else, I'd have waited to see him get his three, and congratulate him. As it was, I went indoors, and didn't hear of his death until long afterwards."

"And you never saw him play the shot?" Trent said thoughtfully.

The Professor turned a choleric blue eye on him. "How the deuce could I?" he said huffily. "I can't see through a mass of solid earth."

"I know, I know," Trent said. "I was only trying to follow your mental process. Without seeing him play the shot, you knew it was his second—you say he would have been putting for a three. And you said, too—didn't you?—that it was a brassie shot."

"Simply because, my young friend"—the Professor was severe—"I happened to know the man's game. I had played that nine holes with him before breakfast often, until one day he lost his temper more than usual, and made himself impossible. I knew he practically always carried the ridge with his second—I won't say he always got the green—and his brassie was the only club that would do it. It is conceivable, I admit," Professor Hyde added a little stiffly, "that some mishap took place and that the shot in question was not actually Freer's second; but it did not occur to me to allow for that highly speculative contingency."

On the next day, after those playing a morning round were started on their perambulation, Trent indulged himself with an hour's practice, mainly on the unsurveyed stretch of the second hole. Afterwards he had a word with the caddy-master; then visited the professional's shop, and won the regard of that expert by furnishing himself with a new mid-iron. Soon he brought up the subject of the last shot played by Arthur Freer. A dozen times that morning, he said, he had tried, after a satisfying drive, to reach the green with his second; but in vain. Fergus MacAdam shook his head. Not many, he said, could strike the ball with yon force. He could get there himself, whiles, but never for certainty. Mr. Freer had the strength, and he kenned how to use it forbye.

What sort of clubs, Trent asked, had Freer preferred? "Lang and heavy, like himsel'. Noo ye mention it," MacAdam said, "I hae them here. They were brocht here after the ahccident." He reached up to the top of a rack. "Ay, here they are. They shouldna be, of course; but naebody came to claim them, and it juist slippit ma mind."

Trent, extracting the brassie, looked thoughtfully at the heavy head with the strip of hard white material inlaid in the face. "It's a powerful weapon, sure enough," he remarked.

"Ay, for a man that could control it," MacAdam said. "I dinna care for yon ivorine face mysel'. Some fowk think it gies mair reseelience, ye ken; but there's naething in it."

"He didn't get it from you, then," Trent suggested, still closely examining the head.

"Ay, but he did. I had a lot down from Nelsons while the fashion for them was on. Ye'll find my name," MacAdam added, "stampit on the wood in the usual place, if yer een are seein' richt."

"Well, I don't—that's just it. The stamp is quite illegible."

"Tod! Let's see," the professional said, taking the club in hand. "Guid reason for its being illegible," he went on after a brief scrutiny. "It's been obleeterated—that's easy seen. Who ever saw sic a daft-like thing! The wood has juist been crushed some gait—in a vice, I wouldna wonder. Noo, why would onybody want to dae a thing like yon?"

"Unaccountable, isn't it?" Trent said. "Still, it doesn't matter, I suppose. And anyhow, we shall never know."

It was twelve days later that Trent, looking in at the open door of the secretary's office, saw Captain Royden happily engaged with the separated parts of some mechanism in which coils of wire appeared to be the leading motive.

"I see you're busy," Trent said.

"Come in! Come in!" Royden said heartily. "I can do this any time—another hour's work will finish it." He laid down a pair of sharp-nosed pliers. "The electricity people have just changed us over to A.C., and I've got to re-wind the motor of our vacuum cleaner. Beastly nuisance," he added, looking down affectionately at the bewildering jumble of disarticulated apparatus on his table.

"You bear your sorrow like a man," Trent remarked; and Royden laughed as he wiped his hands on a towel.

"Yes," he said, "I do love tinkering about with mechanical jobs, and if I do say it myself, I'd rather do a thing like this with my own hands than risk having it faultily done by a careless workman. Too many of them about. Why, about a year ago the company sent a man here to fit a new main fuse-box, and he made a short-circuit with his screw-driver that knocked him right across the kitchen and might very well have killed him." He reached down his cigarette-box and offered it to Trent, who helped himself; then looked down thoughtfully at the device on the lid.

"Thanks very much. When I saw this box before, I put you down for an R.E. man. *Ubique*, and *Quo fas et gloria ducunt*. H'm! I wonder why Engineers were given that motto in particular."

"Lord knows," the captain said. "In my experience, Sappers don't exactly go where right and glory lead. The dirtiest of all the jobs and precious little of the glory—that's what they get."

"Still, they have the consolation," Trent pointed out, "of feeling that they are at home in a scientific age, and that all the rest of the Army are amateurs compared with them. That's what one of them once told me, anyhow. Well now, captain, I have to be off this evening. I've looked in just to say how much I've enjoyed myself here."

"Very glad you did," Captain Royden said. "You'll come again, I hope, now you know that the golf here is not so bad."

"I like it immensely. Also the members. And the secretary." Trent paused to light his cigarette. "I found the mystery rather interesting, too."

Captain Royden's eyebrows lifted slightly. "You mean about Freer's death? So you made up your mind it *was* a mystery."

"Why, yes," Trent said. "Because I made up my mind he had been killed by somebody, and probably killed intentionally. Then, when I had looked into the thing a little, I washed out the 'probably.' "

Captain Royden took up a penknife from his desk and began mechanically to sharpen a pencil. "So you don't agree with the coroner's jury?"

"No: as the verdict seems to have been meant to rule out murder or any sort of human agency, I don't. The lightning idea, which apparently satisfied them, or some of them, was not a very bright one, I thought. I was told what Dr. Collins had said against it at the inquest; and it seemed to me he had disposed of it completely when he said that Freer's clubs, most of them steel ones, were quite undamaged. A man carrying his clubs puts them down, when he plays a shot, a few feet away at most; yet Freer was supposed to have been electrocuted without any notice having been taken of them, so to speak."

"H'm! No, it doesn't seem likely. I don't know that that quite decides the point, though," the captain said. "Lightning plays funny tricks, you know. I've seen a small tree struck when it was surrounded by trees twice the size. All the same, I quite agree there didn't seem to be any sense in the lightning notion. It was thundery weather, but there wasn't any storm that morning in this neighbourhood."

"Just so. But when I considered what had been said about Freer's clubs, it suddenly occurred to me that nobody had said anything about *the* club, so far as my information about the inquest went. It seemed clear, from what you and the parson saw, that he had just played a shot with his brassie when he was struck down; it was lying near him, not in the bag. Besides, old Hyde actually saw the ball he had hit roll down the slope on to the green. Now, it's a good rule to study every little detail when you are on a problem of this kind. There weren't many left to study, of course, since the thing had happened four months before; but I knew Freer's clubs must be somewhere, and I thought of one or two places where they were likely to have been taken, in the circumstances, so I tried them. First, I reconnoitred the caddymaster's shed, asking if I could leave my bag there for a day or two; but I was told that the regular place to leave them was the pro.'s shop. So I went and had a chat with MacAdam, and sure enough it soon came out that Freer's bag was still in his rack. I had a look at the clubs, too."

"And did you notice anything peculiar about them?" Captain Royden asked.

"Just one little thing. But it was enough to set me thinking, and next day I drove up to London, where I paid a visit to Nelsons, the sporting outfitters. You know the firm, of course."

Captain Royden, carefully fining down the point of his pencil, nodded. "Everybody knows Nelsons."

"Yes; and MacAdam, I knew, had an account there for his stocks. I wanted to look over some clubs of a particular make—a brassie, with a slip of ivorine let into the face, such as they had supplied to MacAdam. Freer had had one of them from him."

Again Royden nodded.

"I saw the man who shows clubs at Nelsons. We had a talk, and then—you know how little things come out in the course of conversation—"

"Especially," put in the captain with a cheerful grin, "when the conversation is being steered by an expert."

"You flatter me," Trent said. "Anyhow, it did transpire that a club of that particular make had been bought some months before by a customer whom the man was able to remember. Why he remembered him was because, in the first place, he insisted on a club of rather unusual length and weight—much too long and heavy for himself to use, as he was neither a tall man nor of powerful build. The salesman had suggested as much in a delicate way; but the customer said no, he knew exactly what suited him, and he bought the club and took it away with him."

"Rather an ass, I should say," Royden observed thoughtfully.

"I don't think he was an ass, really. He was capable of making a mistake, though, like the rest of us. There were some other things, by the way, that the salesman recalled about him. He had a slight limp, and he was, or had been, an Army officer. The salesman was an ex-Service man, and he couldn't be mistaken, he said, about that."

Captain Royden had drawn a sheet of paper towards him, and was slowly drawing little geometrical figures as he listened. "Go on, Mr. Trent," he said quietly.

"Well, to come back to the subject of Freer's death. I think he was killed by some one who knew Freer never played on Sunday, so that his clubs would be—or ought to be, shall we say?—in his locker all that day. All the following night, too, of course—in case the job took a long time. And I think this man was in a position to have access to the lockers in this clubhouse at any time he chose, and to possess a master-key to those lockers. I think he was a skilful amateur craftsman. I think he had a good practical knowledge of high explosives. There is a branch of the Army"—Trent paused a moment and looked at the cigarette-box on the table—"in which that sort of knowledge is specially necessary, I believe."

Hastily, as if just reminded of the duty of hospitality, Royden lifted the lid of the box and pushed it towards Trent. "Do have another," he urged.

Trent did so with thanks. "They have to have it in the Royal Engineers," he went on, "because—so I'm told—demolition work is an important part of their job."

"Quite right," Captain Royden observed, delicately shading one side of a cube.

"*Ubique!*" Trent mused, staring at the box-lid. "If you are 'everywhere,' I take it you can be in two places at the same time. You could kill a man in one place, and at the same time be having breakfast with a friend a mile away. Well, to return to our subject yet once more; you can see the kind of idea I was led to form about what happened to Freer. I believe that his brassie was taken from his locker on the Sunday before his death. I believe the ivorine face of it was taken off and a cavity hollowed out behind it; and in that cavity a charge of explosive was placed. Where it came from I don't know, for it isn't the sort of thing that is easy to come by, I imagine."

"Oh, there would be no difficulty about that," the captain remarked. "If this man you're speaking of knew all about H.E., as you say, he could have compounded the stuff himself from materials anybody can buy. For instance, he could easily make tetranitroaniline—that would be just the thing for him, I should say."

"I see. Then perhaps there would be a tiny detonator attached to the inner side of the ivorine face, so that a good smack with the brassie would set it off. Then the face would be fixed on again. It would be a delicate job, because the weight of the club-head would have to be exactly right. The feel and balance of the club would have to be just the same as before the operation."

"A delicate job, yes," the captain agreed. "But not an impossible one. There would be rather more to it than you say, as a matter of fact; the face would have to be shaved down thin, for instance. Still, it could be done."

"Well, I imagine it done. Now, this man I have in mind knew there was no work for a brassie at the short first hole, and that the first time it would come out of the bag was at the second hole, down at the bottom of the dip, where no one could see what happened. What certainly did happen was that Freer played a sweet shot, slap on to the green. What else happened at the same moment we don't know for certain, but we can make a reasonable guess. And then, of course, there's the question what happened to the club—or what was left of it; the handle, say. But it isn't a difficult question, I think, if we remember how the body was found."

"How do you mean?" Royden asked.

"I mean, by whom it was found. One of the two players who found it was too much upset to notice very much. He hurried back to the club-house; and the other was left alone with the body for, as I estimate it, at least fifteen minutes. When the police came on the scene, they found lying near the body a perfectly good brassie, an unusually long and heavy club, exactly like Freer's brassie in every respect—except one. The name stamped on the wood of the club-head had been obliterated by crushing. That name, I think, was not F. MacAdam, but W. J. Nelson; and the club had been taken out of a bag that was not Freer's—a bag which had the remains, if any, of Freer's brassie at the bottom of it. And I believe that's all." Trent got to his feet and stretched his arms. "You can see what I meant when I said I found the mystery interesting."

For some moments Captain Royden gazed thoughtfully out of the window; then he met Trent's inquiring eye. "If there was such a fellow as you imagine," he said coolly, "he seems to have been careful enough—lucky enough too, if you like—to leave nothing at all of what you could call proof against him. And probably he had personal and private reasons for what he did. Suppose that somebody whom he was much attached to was in the power of a foul-tempered, bullying brute; and suppose he found that the bullying had gone to the length of physical violence; and suppose that the situation was hell by day and by night to this man of yours; and suppose there was no way on earth of putting an end to it except the way he took. Yes, Mr. Trent; suppose all that!"

"I will—I do!" Trent said. "That man—if he exists at all—must have been driven pretty hard, and what he did is no business of mine anyway. And now—still in the conditional mood—suppose I take myself off."

[3]

THE CLEVER COCKATOO

"WELL, that's my sister," said Mrs. Lancey, in a low voice. "What do you think of her, now you've spoken to her?"

Philip Trent, newly arrived from England, stood by his hostess within the loggia of a villa looking out upon a prospect of such loveliness as has enchanted and enslaved the Northern mind from age to age. It was a country that looked good and gracious for men to live in. Not far below them lay the broad, still surface of a great lake, blue as the sky; beyond it, low mountains rose up from the distant shore, tilled and wooded to the summit, drinking the light and warmth, visibly storing up earthly energy, with little villages of white and red scattered about their slopes—like children clustered round their mothers' knees. Before the villa lay a long paved terrace, and by the balustrade of it, from which a stone could be dropped into the clear water, a woman stood looking out over the lake and conversing with a tall, grey-haired man.

"Ten minutes is rather a short acquaintance," Trent replied. "Besides, I was attending rather more to her companion. Mynheer Scheffer is the first Dutchman I have met on social terms. One thing about Lady Bosworth is clear to me, though. She is the most beautiful thing in sight, which is saying a good deal. And as for that low, velvety voice of hers, if she asked me to murder my best friend I should have to do it on the spot."

Mrs. Lancey laughed.

"But I want you to take a personal interest in her, Philip; it means nothing, I know, when you talk like that. I care a great deal about Isabel, she is far more to me than any other woman. That's rather rare between sisters, I believe; but when it happens it is a great thing. And it makes me wretched to know that there's something wrong with her."

"With her health, do you mean? One wouldn't think so."

"Yes, but I fear it is that."

"Is it possible?" said Trent. "Why, Edith, the woman has the complexion of a child and the step of a racehorse and eyes like jewels. She looks like Atalanta in blue linen."

"Did Atalanta marry an Egyptian mummy?" inquired Mrs. Lancey.

"Not by any means—priests of Cybele bear witness!"

"Well, Isabel did, unfortunately."

"It is true," said Trent, thoughtfully. "That Sir Peregrine looks rather as if he had been dug up somewhere. But I think he owes much of his professional success to that. People like a great doctor to look more or less unhealthy."

"Perhaps they do; but I don't think the doctor's wife enjoys it very much. Isabel is always happiest when away from him—if he were here now she would be quite different from what you see. You know, Philip, their marriage hasn't been a success—I always knew it wouldn't be. It's lasted five years now, and there are no children. Peregrine never goes about with her; he is one of the busiest men in London—you see what I mean."

Trent shrugged his shoulders.

"Let us drop the subject, Edith. Tell me why you want me to know about Lady Bosworth having something the matter with her. I'm not a physician."

"No, but there's something very puzzling about it, as you will see; and you are clever at getting at the truth about things other people don't understand. Now, I'll tell you no more. I only want you to observe Bella particularly at dinner this evening, and tell me afterwards what you think. You'll be sitting opposite to her, between me and Agatha Stone. Now go and talk to her and the Dutchman."

"Scheffer's appearance interests me," remarked Trent. "He has a face curiously like Frederick the Great's, and yet there's a difference—he doesn't look quite as if his soul were lost for ever and ever."

"Well, go and ask him about it," suggested Mrs. Lancey. "I have things to do in the house."

When the party of seven sat down to dinner that evening, Lady Bosworth had just descended from her room. Trent perceived no change in her; she talked enthusiastically of the loveliness of the Italian evening, and joined in a conversation that was general and lively. It was only after some ten minutes that she fell silent, and that a new look came over her face.

Little by little all animation departed from it. Her eyes grew heavy and dull, her red lips were parted in a foolish smile, and to the high, fresh tint of her cheek there succeeded a disagreeable pallor. There was nothing about this altered appearance in itself that could be called odious. Had she been always so, one would have set her down merely as a beautiful and stupid woman of lymphatic type. But there was something inexpressibly repugnant about such a change in such a being; it was as though the vivid soul had been withdrawn.

All charm, all personal force had departed. It needed an effort to recall her quaint, vivacious talk of an hour ago, now that she sat looking vaguely at the table before her, and uttering occasionally a blank monosyllable in reply to the discourse that Mr. Scheffer poured into her ear. She helped herself from the dishes handed to her; some she refused; she made a fairly good dinner in a lifeless way. It was not, Trent told himself, that anything abnormal was done. It was the staring fact that Lady Bosworth was not herself, but some one wholly of another kind, that opened a new and unknown spring of revulsion in the recesses of his heart.

Mrs. Stone, with whom he had been talking uninterruptedly as he watched, caught his eye.

"We don't notice it," she murmured, quickly.

An hour later Mrs. Lancey carried Trent off to a garden seat facing the lake.

"Well?" she said, quietly, glancing back into the drawing-room.

"It's very strange and rather ghastly," he answered, nursing his knee. "But if you hadn't told me it puzzled you, I should have thought it was easy to find an explanation."

"Drugs, you mean?" He nodded. "Of course everybody must think so. George does, I know. It's horrible!" declared Mrs. Lancey, with a thump on the arm of the seat. "Agatha Stone began hinting at it after the first few days. I told her it was a sort of nervous attack Isabel had been subject to from a child, which was a lie, and of course she didn't believe it. Gossiping cat! She loathes Isabel, and she'll spread it round everywhere that my sister is a drug-fiend. How I hate her!"

"But you do believe it isn't that?"

"Philip, I don't know what to believe. Listen now! The morning after the second time it happened, I asked her what was the matter with her. She said she didn't know; she began to feel stupid and strange soon after dinner began. It had never happened to her before until she came to us here. It wasn't either a pleasant or an unpleasant feeling, she said; she just felt indifferent to everything, and completely lazy. Then I asked her point blank if she was taking anything that could account for it. She was much offended at that; told me I had known her long enough to know she never had done and never would do such a thing. And it is certain that it would be utterly against all I ever knew of her. Besides, she denied it; and, though Isabel has her faults, she's absolutely truthful."

Trent looked on the ground. "Yes, but you may have heard—"

"Oh, I know! They say that kind of habit makes people lie and deceive who never did before. But you see, she is so completely herself, except just at this time. I simply couldn't make up my mind to disbelieve her. And besides, why should she ever start such a practice? I don't see how she would have been drawn into it. If Bell is peculiar about anything, it's clean, wholesome, hygienic living. She was always that way as a girl, but she was studying to be a doctor, you know, when she met her husband, and that made her ever so much worse. She has every sort of carbolicky idea. She never uses scent or powder or any kind of before-and-after stuff, never puts anything on her hair; she is washing herself from morning till night, but she always uses ordinary yellow soap. She never touches anything alcoholic, or tea, or coffee. You wouldn't think she had that kind of fad to look at her and her clothes, but she has; and I can't think of anything in the world she would despise more than dosing herself with things."

"Not any kind of cosmetic whatever? That is surprising. Well, it seems to suit her," Trent remarked. "When she isn't like this, she is one of the most radiant creatures I ever saw."

"I know, and that's what makes it so irritating for women like myself, who look absolute hags if they don't assist Nature a little. She's always been as strong as a horse and bursting with vitality, and her looks have never shown the slightest sign of going off. And now this thing has come to her, absolutely suddenly and without warning."

"How long has it been going on?"

"This is the seventh evening. I entreated her to see a doctor, but she hates the idea of being doctored. She says it's sure to pass off and that it doesn't make any difference to her general health. It's true that she is quite well and lively all the rest of the time; but even if that is so, of course you can see how serious it is for a woman. It means that people shun her. She hasn't realized it yet, but I can see our friends are revolted by the sight of these fits of hers, which they naturally account for in the obvious way. And Bella hasn't any pleasure in life without society —especially men's. But it's come to this, that George, who has always been devoted to her, only talks to her now with an effort. Randolph Stone is just the same; and two days before you arrived the Illingworths and Captain Burrows both went earlier than they had intended—I'm certain, because this change in Isabel was spoiling their visit for them."

"She seems to get on remarkably well with Scheffer," remarked Trent.

"I know—it's extraordinary, but he seems more struck with her than ever."

"Well, he is, but in a lizard-hearted way of his own. He and I were talking just now after you left the dining-room. I had said something about the art of primitive peoples, and he took me aside soon afterwards and gave me more ideas on the subject in ten minutes than I'd ever heard in all my life. Then he began suddenly to speak of Lady Bosworth in a queer, semi-scientific sort of way, saying she was the nearest approach to a perfect female physiology he had ever seen among civilized and educated woman; and he went on to ask if I had noticed her strangeness during dinner. I said, 'Yes,' of course; and he said it was very interesting to a medical man like himself. You didn't tell me he was one."

"I didn't know. George calls him an anthropologist, and disagrees with him about the races of Farther India. George says it's the one thing he does know something about, having lived there twelve years governing the poor things. They took to each other at once when they met last year, and when I asked him to stay here he was quite delighted. He only begged to be allowed to bring his cockatoo, as it could not live without him."

"Strange pet for a man," Trent observed. "He was showing off its paces to me this afternoon. It's a mischievous fowl, and as clever as a monkey. Well, it seems he's greatly interested in these attacks of hers. He has seen nothing quite like them. But he is convinced the thing is due to what he calls a toxic agent of some sort. As to what, or how, or why, he is absolutely at a loss."

"Then you must find out what, and how, and why, Philip. I'm glad Scheffer isn't so easily upset as the other men; it's so much better for Isabel. She finds him very interesting, of course; not only because he's the only man here who pays her a lot of attention but because he really is a wonderful person. He's lived for years among the most appalling savages in Dutch New Guinea, doing scientific work for his Government, and according to George they treat him like a sort of god; he's somehow got the reputation among them that he can kill a man by pointing his finger at him, and he can manage the natives as nobody else can. He's most attractive and quite kind really, I think, but there's something about him that makes me afraid of him."

"What is it?"

"I think it is the frosty look in his eyes," replied Mrs. Lancey drawing her shoulders together in a shiver.

"You share the public opinion of Dutch New Guinea, in fact," said Trent, "Did you tell me, Edith, that your sister began to be like this the very first evening she came here?"

"Yes. And it had never happened before, she declares."

"She came out from England with the Stones, didn't she?"

"Only the last part of the journey. They got on the train at Lucerne."

Trent looked back into the drawing-room at the wistful face of Mrs. Stone, who was playing piquet with her host. She was slight and pretty, with large, appealing eyes that never lost their melancholy, though she was always smiling.

"You say she loathes Lady Bosworth," he said. "Why?"

"Well, I suppose it's mainly Bella's own fault," confessed Mrs. Lancey, with a grimace. "You may as well know, Philip—you'll soon find out, anyhow—the truth is she *will* flirt with any man that she doesn't actively dislike. She's so brimful of life she can't hold herself in —or she won't, rather; she says there's no harm in it, and she doesn't care if there is. Before her marriage she didn't go on in that way, but since it turned out badly she has been simply uncivilized on that point. And her being perfectly clear-headed about it makes it seem so much worse. Several times she has practised on Randolph, and, although he's a perfectly safe old donkey if there ever was one, Agatha can't bear the sight of her."

"She seems quite friendly with her," Trent observed.

Mrs. Lancey produced through her delicate nostrils a sound that expressed a scorn of which there were no words. There was a short silence.

"Well, what do you make of it, Philip?" his hostess

asked at length. "Myself, I simply don't know what to think. These queer fits of hers frighten me horribly. There's one dreadful idea, you see, that keeps occurring to me. Could it, perhaps, be"—Mrs. Lancey lowered her already low tone—"the beginning of insanity?"

He spoke reassuringly. "Oh, I shouldn't cherish that fancy. There are other things much more likely and much less terrible. And there are some things we can do, too, and do at once. Look here, Edith, you know I hate explaining my own ideas until I'm sure there's something in them. Will you try to arrange certain things for to-morrow, without asking me why? And don't let anybody know I asked you to do it—not even George. Until later on, at least. Will you?"

"How exciting!" Mrs. Lancey breathed. "Yes, of course, mystery-man. What do you want me to do?"

"Do you think you could manage things to-morrow so that you and I and Lady Bosworth could go out in the motor-boat on the lake for an hour or two in the evening, getting back in time to change for dinner—just the three of us and the engineer? Could that be worked quite naturally?"

She pondered. "It might be. George and Randolph are playing golf at Cadenabbia to-morrow. I might arrange an expedition in the afternoon for Agatha and Mr. Scheffer, and let Bella know I wanted her to stay with me. You could lose yourself after breakfast with your sketching things, I dare say, and return for tea. Then the three of us could run down in the boat to San Marmette—it's a lovely little place—and be back before seven. In this weather it's really the best time of day for the lake."

"That would do admirably, if you could work it. And

one thing more—if we do go as you suggest, I want you privately to tell your engineer to do just what I ask him to do—no matter what it is. He's an Italian, isn't he? Yes, then he'll be deeply interested."

Mrs. Lancey worked it without difficulty. At five o'clock the two ladies and Trent, with a powerful young man of superb manners at the steering-wheel, were gliding swiftly southward, mile after mile, down the long lake. They landed at the most picturesque, and perhaps the most dilapidated and dirtiest, of all the lakeside villages, where in the tiny square above the landing-place, a score of dusky infants were treading the measures and chanting the words of one of the immemorial games of childhood. While Mrs. Lancey and her sister watched them in delight Trent spoke rapidly to the young engineer, whose gleaming eyes and teeth flashed understanding.

Soon afterward they strolled through San Marmette, and up the mountain road to a little church, half a mile away, where a curious fresco could be seen.

It was close on half-past six when they returned, to be met by Giuseppe, voluble in excitement and apology. It appeared that while he had been fraternizing with the keeper of the inn by the landing-place certain *triste individue* had, unseen by any one, been tampering maliciously with the engine of the boat, and had poured in handfuls of dust into the delicate mechanism. Mrs. Lancey, who had received a private nod from Trent, reproved him bitterly for leaving the boat, and asked how long it would take to get the engine working again.

Giuseppe, overwhelmed with contrition, feared that it

might be a matter of hours. Questioned, he said that the public steamer had arrived and departed twenty minutes since; the next one, the last of the day, was not due until after nine. Their excellencies could at least count on getting home by that, if the engine was not ready sooner. Questioned further, he said that one could telephone from the post office, and that food creditably cooked was to be had at the *trattoria.*

Lady Bosworth was delighted. She declared that she would not have missed this occasion for anything. She had come to approve highly of Trent, who had made himself excellent company, and she saw her way to being quite admirable, for she was in dancing spirits. In ten minutes she was on the best of terms with the fat, vivacious woman of the inn. Trent, who had been dispatched to telephone their plight to George Lancey, and had added that they were enjoying it very much, returned to find Lady Bosworth in the little garden behind the inn, with her skirts pinned up, peeling potatoes and singing "*Il segreto per esse felice,*" while her sister beat up something in a bowl, and the landlady, busy with cooking, laughed and screamed cheerful observations from the kitchen. Seeing himself unemployable, Trent withdrew; sitting on a convenient wall, he took a leaf from his sketch-book and began to devise and decorate a *menu* of an absurdity suited to the spirit of the hour.

It was a more than cheerful dinner that they had under a canopy of vine-leaves on a tiny terrace overlooking the lake. Twilight came on unnoticed. It was already dark when Trent, returning from an inspection of the boat advised that they should return by the steamer if they would make sure of getting home that night; it would take an hour, but it would be safer. And presently there was a long-drawn hoot from down the lake, and a great black mass crowned with a galaxy of yellow lights came moving smoothly through the darkness.

It was as they sought for places on the crowded upper deck that Mrs. Lancey put her hand on Trent's arm. "There hasn't been a sign of it all the evening," she whispered. "What does that mean?"

"It means," murmured Trent, "that we got her away from the cause at the critical time, without anybody knowing we were going to do it."

"Whom do you mean by 'anybody'?"

"How on earth should I know? Here comes your sister."

It was not until the following afternoon that Trent found an opportunity of being alone with his hostess in the garden.

"She is perfectly delighted at having escaped it last night," said Mrs. Lancey. "She says she knew it would pass off, but she hasn't the least notion how she was cured. Nor have I."

"She isn't," replied Trent. "Last night was only a beginning and we can't get her unexpectedly stranded for the evening every day. The next move can be made now, if you consent to it. Lady Bosworth will be out until this evening, I believe?"

"She's gone shopping in the town. What do you want to do?"

"I want you to take me up to her room, and there I want you to look very carefully through everything in the place—in every corner of every box and drawer and bag and cupboard—and show me anything you find that might—"

"I should hate to do that!" Mrs. Lancey interrupted him, her face flushing.

"You would hate much more to see your sister again this evening as she was every evening before last night. Look here, Edith, the position is simple enough. Every day, about seven, Lady Bosworth goes into that room in her normal state to dress for dinner. Every day she comes out of it apparently as she went in, but turns queer a little later. Now is there any other place than that room where the mischief, whatever it is, could happen?"

Mrs. Lancey frowned dubiously. "Her maid is with her always."

"I suppose so; but it doesn't make any difference to the argument. That room is the only place where Lady Bosworth isn't with the rest of us, doing what we do, eating the same food, breathing the same air, exposed to all the same influences as we are. Does anything take place in that room to account for those strange seizures?"

Mrs. Lancey threw out her hands. "I cannot bear to think that Isabel should be deceiving me. And yet I know—it's a dreadful thing—and what else could happen there?"

"That is what we may find out, if we do as I say. You must decide. But remember that you must think of Lady Bosworth as one whom you are trying to save from a subtle evil. You can't shrink from a step merely because you wouldn't dream of taking it in the ordinary way."

For a few moments she stood carefully boring a hole in the gravel with one heel. Then, "Come along," she said, and led the way toward the house.

"Unless we take the floor up," said Mrs. Lancey, seating herself emphatically on the bed in her sister's room twenty minutes later, "there's nowhere else to look. I've taken everything out and pried into every hole and corner. There isn't a single lockable thing that is locked. There isn't a bottle or phial or pill-box of any sort to be found. So much for your suspicions. And all the time I have been working like a negro slave you have done nothing but stare about you, and play with brushes and combs and manicure-things. What interests you about that nail-polishing pad? You must have seen one before surely?"

"This ornamental design on hammered silver is very beautiful and original," replied Trent, abstractedly. "I have never seen anything quite like it."

"The same design is on the whole of the toilet set," Mrs. Lancey observed tartly, "and it shows to least advantage on the manicure-things. You are talking rubbish, Philip. Put the pad away and shut the case as you found it. We shall do no good here, I am sure; you will have to guess again. And yet," she added, slowly, "you are looking rather pleased with yourself."

Trent, his hands in his pockets, was balancing himself on his heels as he stared out of the window of the bedroom. His eyes were full of animation, and he was whistling almost inaudibly.

He turned round slowly. "I'm only guessing again—that's my guessing face. Whose are the rooms on each side of this, Edith?"

"This side, the Stones'; that side, Mr. Scheffer's."

"Then I will go for a walk all alone and guess some more. Good-bye."

"Yes," declared Mrs. Lancey, as he went out, "it's plain

enough you have picked up some scent or other."

"It isn't scent exactly," Trent replied, as he descended the stairs. "Guess again."

Trent was not in the house when, three hours later, a rousing tumult broke out on the upper floor. Those below in the loggia heard first a piercing scream, then a clatter of feet on parquet flooring, then more sounds of feet, excited voices, other screams of harsh, inhuman quality, and a lively scuffling and banging. Mr. Scheffer, with a volley of guttural words of which it was easy to gather the general sense, headed the rush of the company upstairs.

"Gisko! Gisko!" he shouted, at the head of the stairway. There was another ear-splitting screech, and the cockatoo came scuttling and fluttering out of Lady Bosworth's room, pursued by three vociferating women servants. The bird's yellow crest was erect and quivering with agitation; it screeched furious defiance again as it leapt upon its master's outstretched wrist.

"Silence, devil!" exclaimed Mr. Scheffer, seizing it by the head and shaking it violently. "I know not how to apologize, Lancey," he declared. "The accursed bird has somehow slipped from his chain away. I left him in my room secure just before we had tea."

"Never mind, never mind!" replied his host, who seemed rather pleased than otherwise with this small diversion. "I don't suppose he's done any harm beyond frightening the women. Anything wrong, Edith?" he asked, as they approached the open door of the bedroom, to which the ladies had already hurried. Lady Bosworth's maid was telling a voluble story.

"When she came in just now to get the room ready

for Isabel to dress," Mrs. Lancey summarized, "she suddenly heard a voice say something, and saw the bird perched on top of the mirror, staring at her. It gave her such a shock that she dropped the water-can and fled; then the two other girls came and helped her, trying to drive it out. They hadn't the sense to send for Mr. Scheffer."

"Apologize, carrion!" commanded Gisko's master. The cockatoo uttered a string of Dutch words in a subdued croak. "He says he asks one thousand pardons, and he will sin no more," Mr. Scheffer translated. "Miserable brigand! Traitor!"

Lady Bosworth hurried out of her room.

"I won't hear the poor thing scolded like that," she protested. "How was he to know my maid would be frightened? He looks so wretched! Take him away, Mr. Scheffer, and cheer him up." So Gisko was led away to bondage, and the episode was at an end.

It was half an hour later that Mrs. Lancey came to her husband in his dressing-room.

"I must say Bella was very decent about Scheffer's horrid bird," she began. "Do you know what the little fiend had done?"

"No, my dear. I thought he had confined himself to frightening the maid out of her skin."

"Not at all. He had been having the time of his life. Bella saw at once that he had been up to mischief, but she pretended there was nothing. Now it turns out he has bitten the buttons off two pairs of gloves, chewed up a lot of hair-pins, and spoiled her pretty little manicure set. He's torn the lining out of the case, the silver handles are covered with beak marks, two or three of the things he seems to have hidden somewhere, and the polishing pad is a ruin. When Hignett saw him perched on the mirror he had the pad in one hand—I mean, foot—and was busy tearing away the last rags of the leather."

"It's too bad!" declared Mr. Lancey, bending over a shoe.

"I believe you're laughing, George," said his wife, coldly.

He began to do so audibly. "You must admit it's funny to think of the bird going solemnly through a programme of mischief like that. I wish I could have seen the little beggar at it. Well, we shall have to get Bell a new nail-outfit. I'm glad she held her tongue about it just now."

"Why?"

"Because, my dear, we don't ask people to the house to make them feel uncomfortable—especially foreigners."

"Bella wasn't thinking of your ideal of hospitality. She held her tongue because she's taken a fancy to Scheffer. But, George, how do you suppose the little pest got in? The window was shut, and Hignett declares the door was too, when she went to the room."

"Then I expect Hignett deceives herself. Anyway, what does it matter? What I am anxious about is your sister's little peculiarity. As I've told you, I don't at all like the look of her having been quite normal yesterday evening, the one evening when she was away from the house by accident. I wish I wasn't so fond of her, Edith. If it was another woman, she could do what she liked to herself for all I cared."

Mrs. Lancey sighed. "If she had married you she would have been a very different woman."

"I know. It's awful to think of what we've all missed.

If you had married Scheffer, Gisko would have been a very different cockatoo. For of all sad words of tongue or pen— I really am feeling miserably depressed, Edith. What I'm dreading now is a repetition of the usual ghastly performance to-night."

But neither that night, nor any night after, was that performance repeated. Lady Bosworth, free now of all apprehension, renewed and redoubled the life of the little company. And the lips of Trent were obstinately sealed.

Three weeks later Trent was shown into the consulting-room of Sir Peregrine Bosworth. The famous physician was a tall, stooping man of exaggerated gauntness, narrow-jawed and high-nosed. His still black hair was brushed backward, his eyes were deep-set and glowing, his mouth at once sensitive and strong. He was courteous of manner and smiled readily, but his face was set in unhappy lines.

"Will you sit down, Mr. Trent?" said Sir Peregrine. "You wrote that you wished to see me upon a private matter concerning myself. I am at a loss to imagine what it can be, but, knowing your name, I had no hesitation in making an appointment."

Trent inclined his head. "I am obliged to you, Sir Peregrine. The matter is really important, and also quite private—so private that no person whatever knows the material facts besides myself. I won't waste words. I have lately been staying with the Lanceys, whom you know, in Italy. Lady Bosworth was also a guest there. For some days before my arrival she had suffered each evening from a curious attack of lassitude and vacancy of mind. I don't know what it was. Perhaps you do."

Sir Peregrine, immovably listening, smiled grimly.

"The description of symptoms is a little vague. I have heard nothing of this, I may say, from my wife."

"It always came on at a certain time of the day, and only then. That time was a few minutes after eight, at the beginning of dinner. The attack passed off gradually after two hours or so."

The physician laid his clenched hand on the table between them. "You are not a medical man, Mr. Trent, I believe. What concern have you with all this?" His voice was coldly hostile now.

"Lots," answered Trent, briefly. Then he added, as Sir Peregrine got to his feet with a burning eye, "I know nothing of medicine, but I cured Lady Bosworth."

The other sat down again suddenly. His open hands fell upon the table and his dark face became very pale. "You—" he began with difficulty.

"I and no other, Sir Peregrine. And in a curiously simple way. I found out what was causing the trouble, and without her knowledge I removed it. It was—oh, the devil!" Trent exclaimed in a lower tone. For Sir Peregrine Bosworth, with a brow gone suddenly white and clammy, had first attempted to rise and then sunk forward with his head on the table.

Trent, who had seen such things before, hurried to him, pulled his chair from the table, and pressed his head down to his knees. Within a minute the stricken man was leaning back in his chair. He inspired deeply from a small bottle he had taken from his pocket.

"You have been overworking, perhaps," Trent said. "Something is wrong. I think I had better not—"

Sir Peregrine had pulled himself together. "I know very well what is wrong with me, sir," he interrupted, brusquely. "It is my business to know. That will not happen again. I wish to hear what you have to say before you leave this house."

"Very well." Trent took a tone of colourless precision. "I was asked by Lady Bosworth's sister, Mrs. Lancey, to help in trying to trace the source of the disorder which attacked her every evening. I need not describe the signs of it, and I will not trouble you with an account of how I reasoned on the matter. But I found out that Lady Bosworth was, on these occasions, under the influence of a drug, which had the effect of lowering her vitality and clogging her brain, without producing stupefaction or sleep; and I was led to the conclusion that she was administering this drug to herself without knowing it."

He paused, and felt in his waistcoat pocket. "When Mrs. Lancey and I were making a search for something of the kind in her room, my attention was caught by the fine workmanship of a manicure-set on the dressing-table. I took up the little round box meant to contain nail-polishing paste, admiring its shape and decoration, and on looking inside it found it half-full of paste. But I have often watched the process of beautifying finger-nails, and it seemed to me that the stuff was of a deeper red than the usual pink confection; and I saw next that the polishing-pad of the set, though well-worn, had never been used with paste, which leaves a sort of dark incrustation on the pad. Yet it was evident that the paste in the little box had been used. It is useful sometimes, you see, to have a mind that notices trifles. So I jumped to the conclusion that the paste that was not employed as nail-polish was employed for some other purpose; and when I reached that point I simply put the box in my pocket and went away with it.

I may say that Mrs. Lancey knew nothing of this, or of what I did afterwards."

"And what was that?" Sir Peregrine appeared now to be following the story with an ironic interest.

"Naturally, knowing nothing of such matters, I took it to a place that called itself 'English Pharmacy' in the town, and asked the proprietor what the stuff was. He looked at it, took a little on his finger, smelt it, and said it was undoubtedly lip-salve.

"It was then I remembered how, when I saw Lady Bosworth during one of her attacks, her lips were brilliantly red, though all the colour had departed from her face. That had struck me as very odd, because I am a painter, and naturally I could not miss an abnormality like that. Then I remembered another thing. One evening, when Lady Bosworth, her sister, and myself were prevented from returning to the house for dinner, and dined at a country inn, there had been no signs of her trouble; but I had noticed that she moistened her lips again and again with her tongue."

"You are observant," remarked Sir Peregrine, dispassionately, and again had recourse to his smelling-bottle.

"You are good enough to say so," Trent replied, with a wooden face. "On thinking these things over, it seemed to me probable that Lady Bosworth was in the habit of putting on a little lip-salve when she dressed for dinner in the evening; perhaps finding that her lips at that time of day tended to become dry, or perhaps not caring to use it in daylight, when its presence would be much more easily detected. For I had learned that she made some considerable parade of not using any kind of cosmetics or artificial aids to beauty; and that, of course, accounted for her carrying it in a box meant for manicure-paste, which might be represented as merely a matter of cleanliness, and at any rate was not to be classed with paint and powder. It was not pleasant to me to have surprised this innocent little deception; but it was as well that I did so, for I soon ascertained beyond doubt that the stuff had been tampered with and drugged.

"When I left the chemist's I went and sat in a quiet corner of the Museum grounds. There I put the least touch of the salve on my tongue, and waited results. In five minutes I had lost all power of connected thought or will; I no longer felt any interest in my own experiment. I was conscious. I felt no discomfort, and no loss of the power of movement. Only my intelligence seemed to be paralyzed; and that did not trouble me in the least. For upwards of an hour I was looking out upon the world with the soul of an ox, utterly placid and blank."

Trent now opened his fingers and showed a little round box of hammered silver, with a delicate ornamentation running round the lid. It was of about the bigness of a pill-box.

"It seemed best to me that this box should simply disappear, and in some quite natural, unsuspicious way, merely to remove the salve would have drawn Lady Bosworth's attention to it and set her guessing. She did not suspect the stuff as yet, I was fully convinced, and I thought it well that the affair of her seizures should remain a mystery. Your eyes ask why. Just because I did not want a painful scandal in Mrs. Lancey's family—we are old friends, you see. So the problem was to make the box and its contents disappear in a manner which would appear completely accidental, and suggest no ideas of any sort to Lady Bosworth or any one else. That I managed to do; and now here I am with the box, and neither Lady Bosworth nor any other person has the smallest inkling of its crazy secret but you and I."

He stopped again and looked in Sir Peregrine's eyes. They remained fixed upon him with the gaze of a statue.

"It was plain, of course," Trent continued, "that some one had got at the stuff immediately before she went out to Italy, or immediately on her arrival. The chemical operation of combining the drug with the salve would hardly have been performed during the journey. But the attacks began on the first evening there, two hours after her reaching the house. Therefore any tampering with the salve after her arrival was practically impossible. When I asked myself who should have tampered with it before Lady Bosworth left this house to go out to Italy, I was led to form a very unpleasant conjecture."

Sir Peregrine stirred in his chair. "You had been told the truth—or a part of the truth—about our married life, I suppose?"

Trent inclined his head. "Three days ago I arrived in London, and showed a little of this paste to a friend of mine who is an expert analyst. He has sent me a report, which I have here." He handed an envelope across the table. "He was deeply interested in what he found, but I have not satisfied his curiosity. He found the salve to be evenly inpregnated with a very slight quantity of a rare alkaloid body called purvisine. Infinitesimal doses of it produce effects on the human organism which he describes, as I can testify, with considerable accuracy. It was discovered, he notes, by Henry Purvis twenty-five years ago; and you will remember, Sir Peregrine, what I only found out by inquiry—that you were assistant to Purvis about that time ago in Edinburgh. Where he had the Chair of medical jurisprudence and toxicology."

He ceased to speak, and there was a short silence. Sir Peregrine gazed at the table before him. Once or twice he drew breath deeply, and at length began to speak with composure.

"I shall not waste words," he said, "in trying to explain fully my state of mind or my action in this matter. But I will tell you enough for your imagination to do the rest. My feeling for my wife was an infatuation from the beginning and is still. I was too old for her. I don't think now that she ever cared for me greatly; but she was too strong-minded ever to marry a wealthy fool, and I had won a high position and a fortune. By the time we had been married a year I could no longer hide from myself that she had an incurable weakness for philandering. She has surrendered herself to it with less and less restraint, and without any attempt to deceive me on the subject. If I tried to tell you what torture it has been to me, you wouldn't understand. The worst was when she was away from me, staying with her friends, and I could not know what was happening. At length I took the step you know. It was undeniably an act of baseness, and we will leave it at that, if you please. If you should ever suffer as I do, you will modify your judgment upon me. I knew of my wife's habit, discovered by you, of using lip-salve at her evening toilette. On the night before her departure I took what was in that box and combined it with a preparation of the drug purvisine. The infinitesimal amount which would pass into the mouth after the application of the salve was calculated to produce for an hour or two the effects you have described, without otherwise doing any harm. But I knew the impression that would be produced upon normal men and women by the sight of any one in such a state. I wanted to turn her attractiveness into repulsiveness, and I seem to have succeeded. I was mad when I did it. I have been aghast at my own action ever since. I am glad it has been frustrated. And now I should like to know what you intend to do."

Trent took up the box. "If you agree, Sir Peregrine, I shall drop this from Westminster Bridge to-night. And so long as nothing of the sort is practised again, the whole affair shall be buried. Yours is a wretched story, and I don't suppose any of us would find our moral fibre improved by such a situation. I have no more to say."

He rose and moved to the door. Sir Peregrine rose also and stood with lowered eyes, apparently deep in thought. Suddenly he looked up.

"I am obliged to you Mr. Trent," he said formally. "I may say, too, that your account of your proceedings interested me deeply. I should like to ask a question. How did you contrive that the box should disappear without its owner seeing anything remarkable in its absence?"

"Oh, easily," Trent replied, his hand on the door-knob. "After experimenting on myself, I went back to the house before tea-time, when no one happened to be in. I went upstairs to a room where a cockatoo was kept—mischievous brute—took him off his chain, and carried him into Lady Bosworth's room. There I put him on the dressing-table, and teased him a little with the manicure things to interest him in them. Then I took away one of the pairs of scissors, so that the box shouldn't be the one thing missing, and left him shut in there to do his worst, while I went out of the house again. When I went he was ripping out the silk lining of the case, and had chewed up the silver handles of the things pretty well. After I had gone he went on to destroy various other things. In the riot that took place when he was found the disappearance of the little box and scissors became a mere detail. Certainly Lady Bosworth suspected nothing.

"I suppose," he added, thoughtfully, "that occasion would be the only time a cockatoo was of any particular use."

And Trent went out.

4

THE VANISHING LAWYER

WHAT made the Gayles affair such an especially bad business was the culprit's standing in his profession and in the eyes of the world. The firm of Gayles & Sims had a position as family solicitors that was second to none, and its head was a very important person indeed.

So it was that John Charlton Gayles, after the fact of his disappearance became known, was one of the most badly wanted men who had ever attracted the attention of the police. According to the information furnished by his partner, he had always had the sole control of the firm's accounts and financial business. An enormous amount of property entrusted to his care could not be traced; and neither could Mr. Gayles, of whom nothing had been seen or heard since he retired to his bedroom one Tuesday night in May. During the following two days matters had been brought to the notice of Mr. Sims which made it clear that there was a great deal requiring explanation from the senior partner; and on the Friday it was decided to give information to the police of his disappearance and of the firm's predicament.

Philip Trent, at the opening of his first article as the *Record's* special investigator of this unusual case, dwelt upon the rock-ribbed respectability of the missing man.

"It is a safe statement," he wrote, "that no lawyer has ever enjoyed a more spotless reputation. He has for some years been chairman of the Law Society's Disciplinary Committee, whose duty is to examine and act upon cases of professional misconduct. In his own life he has always been a model of probity and high principle.

"On Tuesday last Mr. Gayles returned by an early train after a long week-end at Preakness, and drove from Victoria to his office in Lincoln's Inn Fields. This, at least, was his own account of how he had spent his time; but it is now established that nothing was seen of him that week-end at the hotel where he always stayed in Preakness. He did a normal day's work, and a little after six o'clock went home to his house in Castle Terrace, Knightsbridge. At 9.30, as usual, he went to bed; for Mr. Gayles believed in very early hours both night and morning.

"He was not called next day, as he preferred to rise at his own time, and often did so before the servants were stirring. But at eight, his hour for breakfast, he did not appear; and when his butler went to call him, he found no sign anywhere of Mr. Gayles. His bed had been slept in, and he had washed and shaved in the bathroom opening out of the bedroom. It would seem that he left the house before seven, the servants' time for rising, and that he did not go out by either of the house doors, which were still bolted inside. Mr. Gayles had his bedroom on the ground floor; it opens on the garden by way of a french-window, and through this, it is surmised, he went to the end of the garden and out by a door in the wall, which was found unlocked with the key in its place. This door gives on a narrow blind alley leading into Knightsbridge, where an early bus or cab could have been taken. Mr. Gayles, an old-fashioned man in many ways, did not own a car and had never learnt to drive one.

"His partner, Mr. Sims, when told of his disappearance was completely mystified. Why Mr. Gayles, the sanest of men, should have chosen so to absent himself without a word to any one was quite incomprehensible; but Mr. Sims was naturally unwilling to take any hasty action which might prejudice the reputation of the firm. When facts came to light, however, which made Mr. Gayles's presence desirable, to say the least, the police were called in. After a day of investigation they are believed to be still at a loss.

"Mr. Gayles recently drew from his bank a large sum in cash, being the whole of the amount standing to his credit."

The photograph accompanying this article showed a firm, grave face, of which the most striking details were the bushy brows over dark-rimmed glasses, the rather heavy jowls, and, by contrast, the hair not yet at all receded from the forehead. This was from a Press picture of the high table at a City banquet; for Gayles, as far as could be discovered, had never been photographed on his own account.

Trent had added little to the bare facts given to the newspapers from Scotland Yard. He set out now to follow his own hunting nose; and on the morning of the appearance of this article he had an interview at the firm's office with the junior partner. Mr. Sims was a man in the forties, smart, worldly, and with competence stamped on his hard, clean-shaven face. He looked jaded and harassed.

"You want to hear about Gayles as a personality?" Sims said. "Well, I thought that if anybody knew John Gayles, I did. I would have trusted him with every shilling I had in the world. And now we find he has gambled away his own fortune and God knows how much of other people's money. So much for being a very reserved character! Gayles was always that; and after his wife's death he became very much more so. He was devoted to her—even he couldn't help showing that—and it wasn't until after she died, as far as we can make out, that this Stock Exchange mania got hold of him. It was a distraction, perhaps; anyhow, it seems to have begun the year after she died."

"I am told he was a Cambridge man," Trent said. "Did you ever hear of his doing any gambling in those days? It's one of the tastes that can be acquired at the Universities, I know."

"Oh no! Far from it. His father—the founder of the firm—was very proud of Gayles's Cambridge record. He carried off two prizes, I remember, and got an excellent degree, besides being President of the Union. I never heard of his making a bet in his life."

"Did he take any interest in sport or games?"

"Not the faintest. He never seemed to need exercise himself."

"Was his health good, then?" Trent asked.

"Why, he never looked healthy, because of that pale face of his," Sims said. "But as a matter of fact, I never knew him have an illness until the time when he took a holiday five years ago. He used always to go abroad for a month in the summer, not having letters forwarded. Well, this time, when the month was up, instead of Gayles came a post card from him saying he was obliged to prolong his holiday for a week or two. There was no address on the card, but it was postmarked Freiburg in Breisgau. This was very unlike Gayles, because he had always been keen to get back to his work—that and his garden at home. When he did return, it came out that he had travelled straight to Freiburg, arrived there feeling very ill, and been sent straight into the Heiliggeist Hospital with scarlet fever."

"Then was he there all by himself all that time?"

"Absolutely. He only sent me that one disinfected post card, and remained there till he was out of quarantine. He had had it badly, and all his hair had fallen out. He was wearing a wig, a very expensive one he said it was, but it never looked like his own hair. He was evidently feeling very disgusted about it; and he said he wished never to have it referred to again. It wasn't, either; it didn't do to annoy Gayles. I suspect he had been rather proud of having a thick crop of dark hair at his age."

"And didn't the illness mark him in any other way?"

"Only that it had affected his eyes—he had to wear tinted glasses all the time. But his health recovered completely, in spite of the fact that he never took a proper holiday after that. He had had enough of long holidays, he said; and he made up for it by spending most of his week-ends inhaling the sea-air at Preakness."

"Why at Preakness?" Trent wondered. "I barely know its name, and I've never met any one who has been there."

Sims made a grimace. "You wouldn't. It's on a branch off the main line to Mewstone, and once when I was there I ran over in my car to have a look at Preakness. Gayles always said it was the quietest spot on the South Coast, and I should say he wasn't far wrong. Five minutes of it was ample for me. I believe the inn Gayles stayed at is good enough, though—people go there for the trout-fishing. Anyhow, it did Gayles good. The only thing he has ever had wrong with him since that illness is neuralgia, which he began to suffer from intermittently some time ago. Now and then he would come to the office with his jaws tied up in a scarf—he was that way the last time he was here."

Trent considered a few moments. "His hair was entirely gone, you say. I suppose you never saw him without his wig."

"No, not I. Some of the staff have done, though. There's Willis, the clerk who went to his room to take letters at eleven each morning. Once or twice he has caught Gayles with his wig off at the glass over by the window. Of course, Willis had the sense to pretend not to have seen, and Gayles had shoved it on again in a moment. Then there's the office boy who had to take in Gayles's cup of tea at 4.30. He caught him once in just the same way, Willis told me."

Trent smiled. "Would you describe Gayles as at all an eccentric man?" he said as he got up to go.

"Oh no," Sims said, rising also to his feet. "He was much like a hundred other lawyers of fifty-five to look at—more old-fashioned and black-coated than some, perhaps; but that's all. And he was a perfect devil for punctuality and system in the office. But many of us are like that, and all of us ought to be. And it is just that, you see, Mr. Trent, that makes this affair so completely bewildering. Gayles was almost inhumanly correct. It's what makes me wonder"—Sims lowered his voice impressively here—"if there can have been anything wrong with him mentally after all. Well, good-bye. Look me up again if you want to ask about anything more."

Trent had no difficulty, later in the day, in prevailing on Perfitt and his wife, the butler and cook-housekeeper in the Gayles household, to talk about their employer's disappearance, and to allow an inspection of the bedroom from which the bird had so mysteriously flown. They found a gloomy enjoyment in their connection with fraud on such a scale, and the collapse of such a reputation. None of the four servants had had much liking for Gayles, but they had esteemed him a just man and a tower of respectability. It was, Mrs. Perfitt said, like as if the world had turned upside down to think of Mr. Gayles having took money, and being in hiding from the police.

The bedroom was a large, airy, rather monastic apartment, with a small shelf of bedside books as its only humane feature. This, thought Trent, would be Gayles's idea of light reading. His roving eye fell upon *Serjeant Ballantine's Experiences; Anomalies of the Law of England; Stories from the Law Reports; Life in the Law.* Fiction was represented by *The Pilgrim's Progress,* with the excellent illustrations of J. D. Watson.

A little chilled by this glimpse into the mental privacy of John Gayles, Trent turned to the french-window, still open upon a beautifully tended garden. Beds of tulips in luxuriant variety flanked the smooth lawn. Gayles, it could be seen, was an enthusiast. Companies of different blooms were arrayed in a carpet-work of diagonal stripes. Mr. Gayles, said the butler, did most of the work himself, in the early morning or after office hours; when he was not planting and trimming he would just sit and look at them.

A garden-book lay open on a table by the window, and Trent looked down on a list of tulips, in the order of the time of their flowering. Albino; Bronze Knight; Sieraad van Flora; Mewstone Glory; Rijnland; Pollux; Mr. Zimmerman; Malicorne—so the list went on. With what a wrench must Gayles have torn himself away from all this! In a corner of the room stood a strange-looking standard lamp, topped by a metal cowl with wires attached, and stamped with a maker's name and the words "Ultra-Violet Ray." Gayles used it, the butler said, for his neuralgia.

There was a bathroom, with the usual outfit of toilet accessories, opening out of the bedroom. None of these things, nor, as far as Perfitt could say, any clothing or requisites of travel, had been taken away by Gayles. He seemed to have taken nothing but the clothes he stood up in—those he had worn the day before. This was as much as an inquirer without authority could gather from the household of the much-wanted man.

Three days later Trent was closeted with Chief-Inspector Murch in his bare little office at Scotland Yard; a room which the visitor knew well. He had even contributed to its scanty decoration a charcoal sketch of Mrs. Murch, which beamed from above the fireplace.

"Yes," Mr. Murch said as he stuffed tobacco into a

pipe. "We have been in communication with the police at Freiburg. What to make of it I don't know; and I can't think what put you on to suggesting this line. Nor how it's going to help us, either. But the fact, for what it's worth, is that the whole story about Gayles having scarlet fever in Freiburg is simply a lie."

Trent jumped to his feet. "Three ringing cheers! And just what did you hear from the police there?"

Mr. Murch got his pipe going, then said, "They're very thorough; very anxious to be helpful, too. They say there was no Englishman, or any other foreigner, in that hospital with scarlet fever or with anything else all that summer. Not only that, but there wasn't a single case of scarlet fever in the town all that year. So there you are—Gayles cooked up the whole thing. Presumably he did go there, because of the post card; but nobody calling himself Gayles stayed at any of the hotels at that time. And now, what about it?"

"It depends," Trent said, "on the answer to another question. Do you know when he began helping himself to his clients' money?"

The inspector took up some typewritten sheets from a wire basket. "I can give you an outline of what has been found out so far. He started speculating on a large scale about nine years ago, and at first he made a lot of money. After that he had a run of serious losses, and he appears to have got through the whole of his private fortune four years after he began; anyhow, it was then that he took his first fatal step. He was a trustee of various settlements and other funds. He started with one of £17,000, which he converted for his own use and benefit; lost that, and went on going deeper and deeper, in the hope of getting square again. All the victims received their incomes regularly, so they naturally never suspected they were being paid out of stolen capital. You can see how easy it is, when every one has absolute confidence in a man's integrity. First and last, nearly £200,000 had gone by the time Gayles did his disappearing act. Some of it, no doubt, he had stowed away somewhere where he could get at it under another name. The rest went down the drain. That's the story, put short. It has taken some getting at, because he employed a number of different brokers."

"Thank you," Trent said. "It is just as I expected."

"You mean about the time when he went wrong?"

"Yes, first we hear that he had scarlet fever five years ago. Now we hear that he began gambling nine years ago, and that ruin was staring him in the face after four years of it. You see? The Freiburg trick was staged just about the time when he had yielded to temptation, or was just going to, perhaps."

Mr. Murch looked at Trent consideringly. "Well, if you will tell me why," he said slowly. "I suppose you are not suggesting he could have lost his hair any other way than by having a severe illness somewhere. And why should that have had anything to do with his starting out as a wrong 'un? I agree that he had been preparing his get-away a long time. The Perfitts say it was some years ago—they don't remember exactly—that he took to sleeping in that convenient ground-floor room. And we know now why he never took a holiday apart from week-ends—a show-up might come at any time, if he wasn't on the spot to stave it off. I must say he managed very well. He knew Sims wouldn't have any grounds for calling us in at first, so that the trail was stone-cold by the time we started. We don't know when he left the house, and we haven't a clue to where he went, and the watch-out for him at home and abroad has been absolutely fruitless so far."

"Yes, he certainly showed good judgment. But I should keep Freiburg in mind if I were you. Did you find anything out of the way when you went through Gayles's place?"

"Nothing—except that in the bathroom, among the little bottles over the basin, there was one of spirit gum. And I don't see what he could have wanted with that. He couldn't have imagined he could get away with a false beard or moustache."

"Perhaps he put it there to make it more difficult. You must have been meant to find it."

"That's just the kind of thing," the inspector said, "you can't be so sure about. A criminal will often mess up the cleverest plan by some idiotic piece of carelessness—you know that as well as I do."

"Just so. Well, I hope the Freiburg myth seems to you worth pondering about—it does to me. Now I must be off—and I say, if I *should* manage to beat you to Gayles, I will let you know at once. The word will be Snowdrop."

"Well, it's nice to see you again, Phil," Eunice Faviell said. "I wish it happened oftener. What did you want to see me about? You aren't here on account of my beautiful eyes, I know."

She was receiving Trent in her dressing-room at the Siddons Theatre, after the first act of that vivacious comedy *Beautiful Soup*, and she was delicately adjusting, before her glass, the coronet she was to wear in the second act.

"It was to get some advice about beauty treatment, at least," Trent said.

"Beauty treatment!" she stared at him. "My dear, do you want to have your face lifted, or your silhouette improved? I can put you on to a friend of mine who has just had ten pounds carved off below the waist-line—or perhaps I hadn't better, as no one is supposed to know. But really, Phil, you will do as you are for a few years yet. You mustn't lose heart about your figure."

"I don't. I want to know about something quite different. The question is whether a man can disguise his complexion in such a way that it will look natural by daylight and not be detected at all."

Eunice reached to a row of small bottles on a shelf by the mirror. "You could do it with this wash," she said. "It will change that light ginger-bread colour of yours to an interesting paleness, and if you renew it two or three times a day it will look all right to any one who doesn't know you. But with any one who does, it would be very hard to change your complexion so that he couldn't tell it was faked. And now will you tell me why you should be thinking of trying to look like a turnip?"

"But I wasn't thinking of myself at all. I never do—you know that. The man I have in mind is a white-faced man."

"If that's his type," Eunice said, "you can get lotions which claim to give you a healthy tan that you haven't deserved. But it never looks as good as the real thing, and, like the other, it wouldn't deceive his friends. The only convincing way for a pale man to get brown is nature's way."

"I see. Well, that clears up my uncertainties, Eunice; and you have given me something to think about."

"Miss Faviell, please," came a yelp and a knock at the door.

One evening a week later Inspector Murch was much moved on receiving a telegram in these words:

SNOWDROP WHAT TRAIN SHALL I MEET TOMORROW PRINCES STREET REPLY TRENT NORFOLK HOTEL MEWSTONE.

Mr. Murch, knowing Trent well enough to be sure that this meant business, consulted a time-table and replied at once. Next morning at 10.45, on the platform of the Prince's Street Station at Mewstone, he was greeted by Trent.

"I can see by the look in your eye that you have got something," the inspector said as they went through the barrier.

"When I say Snowdrop, I mean Snowdrop."

"All right. Where do we go from here? And why Mewstone?"

"We go to the Botanic Gardens," Trent said as they went briskly up the station approach. "They are said to be among the finest in the country—and Gayles, you know, loved flowers. You may not know that he had among his tulips one named after this place. It's famous for them, I find. Then there is the immortal question, 'Where does a wise man hide a leaf?' Answer, 'In the forest.' And where does a retired—or retiring—professional man hide himself? In Mewstone, of course—it's swarming with them. Above all, Mewstone is not very far from Preakness, and you take the same train from Victoria for both of them. So I decided to pay a visit to Mewstone; and yesterday I saw Gayles in the Botanic Gardens. When he went off to his hotel for lunch, I went there too, and took a room. I have made a few discreet inquiries there; also at Preakness.

"Now I will tell you a few things I guessed about Gayles. The first is that, during that long holiday five years ago, wherever he spent it, he employed his time learning to drive a car."

"Ha!" Mr. Murch ejaculated.

"Anyhow, he drives quite well now. He went on improving, I dare say, during those solitary week-ends of his, most of which he did *not* spend at Preakness, as you'll find if you look up the register at the Pitt's Head inn there, where he was supposed to stay. It's true he went there fairly often; but Mewstone is the place for hiring cars.

"In other ways he got ready for the smash, if it should become inevitable. For five years he wore his wig and his conspicuous glasses. He took to sleeping on the ground-floor.

"In time things went from bad to worse, and at last exposure was very near. So Gayles took his final measures. He developed neuralgia, and bought an ultra-violet sun-ray lamp to cure it. It is true that the deep infra-red is what they use for neuralgia; but the ultra-violet is excellent for another thing—it cures you of being pale. Gayles used it, I imagine, each morning before breakfast. In a fortnight, say, he had a fine natural brown-red colour. As soon as it began to appear, he took to whitening his face with liquid powder or some such stuff, and he kept it on till bedtime.

"Then he went for his last long week-end. Early on the Friday evening he took a taxi from the office, with his suitcase, to Victoria. We know that; what follows is guesswork. At the station he took a dressing-room, perhaps, washed his face, shed his wig and glasses, and changed into different—very different—clothes. Also he trimmed his eyebrows close, and put the loose hair in an envelope. Then he left Victoria, when the rush-period was on, and nobody paid any attention to him. He proceeded to make a call on Mr. H. T. Wyman, of 37 Yarborough Place, who performed on him the simple and swift operation of lifting his face."

"What!" shouted Mr. Murch, exploding in a laugh; then added soberly, "Well, go on."

"I got the idea of it," Trent said, "from a chance remark made by a friend whom I was consulting about changing one's complexion. Then I inquired for the names of the principal experts who do that operation, and started to look them up; and at the second shot I found Wyman. He will tell you that at 5.30 that day he did the job for a man named Davies, who had made the appointment by phone some days before—an elderly sportsman with a very brown face, in light grey tweeds and a rather larky striped tie.

"Gayles returned to the station and took the dining-car express, not to Preakness, but to Mewstone. He had nothing to show on him but some stitches behind his ears, and he looked about half his age. On arriving, he went to the Norfolk hotel and took a room in the name of E. G.

Fairhurst, saying that he would probably be staying some months if he liked the place. He has stayed there ever since."

"That's wrong, anyhow," snapped the inspector. "On the following Tuesday—"

"Let me tell you what he did on the following Tuesday. He left for London by the 7.35 a.m., on which he had booked a compartment for himself. He said he was going to bring his car down to Mewstone, and took a place for it in the hotel garage. In the compartment he changed into the Gayles outfit, whitened his face, and resumed his wig; also he stuck on his eyebrows the clippings he had kept, using that spirit gum which he afterwards left about to keep you guessing. Before reaching London he tied up his jaws in a scarf because of his neuralgia, which had taken the unusual form of much improving the shape of his face. Then he was ready for what was to be positively the last appearance of J. C. Gayles. After his day at the office he went home, and retired at 9.30. As soon as he was in the room, he floundered about in the bed for a little, then changed back into the personality of E. G. Fairhurst, put the Gayles clothes into his suitcase, walked out with it through the garden, and went off to some garage where he had been keeping a car for some time—under his new name, no doubt.

"And so, you see, he drove straight down to Mewstone, arriving, according to the night porter, about 1.30, saying he had had a break-down; garaged the car, went up to bed, and had six or seven hours of refreshing slumber after a busy day. He had been in regular residence at the hotel for five days before Gayles was missed from his home, and a week before his disappearance was reported in the papers. Looking as if he had never put his nose inside an office in his life, too. He must have thought the position fairly safe."

"Devil doubt it," agreed Mr. Murch. "He had worked hard enough."

By this time they had arrived at the Botanic Gardens, and Trent led the way to a seat in that well-wooded, smooth-turfed and gorgeous-bedded park. "That is how the fake was managed, I believe," he said. "Some of it is conjecture, of course; but does it seem to you to hang together?"

The inspector lay back with his arms along the top of the seat, and reflected. "If you have really got Gayles, it would account for everything. If you have got him, it's a fine piece of work, and you can say I said so."

"I said Snowdrop," Trent reminded him. "Take a look at the man over there." His glance indicated a typical Mewstone resident, brown-red of face, leisurely of mien, rather gaily plus-foured and stockinged, on a seat about twenty yards from them on the opposite side of the walk. This person had bared his head to the gentle breeze, and was contentedly eyeing the great bank of tulips that faced him beyond the path. Mr. Murch stared, then turned to Trent.

"I don't see it," he said curtly. "Why, that man's hair is as genuine as your own. Dammit, look at it! And he isn't more than forty at the outside—I'd say thirty if he wasn't going grey."

"That," Trent said, "is what Wyman does for you. As for his hair, of course it's genuine, because he never lost it. He wore a wig on top of it for those five years."

The inspector snorted. "Then you haven't heard that Gayles has been seen without his wig, and that he is as bald as a coot."

"Oh yes; Sims told me that. But on those occasions, you see, Gayles was wearing a sham bald head, such as you've often seen on the stage. Now and then, when he meant to be caught that way, he would wear his bald pate, and the wig over that. He was seen so only for a moment, with the light behind him, and the effect was quite convincing. All the same, it was just that that gave me my first idea about the whole fraud. He was always seen by people whose duty it was to come into his room at that precise moment. You know that he insisted on the strictest punctuality. When I realized that he would naturally be most careful to have his wig in place at those times, the great idea began to dawn on me. At last I saw that he had planned to disappear by shedding a few things that were not genuine, and giving himself an entirely new appearance that any one could see *was* genuine. Quite a good notion, I thought."

The inspector sighed. "All right; you win. But how am I going to arrest a man I can't identify? I have only known him as he was before he absconded. The real hair, and the eyebrows, and the shape of the face—they make all the difference."

Trent took from his pocket an envelope, and drew out two slips of paper. "Here are two portraits cut from unmounted group-photographs of the Committee of the Cambridge Union Society, taken in Gayles's third year, before his eyebrows began to thicken. I had them sent to me by Hurst & Bingham, the firm who took them; they keep negatives of that kind in case they're wanted for memoirs or biographies. The serious-looking person in this print is the Librarian of the Union. In the other, taken six months later, you see him again as President. Pretty good likenesses, don't you think?"

Mr. Murch gazed at the young-old face in the two prints, then at the old-young face of the man on the neighbouring seat. He shook hands with Trent in silence, then rose, walked over to his unsuspecting victim, and touched him lightly on the shoulder.

Two months later John Charlton Gayles, found guilty on all counts of the indictment, was sentenced to fourteen years' penal servitude.

[5]

THE INOFFENSIVE CAPTAIN

"INSPECTOR Charles B. Muirhead. Introduced by Chief Inspector W. Murch." Trent was reading from a card brought to him as he sat at breakfast. "I had no idea," he remarked to his servant, "that Mr. Murch was introducing a new kind of policeman. What does he look like, Dennis?"

"He might be anything, sir. A very ordinary-looking man, I should say."

"Well, that's the highest compliment you could pay a plain-clothes officer, I suppose."

Trent finished his coffee and stood up. "Show him into the studio. And if he should happen to arrest me, telephone to Mr. Ward that I am unfortunately detained and cannot join him this evening."

"Certainly, sir."

The two men who came together in Philip Trent's studio looked keenly at each other. The police officer, who did not much approve of the mission on which he had been sent, was not reassured by what he saw. Trent was at this time—it was a few years before the unravelling of the Manderson affair came to change his life—a man not yet thirty, with an air of rather irresponsible good humour and an easy, unceremonious carriage of his loose-knit figure that struck his visitor as pleasing in general, but not in keeping with great mental gifts. His features were regular; his short, curling hair and moustache, and, indeed, his whole appearance, suggested a slight but not defiant carelessness about externals.

Mr. Muirhead, knowing nothing of modern painters, thought this quite right in an artist, but he wondered what could have led such a man to interest himself in police problems.

As for Inspector Muirhead, he was a lean, light-haired, upstanding man with a scanty yellow moustache, dressed in an ill-fitting dark suit, with a low collar much too large for his neck. The only noticeable things about him were an air of athletic hardness and a pair of blue eyes like swords. He looked like a Cumberland shepherd who had changed clothes with a rent-collector.

"I am very glad," said Trent, "to meet any friend of Inspector Murch's. Sit down and have a cigar. Not a smoker? So much the worse for the criminal class—you look as if your nerves were made of steel wire. Now, let me hear what it is you want of me."

The hard-featured officer squared his shoulders and put his hands on his knees. "Inspector Murch thought you might be willing to help us unofficially, Mr. Trent, in a little difficulty we are in. It concerns the escape of James Rudmore from Dartmoor yesterday afternoon."

"I hadn't heard of it."

"It's in the papers to-day—the bare fact. But the details are unusual. For one thing, he's got clear away, which has happened only in a very few cases at Dartmoor. Rudmore did what others have done—made a bolt from one of the gangs doing outdoor labour, taking advantage of a mist coming on suddenly. But instead of wandering on the moor till he was taken again, as they mostly do, he got on a road some miles from the prison, where he had the luck to meet a motor-car going slowly in the mist. He jumped out in front of the car, and when the chauffeur stopped it Rudmore sprang at him and gave him a knock on the head with a stone that stunned him. The car belongs to an American gentleman and his wife, by name Van Sommeren, who were touring about the country."

"Gratifying for them," remarked Trent. "They will feel the English are not making strangers of them—that we are taking them to our bosom, as it were."

"Mr. Van Sommeren drew a revolver," pursued the detective stolidly, "and shot twice before Rudmore closed with him. He managed to get hold of the weapon after a struggle, and so had them at his mercy. He was hurt slightly in the arm by one of the shots, Mr. Van Sommeren thinks. Rudmore made him give up his motor-coat and cap, and all he had in his pockets; also the lady's purse. Then he put on the coat and cap over his convict dress and drove off alone, going eastward. The others waited till the chauffeur was all right again, then made the best of their way along the road on foot. It was hours before they got to Two Bridges and told their story."

"He managed it well," Trent observed, lighting a pipe. "Decision and promptitude. He ought to have been a soldier."

"He was," returned Mr. Muirhead. "He had been, at least. But the point is, where is he now? We now know that he drove the car as far as Exeter, where he abandoned it outside the railway station, taking with him two large suitcases and a dressing-bag. There can be no doubt that he came on by train to London, arriving last night. He has particular business here, as well as friends who would help him. Do you remember the Danbury pendant affair, Mr. Trent? It's nearly two years ago now."

"I don't. Probably I was not in England at the time."

"Then I may as well tell you the story of it and the Rudmores. You must know it if you're to assist us. Old John Rudmore was for many years a doctor in very good practice in Calcutta—had been an army doctor at first. He was a widower, a man of good family, highly educated, very clever and popular. His only son was James Rudmore, who was a lieutenant in a Bengal cavalry regiment, very much the same sort of man as his father. There was a daughter, too—a young girl. Six years ago, when James was twenty-three, something happened—something to do with old Rudmore, it is believed. It was kept dark quite successfully, but the word went out against the Rudmores. The old man threw up his practice, and the son sent in his papers. All three of them came home and settled in London. The Rudmores had influential connections, and Jim got a soft job under the Board of Trade. His sister went to live with some relatives of her mother's. The father made his headquarters in bachelor chambers in Jermyn Street. He travelled a good deal and was interested in mining properties. He seemed to have amassed a great deal of money, and it was believed he made his son a considerable allowance."

"Was there supposed to be anything wrong about the money?"

"That we don't know; but what happened afterward makes it seem likely. Well, James Rudmore went the pace considerably. He got into a gambling, dissipated set, and wasn't particular about what friends he made. He was intimate with some of the shadiest characters in sporting circles—people we'd had an eye upon more than once. He was a reckless, desperate chap, with a dangerous temper when roused, and he was well on his way to being a regular wrong 'un when the affair of the pendant happened; but he was very clever and amusing, and had a light-hearted way with him; a gentleman all over to look at, and hadn't lost caste, as they say."

Trent nodded appreciatively. "You describe him to the life. I should like to have known him."

"One day there was a big garden party at Danbury House, and he was there helping with some sort of entertainment. Lady Danbury was wearing the pendant, which was a famous family jewel containing three remarkable diamonds and some smaller stones. It was late in the afternoon before she found that the chain it was attached to had broken and the pendant was gone. By that time many of the guests had gone, too, and James Rudmore among them. A search was begun all over the grounds, but it hadn't gone far when one of the maids, hearing of the loss, came forward with a statement. It seemed she had been philandering with one of the men servants in a part of the grounds where she'd no business to be; the countess had been receiving people there, but it was deserted at the time. The man's eye was caught by something on the grass, and the girl, going nearer to it, recognized the pendant. Just as she was hurrying forward to pick it up, they heard steps on the path, and thinking it might be one of the upper servants, who would make trouble about her being out there, they both stepped behind a clump of shrubbery. They saw James Rudmore come round the corner of the path. He was alone and seemed to be looking for something on the ground. He caught sight of the pendant and stood gazing at it a moment. Then he picked it up and, holding it in his hand, went on toward the place where the company were. That was all that the two saw. Naturally, they thought he was carrying the thing straight to the countess; it never occurred to them that a man of young Rudmore's appearance would steal it."

"It was a silly thing to do," Trent remarked.

"He was in a tight place," explained the detective. "It came out afterward that he was deeply in debt and had just dropped a good sum on the Stock Exchange. He wanted money desperately."

"He had one resource," suggested Trent. "I have heard it described as tapping the ancestor."

"The ancestor," said Mr. Muirhead with a hard smile, "was away on his travels, looking into some East African mining proposition, and apparently couldn't be got at. Besides, as you'll see, tapping him might not have been much good; and James no doubt knew that, for their relations were always very close and confidential. But as I was saying: The two witnesses told their story about the finding of the pendant. An hour afterward I was out after James with a warrant in my pocket. About nine o'clock I arrested him as he walked into the hotel where he lived. He denied the charge with a show of astonishment and indignation, but he made no resistance. The pendant was not on him then, and it was never found. I took him away in a taxicab. In Panton Street he gave me a blow on the jaw that knocked me out, jumped from the cab, and darted round the corner into Whitcomb Street.

There he ran into the arms of a constable, who held him; he fought savagely, and was only secured by the help of two men. He didn't get away again."

"Until yesterday," Trent observed. "Where had he been between leaving Danbury House and returning to his hotel?"

"Apparently at a club in the Adelphi, where he played billiards for an hour and then dined. His story was that he'd walked there straight from Danbury House and gone straight from there to his hotel. It couldn't be shown that he'd been anywhere else; but nobody knew exactly when he had left Danbury House. His line at the trial was that he knew absolutely nothing of the pendant and that it was a plot to ruin him. The case against him was unanswerable, and the assaults on the police, of course, made the matter much worse. He was sent to penal servitude."

"Then you think he has his booty hidden somewhere, waiting for him to take it when he comes out?"

"Sure of it," the detective replied. "Doesn't it stand to reason? He was ruined anyway, and the assaults which his temper had led him into made a heavy sentence certain. He might as well have something to show for it when it was all over."

"Just so. Well, then, inspector, where do I come in?"

Mr. Muirhead drew out a pocket-book.

"Three weeks before his escape James Rudmore, who had been a model prisoner from the first, was allowed the privilege of writing a letter, in accordance with the regulations. He wrote to his father. Now it so happened that old Rudmore had then been himself in jail six months or more. I had arrested him, too. The charge was fraudulent bankruptcy, and it was as clever a piece of crooked work as ever came into court, I should think. I took him at his rooms, and he went like a lamb; pleaded guilty and took his dose without any fuss."

"A philosopher," said Trent. "So he never got the letter from James."

"Certainly not. James Rudmore was informed, in accordance with the regulations, that his letter could not be forwarded, the reason being withheld. He then asked to have it back; and that was a mistake, for the governor of Dartmoor had already taken it into his head that there was something more than met the eye in the letter, and that made him certain of it. He believed it contained a secret message telling old Rudmore where the pendant was. Why he thought so I don't myself know; but it was likely enough, of course. The letter was forwarded to Scotland Yard and has been gone over carefully by the experts. They can make nothing of it."

"That is probably just because they are experts," Trent commented. "You want a really scatter-brained man—or shall we call him a man of tropically luxuriant mental gifts?—such as myself, for example, to deal with the little dodges of people like the Rudmores. I know now what it is your people want of me. They think the hiding-place of the jewel is described in that letter, and that if they can discover it, and mount guard over it, they will soon get James. I am to give an opinion on the letter. There is nothing I should like better. Where is it?"

The inspector, without reply, drew a folded paper from his pocket-book and handed it to Trent. He read the following, written in a firm and legible handwriting:

My dear Dad:

I am writing to you, the first time I am allowed, to say how sorry I am for all the misery my disgrace must have caused you. When I was made a scapegoat, it was the thought of how you would feel the dishonour to our name that hurt me most.

I wish I could have seen you just once before I was put away here. But you, at least, will never have doubted my innocence, I know. It would be the end for me, indeed, if when I were free again I should find even your door closed against me.

I am strong and well; in better health than I have been for years. Most of the time I have been set to what is really navvy's work in the open air, reclaiming waste land. At first it was fearfully hard work, and I used to wish I had a hinge in my back, and as many arms as the idol, whose name I forget, on your mantelshelf. But I soon got hardened. I have not lived an out-of-door life regularly for some years, and it has made me a new man. I feel trained to a hair. I did have one bad bout of fever, though, before I got fit. I fancy the climate here is rather hard on one if one has malaria in one's system, and isn't up to the mark; the country looks and smells rather like the Gelderland country round Apeldjik, where you remember I was laid up three years ago. But this was a much worse attack. I was light-headed for days, and felt like dying. Isn't it somebody in Shakespeare who talks about "the wretch whose fever-weakened joints buckle under life?" I felt exactly like that.

I would like to tell you about the life we lead here, and my opinion of the system, but all I write has to pass under the officials' eyes, and "sie würden das nicht so hingehen lassen," as old Schraube used to say.

I send this to the old rooms in Jermyn Street, trusting it will reach you. Good-bye.

Your loving son,
Jim.

Trent read this through carefully once. Then he looked at Inspector Muirhead with a meditative eye. "Well?" demanded that officer.

"This," said Trent, "is what judges in lawsuits call a very proper letter; meaning, usually, a letter with a faint flavour of humbugging artificiality about it. I don't like the note of its pathos and I think there's some hanky-panky about it somewhere. It contains one passage which must be an absolute lie, I should say."

"I don't know which you mean," the inspector replied, "but all the statements about himself in prison are true enough. He did have a bad illness—"

"Yes, naturally all those are true; he knew the letter would be read by the authorities, of course. I didn't mean anything of that sort. Look here, I should like to spend some time with this in a reference library. Will you meet me outside the British Museum one hour from now?"

"Right, Mr. Trent!" The detective rose quickly. "You'll find me waiting. There may be no time to lose."

But it was the inspector who found Trent awaiting him fifty minutes later, with a taxicab in attendance.

"Jump in," said Trent. "The man knows where to go. I didn't take very long after all. I even had time to dash up into Holborn and buy this." He produced a stout screwdriver from his pocket.

"What on earth for?" inquired Mr. Muirhead blankly as the cab rushed westward. "Where are we going? What have you made of the letter?"

"Inquisitive!" Trent murmured, shaking his finger at him gravely. His eyes were shining with suppressed elation and expectancy.

"What is the screwdriver for? Well, you surely will

admit that it is prudent to be armed when going after a dangerous man. I got it of Lake and Company, so I am going to call it Excalibur. Come, inspector, I ask you as a reasonable man, what else could one call it? Then, as to where we are going—we are going to Jermyn Street."

"Jermyn Street!" Mr. Muirhead was staring at his companion as at some strange animal. "You think the stuff is there?"

"I think the letter says it is—or was—hidden in old Rudmore's rooms."

"But I told you, Mr. Trent, old Rudmore was hundreds of miles away when the theft took place. His rooms were locked up."

"Yes, but isn't it likely James had a key to them? You told me they were on terms of great mutual confidence. The father was quite likely to leave a key with his son, in case it should prove useful—and a latch-key to the front door, too, I dare say."

The inspector nodded gloomily. "Yes—it's quite likely. Then I suppose your idea is, he just walked round to Jermyn Street with the pendant, let himself in, went upstairs to his father's rooms, tucked the thing away, and then strolled on to the club. . . . Certainly it's possible. Only nobody happened to think of it."

"I don't know that anything would have been found if anybody had, with all regard and reverence to you and your friends, inspector, I doubt if anything could have been done without the indications in this letter."

"Well, what does—"

"No! Here we are in Jermyn Street. What number, inspector? 230—right!" Trent leaned out of the window and instructed the driver. The cab drew up before a shoemaker's shop of such supreme distinction that only three unostentatious pairs were placed, as if they had been left there by accident, in the window. To the left of the shop was a closed private door for the use of those living in the chambers above.

The inspector's ring was answered by an extremely corpulent, mulberry-faced man with snowy side-whiskers and smooth, white hair. His precision of dress and manner, with a certain carriage of the body, proclaimed the retired butler.

"Well, Hudson, have you forgotten me?" asked the detective pleasantly, stepping into the well-kept but gloomy little hall. The stout man hesitated, then said, "Bless my soul! It's the officer who came to take Mr. Rudmore." His face lost something of its over-ripe appearance, and he added, as he closed the door, "I do hope it's not another business of that sort. My house will be getting the name of—"

"Now don't you worry yourself," the man of authority advised him. "I'm not after anybody in your house. I only want to know if the rooms that old Rudmore had are occupied at present."

"They are, inspector. They were taken, shortly after that unfortunate affair, by Captain Ainger, who has them still—a military gentleman, invalided home from India, I believe; a very pleasant, quiet gentleman—"

"Is he at home now?"

"Captain Ainger never goes out until luncheon-time."

"Then we want to see him. Don't you trouble to come up, Hudson; stairs don't agree with you, I can see that. It's the second floor, I remember."

"Second floor, and the door on the left. And I do hope, gentlemen—" Hudson withdrew, murmuring vague apprehension, and ponderously descended to the basement floor as Mr. Muirhead, followed by Trent, went up the narrow stairs.

"I thought it better," said the inspector, pausing on a stair, "to go up unannounced. He can't say he won't see us if we just walk in and make ourselves pleasant."

As the two men reached the first landing they heard the sound of a door closed gently on the one above and of light-stepping feet. A tall girl, in neat and obviously expensive tailor-made clothes, appeared at the head of the short stairway and, apparently not seeing them, stood for a moment adjusting her hat and veil. Mr. Muirhead uttered a growling cough from below, at the noise of which the young lady started slightly and hurried down the stairs. In the half-light on the landing, they received, as she passed them, an impression of shining dark hair and barely perceptible perfume. Trent looked after her meditatively as she went swiftly along the ground floor passage and let herself out.

"Smart woman," observed the inspector appreciatively, as the front door slammed.

"A fine example of healthy modern girlhood," Trent agreed. "Did you see the stride and swing as she went to the door? From the cut of her clothes I should say she was American."

There was a note in his voice which made the other look at him sharply.

"And," pursued Trent, returning his gaze with an innocent eye, "I suppose you noticed her feet and ankles as she stood up there and as she came downstairs."

"I did not," returned Mr. Muirhead gruffly. "What was there to notice?"

"Only the size," said Trent. "The size—and the fact that she was wearing a man's shoes."

For an instant the inspector glared at him wild-eyed; then turned and plunged without a word down the stairway. He reached the door and tore at the handle.

"It's locked! Double-locked from outside! Here, Hudson!" he bellowed, and swore loud and savagely as the fat man was heard shuffling across the passage in the basement below and labouring heavily up the stairs. "Give me your latch-key!" he commanded, as Hudson, with a staring housemaid in his wake, appeared, trembling and gasping. For a few moments, filled with vivid language by the enraged officer, the man fumbled at a trousers pocket. At last he produced his key. Mr. Muirhead seized it and endeavoured to thrust it into the keyhole. After half a dozen vain attempts he resigned the key to Hudson, who grasped the situation at the first try.

"I'm afraid whoever double-locked it has left the key in on the other side," he panted. "This'll never go in till the other's taken out."

Mr. Muirhead suddenly recovered his calm and stuck his hands in his pockets. "He's done us," he announced. "He could reach Piccadilly in fifteen seconds from here, without hurrying. It's a clean getaway. Probably he's bowling off in a taxi by now. Hudson, why the devil didn't you say there was a lady with the captain? I'd never have let him pass me if I'd known he was coming from these rooms."

"I never knew there was any one with him, indeed,

inspector," quavered the old man, his mind wrestling feebly with the confusion of genders. "I expect it was this girl let her in."

"How was I to know there was anything wrong?" cried the domestic, bursting into tears. "She spoke like a perfect lady and sent me up with her card and all. I never thought till this minute—"

"All right, all right, my girl," said the inspector brusquely. "You'll get into no trouble if you're straight. Hudson, I want your telephone. In the back room here? Right! And you'd better hail somebody next door and get your door opened."

The detective disappeared into the room and Hudson shuffled down the passage to the back of the building, still in a dazed condition. "What, I don't see," he mumbled, "is where she, or he, or whoever it was, got the key from." And as he said it, Trent, who had been leaning against the wall with a face of great contentment, suddenly turned and fled lightly up the stairs.

Captain Ainger's door opened easily. Captain Ainger himself, a small, crop-headed man, lay upon a sofa near the window of his tastefully furnished sitting-room. As Trent burst in a look of relief came into the captain's bewildered eyes. The rest of his face below them was covered by an improvised gag made out of a tobacco pouch and a tightly-knotted silk scarf. His ankles were tied together and his arms lashed to his sides with box cord.

He looked wretchedly uncomfortable.

Five minutes later, in answer to a call from Trent, Mr. Muirhead closed his conversation with Scotland Yard and came upstairs. He found Captain Ainger sitting in an armchair, restoring his physical tone with a deep glass of whisky and soda. To Trent's account of how he had found that ill-used officer the detective answered only with a grim nod. Then, "I suppose it was your latch-key, sir," he said to the victim.

"Yes," replied the little captain, "she took my latch-key—he did, I mean. Tell you just how it was. She sent up her card—his, I should say—well, it was a woman's card, anyhow. I put it up here." He rose and took a card from the mantelshelf.

Mr. Muirhead glanced at it with curiosity. "Of course!" he exclaimed.

"Mrs. Van Sommeren's card, is it?" asked Trent from his chair by the window.

"It is."

"And Mrs. Van Sommeren's clothes and hat, and Mrs. Van Sommeren's little bag, and Mrs. Van Sommeren's own particular perfume—they all went by us just now," Trent remarked, "in company with (I expect) Mr. Van Sommeren's shoes and Mr. James Rudmore's wig. Probably he was a little excited at seeing you, inspector, awaiting him at the bottom of the stairs. It needed some nerve for him to stand there fixing his veil without a quiver, and to trip downstairs right into your yearning embrace, as one may say."

Annoyance, self-reproach, menacing resolve, and appreciation of the comic side of the episode—all these things were in the inspector's eloquent answering grunt.

"If only he had remembered to walk along the lower passage like a lady, instead of like a champion lightweight," Trent resumed, "I don't believe the meaning of the shoes would have burst upon me as it did. I daresay his hold on himself began to go when he saw the street door and safety six steps in front of him. Yet that latch-key business was pretty coolly done. Jim is certainly a gifted amateur. But you were telling us"—he turned to the obviously mystified captain—"how she made her appearance."

"The message with the card," resumed Captain Ainger who still preserved his pained expression, "was that she would be obliged if I would answer an inquiry on a family matter. It made me feel curious, so I said I would see her. She had on a very thick veil—he had, I mean."

"Why not stick to 'she,' Captain," Trent suggested. "We should get on quicker, I think."

"Thank you," said the veteran gratefully, "I believe we should. The whole thing is so confusing, because she talked just like a woman from beginning to end. Where was I? Ah, yes! I couldn't see her face very well, but her voice and style were those of a well-bred woman. She told me that a year ago she had lost a brother who was very dear to her, and that in his death-bed he had laid what she called a sacred charge upon her. It seemed he had been befriended at some critical time, when he was in India, by an English officer of my name, of whom he had lost sight for many years. He wished her, if possible, to find out that officer and place in his hands a memento, something which had belonged to himself, in token of his undying gratitude. She had made inquiries and had found me in the first place, but understood there were others of my name in the army list."

"How did Rudmore get hold of your name, I wonder?" mused the inspector. "He only got away from Dartmoor yesterday."

"That wouldn't have been difficult for his sort of man," Trent replied. "Very likely he got it out of the housemaid who opened the door, before sending up the message."

The captain cursed the absent malefactor feebly and took another drink from his tumbler. "I confess I was rather touched. Of course, I've usually done a man a good turn when it lay in my power, but I couldn't remember having played Providence to an American at any time. So I asked what his name was. She said their name was Smith. Well, you know, I must have run across about fifty Smiths, and I told her so. Then she said she had a photograph of him with her. She took it out of her bag. It was a picture of a good-looking, youngish chap, with the name of a Philadelphia firm on the mount."

"Van Sommeren's photograph," murmured Trent. "She carried it about with her. You didn't tell me they were on their honeymoon, inspector."

"I felt sure I'd never seen the man," continued Captain Ainger, "but I took it to the window to have a good look. And the moment my back was turned she leaped on me and garotted me. There wasn't a chance for me. She was as strong as a tiger, and I'm pretty shaky from a long illness. When I was about at my last gasp she gagged me with that infernal thing, then dragged me into the bedroom and tied me up with my own cord. When I was trussed properly she went through my pockets and took my latch-key, then she carried me back to the bedroom door. She said she was so sorry to be giving me all this trouble and that she always wished women were not so dependent upon men for everything. She put her veil up a little way and helped herself to a whisky and soda and lighted one of my cigars. After that she took a screw-driver out of her bag and went to work at something behind me. I don't know in the least what she was doing; I couldn't move. It took about five minutes, I should say. Then she skipped to the window with something that looked like a wad of cotton-wool in her fingers and began gloating over something I couldn't see. She stood there a long time, smoking and looking out, and then all at once she gave a start and stared down into the street. Just after that I heard the front-door bell ring. And then she—well, she went." The captain's bronzed face went slowly scarlet to the roots of his hair.

"She said good-bye, surely," murmured Trent, looking at him attentively.

"If you must know," burst out the captain with his first show of fierceness, "she said she didn't know how to thank me, and that I was a dear, and might she give me a kiss? So she—she did it." Here his narrative dissolved into unchivalrous expressions. "And then she went out and shut the door. That's all I can tell you." He wearily resorted to his tumbler again.

Trent and the inspector, who had prudently avoided catching each other's eyes during the last part of the story, now conquered their feelings. "What I want to know now," the detective said, "is where the stuff was hidden here. Can you go straight to the place, Mr. Trent, or should we have to search?"

Trent took the convict's letter from his pocket. "Let me tell you how I got at it first," he said. "You will be interested, Captain, you read it." He handed the document to the soldier and gave him a brief account of the circumstances regarding it.

The captain, now highly interested, read it through carefully twice, then handed it to Trent again. "I don't believe I should make anything out of it in a thousand years," he said. "It seems straight enough to me. I should call it an interesting letter, that's all."

"This letter," said Trent, regarding it with a look of unstinted appreciation, "is the most interesting, by a long way, that I have ever read. It tells us, not, I think, where the pendant was hidden, but where the diamonds of the pendant were hidden by Jim Rudmore before his arrest. What Jim did with the setting I don't know, nor does it matter much. But the diamonds were concealed here; and they are now again, I am afraid, in the possession of Jim."

Inspector Muirhead made an impatient movement. "Come to the point, Mr. Trent," he urged. "What did you pick up from that letter? Where was the stuff hidden?"

"I will tell you first the things I picked up, and how. The first time I read the letter—in your presence, inspector—I checked at the statement that 'the country looks and smells like the Gelderland country around Apeldjik.' When one reads that, it naturally occurs to one's mind that Dartmoor is practically a mountain district, whereas Gelderland is a part of Holland, most of which country is actually below the sea level."

"It didn't occur to *my* mind," observed Captain Ainger.

"Therefore," pursued Trent, unconscious of him, "any similarity of look or smell would be rather curious, don't you think? Possibly that was what struck the governor of the prison and aroused his suspicions of the letter.

Well, the next thing that pulled me up was the Shakespearean reference. I knew I'd read it in Shakespeare, and yet I felt it was wrong somehow. There were some words missing, I thought. Besides, it didn't look like a prose passage; yet it didn't fit into the decasyllabic form, or any other metre. . . . The only other notion that occurred to me at first glance was that it was an odd thing to quote a German phrase where an English one would have been just as good.

"Then I took the letter to the British Museum library and sat down to the problem in earnest. I said to myself that if there was any cipher in it, it was probably impossible to get at it. But I thought it more likely that the message, if any, was conveyed in the words as they stood. So I asked myself what were the signals that it hung out to a man who would be trying to read some inner meaning into it. What things in it were, by ever so little, out of the common, so that the reader would say to himself, 'This may be a pointer'? And I had to remember that both the Rudmores were said to be clever and cultivated men, who understood each other well.

"Now, to begin with, I thought that 'the idol, whose name I forget, on your mantelshelf,' was the sort of thing Rudmore *père* would have pondered over. Of course we've all seen those little images of the Hindu goddess with ten arms. Jim Rudmore, who had lived in India for years, said he had forgotten her name. That might possibly be meant to draw attention to the name."

"It's Parvati—heard it thousands of times," the captain interjected.

"Yes, I found that name when I looked up the Hindu mythology. But there's another, by which she is known in Bengal, where the Rudmores had had their experience of India. There, my book told me, the people call her Doorga. So I noted down both names. . . . Very well; now the next passage that seemed out of the ordinary was that about 'the Gelderland country round Apeldjik.' The first thing I did was to look up Apeldjik in the gazeteer. It mentioned no such place; the nearest thing to it was a town called Apeldoorn, which was in Gelderland sure enough. Then I got a big map and went through Gelderland from end to end. As I expected, it was as flat as a board, and there was no sign of Apeldjik. But I found several towns in Holland ending in 'djik,' which shows you what a conscientious artist Jim is. Now if he had really been ill at Apeldoorn, as I expect he had been, his father would have got a hint at once. I wrote down Apeldoorn, and then I began to see light."

Mr. Muirhead rubbed his nose with a puzzled air. "I don't see—" he began.

"You will very soon. Next I turned to the odd-looking quotation from Shakespeare. On looking up 'joints' in the Cowden-Clarke Concordance, I found the passage. It's in *Henry IV.*, where Northumberland says:

"And as the wretch, whose fever-weaken'd joints,
Like strengthless hinges, buckle under life . . .

"What do you think of that?"

The inspector shook his head.

"Well, then, look at the German phrase. *Sie würden das nicht so hingehen lassen* means 'They would not allow that,' or 'They would not pass that over,' or something of that sort. Now suppose a man looking for a suggestion or hint in each of those German words."

Mr. Muirhead took the letter and conned the words carefully. "I'm no German scholar," he began, and then his eyes brightened. "Those missing words—" he said.

"Like strengthless hinges," Trent reminded him.

"Well, and here"—the inspector tapped excitedly upon the word *hingehen*—"you've got 'hinge' and 'hen' in English."

"You're there! Never mind the hen; she's not there on business. Lastly, I'll tell you a thing you probably don't know. *Schraube* is the German word for 'screw.'"

Mr. Muirhead gave his knee a violent blow with his fist.

"Now then!" Trent tore a leaf from his notebook. "I'll put down the words we've got at that were hidden." He wrote quickly and handed the paper to the inspector. Both he and Captain Ainger read the following:

Doorga.
Doorn.
Hinges.
Hinge.
Screw.

"Also," Trent added, "the word 'door' occurs twice openly in the body of the letter, and the word 'hinge' once. That was to show old Rudmore he was on the right track, if he succeeded in digging out those words. 'Good!' says he to himself. 'The loot is hidden under a screw in a hinge on a door somewhere. Then where?' He turns to the letter again and finds the only address mentioned in it is 'the old rooms in Jermyn Street.' And there you are!"

Trent took his screw-driver from his pocket and went to the open door leading into the captain's bedroom.

"Naturally it wouldn't be the outer door, as to get at the hinges one would have to have it standing open." He glanced at the hinges of the bedroom door. "These screws"—he pointed to those on the door-post half of the upper hinge—"have had their paint scratched a little."

In a minute or two he had removed all three screws. The open door sank forward slightly on the lower hinge and the upper one came away from its place on the door-post. Beneath it was a little cavity roughly hollowed out in the wood. Silently the inspector probed it with a penknife.

"The stones are gone, of course," he announced gloomily.

"Certainly, gone," Trent agreed. "The stones were in that little piece of cotton-wool the captain saw him handling."

Mr. Muirhead rose to his feet. "Well, I don't think they'll go far." As he took up his hat there was a knock at the door and Hudson entered panting, a sharp curiosity in his eyes.

"A messenger boy just brought this for you, inspector," he wheezed, handing a small package to the detective. It was directed in a delicate, sloping handwriting to "Inspector C. M. Muirhead, C.I.D., care of Captain R. Ainger, 230 Jermyn Street."

Hastily the inspector tore it open. It contained a small black suede glove, faintly perfumed. With this was a scrap of paper, bearing these words in the same writing:

"Wear this for my sake.—J. R."

[6]

TRENT AND THE FOOL-PROOF LIFT

ONE of the commonest forms of fatal accident, in the life of the town, is falling down a lift-shaft. Every coroner of large urban experience has dealt with cases by the score, whether due to short-sight, negligence, faulty construction, or defective safety mechanism. And there is another possibility.

One perfect day in June M. Armand Binet-Gailly, who held an important agency in the wine trade, left his office in Jermyn Street rather earlier than usual, and strolled homewards through the Parks to his bachelor flat at 42 Rigby Street. This was a tall old house, "converted" from the errors of its pre-Victorian youth. There were five flats, and M. Binet-Gailly's was the second above the ground-level. About 5.30—so went his statement to the police—he entered by the front door, which always stood open during the daytime, and went to the lift at the end of the hall. The lift was not at the ground floor, as he could see through the lattice gate; and he pressed the button which should bring it down. But nothing happened.

M. Binet-Gailly was very much annoyed. A portly

man, he did not relish the prospect of climbing two flights of stairs on a warm day when he had paid for lift service. He aimlessly seized and shook the handle of the lattice gate. To his amazement, the gate slid aside as if the lift were in place. It should, of course, have been impossible to move it unless the lift were there. The whole system was out of order, he thought. He put his head into the shaft and looked upwards. There was the lift; so far as he could judge, at the top floor. Then, as he drew back his head, his eye was caught by something at the bottom of the shallow well in which the lift shaft ended. There was a strong electric ceiling lamp always alight at this dark end of the hall; and it showed M. Binet-Gailly quite enough.

Like most of his countrymen, he had served in arms, and things of this kind did not upset him. Plump though he was, he began to clamber down into the well; then he bethought himself. Certainly there could be no life in that crumpled bundle of humanity. The thing to do was to leave it untouched until the arrival of the police. M. Binet-Gailly went to the door communicating with the basement, and bellowed downstairs for Pimblett, the caretaker. 42 Rigby Street, though distant by little more than the breadth of Oxford Street from the elegance of Mayfair, did not rise to the luxury of a uniformed porter, and neither Pimblett nor his wife was usually to be seen after the morning job of cleaning the hall and staircase was done.

Pimblett, who also had served in arms, and had seen more dirty work than had M. Binet-Gailly, took in the situation at a glance. Wasting no words, he strode to the hall telephone and rang up the police station. Both men then mounted the stairs to find which gate it was through which the unknown—for the face of the corpse could not be seen—had plunged to his death. On the floor immediately above M. Binet-Gailly's they found the gate drawn back. On this floor was the flat occupied by Mr. Anthony Villiers Maxwell—a young man of sporting tastes—and his valet. M. Binet-Gailly proposed ringing the bell of the flat to make inquiries; but Pimblett remarked that the police would prefer to have all that left to them.

An hour later M. Binet-Gailly, sipping a glass of Campari in his own rooms, discussed with his own servant, by name Aristide, what he had just learnt of this mysterious affair. The dead man had turned out to be his own landlord, Mr. Stephen Havelock Hermon, who had bought the house a few years before, and had installed his nephew, Anthony Maxwell, in the flat above-stairs on its falling vacant soon afterwards. There had been some slight lack of sympathy between M. Binet-Gailly and Mr. Hermon, owing to the fact that Mr. Hermon had among his eccentricities a passionate hatred of liquor in every form, and when he purchased the place had not concealed his chagrin on finding that one of the sitting tenants was engaged in the wine trade, which Mr. Hermon preferred to call the drink-traffic.

No one in the building had seen Mr. Hermon enter it that afternoon. No one had seen him at all before the finding of his body. No one had known of his intention to come to the house. Mr. Clayton Haggett, the famous surgeon, who had the top flat, had not been at home; his housekeeper had heard no ring. Anthony Maxwell also had been out, and his valet had had the afternoon "off." Aristide could vouch for it, as he had already informed the police that no one had called at M. Binet-Gailly's. Mr. Lucian Corderoy, the eminent dress designer, and his wife had both been at his shop in Malyon Street, and their "daily" servant was never in the place after twelve noon. As for Sir George Stower, the Keeper of Phœnician Antiquities at the British Museum, he was enjoying a hard-earned holiday at Margate, and his flat on the ground floor had been shut up for some days past.

"But naturally," remarked Aristide, fingering a swarthy chin, "the old gentleman wished to call upon his nephew."

"It is very probable," M. Binet-Gailly agreed. "He was devoted to that young animal, and they say he had no other relative living. The nephew will be his heir, no doubt, and he will make the money roll a little faster than the uncle ever did."

"Ah! When one is young," observed Aristide sentimentally.

"And when one is a waster by nature," M. Binet-Gailly added. "Well, Aristide, it is time for me to dress."

Philip Trent, in his first outline of the case for the readers of the *Record*, had given these facts about the other tenants of the building. "It is naturally assumed (he wrote) that Mr. Hermon had called, as he often did, to see his nephew, to whom he is said to have been much attached. His ringing at the door had been resultless, and he had turned away to go down by the way he had come. He had opened the gate, believing the lift to be in position there—and stepped out into emptiness. He was known to be extremely short-sighted. His neck, so says the police surgeon, was broken, and there were other injuries that must have been immediately fatal. When his body was found, he had been dead not more than an hour.

"This is very simple; but it leaves all the important questions unanswered.

"Why was not the lift where he expected it to be? He had only just left it; and according to the information gathered by the police there had been no one leaving or entering any of the flats since the early afternoon, when Mr. Clayton Haggett and Mr. Maxwell went out.

"Why was it at the top floor?

"How was it that he had been able to open the gate, which should have been locked automatically the moment the lift moved from that floor?

"Why was the gate on the ground floor unlocked? Why indeed? Conceivably the mechanism of the upstairs gate had gone wrong, so that Mr. Hermon could open it; but the gate at the bottom could not be opened by a dead man.

"Why were all the other gates in working order—the top gate, where the lift was, unlocked; the other two locked?

"On this very vital point I have had some conversation with the expert who was sent to investigate by the firm which built and installed the lift. The mechanism, he told me, was tested by the makers at monthly intervals, and had been in perfect order at the last examination, ten days before. The system was as nearly fool-proof as it could be. 'But,' he added, 'it isn't tool-proof. Any engineer could see with half an eye that both those locks have been forced.'

"Here are the elements of a very sinister mystery.

Some one who was not Mr. Hermon forced the ground-floor gate. Presumably he forced the other. The only persons known to have been in the house from three o'clock onwards were the caretaker in the basement, the French manservant in M. Binet-Gailly's flat, and the housekeeper in Mr. Haggett's. Did some one enter the house before Mr. Hermon; or did some one accompany him? To this point the inquiries of the police are being directed—so far, I believe, without result.

"If Mr. Hermon was a victim of violence, it is hard to think that any feeling of ill-will could have been at work. It is true that he was a man of strong opinions, often violently expressed in public controversy—the hard knocks exchanged between him and his tenant, Mr. Clayton Haggett, in their dispute over vivisection last year will be remembered. But he was always a fair and even a chivalrous fighter, on the friendliest footing with opponents to whom he was personally known. His nature was kindly and generous, his great wealth was largely devoted to works of benevolence; the hospital endowments made by him as memorials to his late wife are but a part of his service to humanity."

Trent did not try to intrude on the sorrow of Anthony Maxwell; but he had from the young man's valet, Joseph Weaver, some material information. He learned that the nephew felt his loss very deeply indeed; that he did not look like the same man. He had, Weaver said, a feeling heart. A little wild he might have been—young gentlemen would be young gentlemen—but he had what they call a nice nature. He owed everything to Mr. Hermon, who had been a father to him after his parents died when he was a child. Naturally he was very much upset.

Trent reflected privately on the deceitfulness of appearances; for he knew Anthony Maxwell by sight, and would not have said that either his eye, his mouth, or his bearing proclaimed the niceness of his nature. Perhaps Weaver was being loyal to his employer. He did not look particularly loyal; but then he did not look anything to speak of. He had the expressionlessness of his calling. His quiet voice, neat clothes, and sleek black hair suggested nothing but discretion. Trent asked a question.

Mr. Hermon, Weaver said, came up fairly often on business from his place in Surrey, and when he did so always visited his nephew. Sometimes he came on purpose to see him. No; Mr. Maxwell had not been expecting him on the day of the accident; he had given no notice that he was coming. If he had done so, Mr. Maxwell would naturally have been at home. Weaver thought it unlikely that Mr. Hermon had been intending to call on any of the other tenants. He did do so from time to time, to talk about some matters of repairs or other landlord's business; but that would always be by appointment, and not during the working day. All the tenants, Weaver pointed out, were busy men, with the exception of Mr. Maxwell; they would seldom be at home until the evening.

Yes; Mr. Hermon attended personally to the management of all his house property in the West End. There was a good deal of it, and it gave him occupation. No; he was not what they call a hard landlord; quite the contrary, Weaver would say. Mr. Hermon liked to do things for people, being a very generous man, as Weaver had good reason to know.

"You mean that he was generous to you," Trent suggested. "A present for you when he called here—that sort of thing?"

"Mr. Hermon always behaved like a gentleman," Weaver said demurely. "But I meant more than that, sir. You see, I was two years in his service before I came to Mr. Maxwell; that is how I came to know so much about his habits, and to appreciate his kindness. Then when Mr. Hermon went on a tour round the world, he suggested I should go to Mr. Maxwell, who was not satisfied with the valet he had then; and I have remained in his service since then—about nine months ago it would be."

When Trent went to talk it over with his friend Chief-Inspector Bligh, he found that officer cheerfully interested in what he described as a very nice case.

"There's nothing easy," he said, "about it so far. Of course, it's a murder—that's certain. You have heard what the lift company's man says. And, of course, it was meant to look as if it might be an accident."

"Then how about the ground-floor gate being forced as well as the other? That doesn't look like an accident."

"Well, what does it look like?" Mr. Bligh wanted to know.

"It looks to me as it looks to you, I suppose. When the old man had been pushed into the lift shaft, the murderer realized that something had gone wrong with his plan. Hermon had had something on him that might give the murderer away if it was found on the body. The only thing for him to do was to run downstairs, prise open the bottom gate, and take what he wanted off the body. If Pimblett or anybody appeared while he was doing so, he could say he had seen the old man open the gate and fall down the shaft, and had rushed down and forced the gate to see if he was still alive."

The Inspector nodded. "Yes; that's the idea. And he did get what he wanted, presumably; and nobody did see him. Of course, it's the sort of place where nobody is about most of the time, and the man who did the job knew that."

"Well, how about the people who live here? Are they all above suspicion?"

"There is no such thing," Mr. Bligh declared, "as being above suspicion—not if I do the suspecting. And it just happens that most of them haven't an alibi. The Museum man has, of course; his flat was shut up, and is still. And the Corderoys were at their dress-shop till after six. But the Frenchman was alone when he came in and reported having found the body; and his story of how he found it, and what time he entered the house, is quite unsupported. Maxwell says he lunched at his flat, went out immediately afterwards, and spent all the afternoon at Lord's watching Lancashire take a licking from Middlesex; then went to his club with some other bright boys, had drinks, and came home to dress for dinner. But Lord's is a place you can dodge out of and return to later, and it's no distance for a car to Rigby Street. Then there's Clayton Haggett, the surgeon. He had lunch in his flat too, after a morning at the hospital; went down to his car at 2.30, had an operation at a nursing-home and another at a private house; finished by 4.15, had a cup of tea, and then spent two hours driving about down Richmond way—just to take the air, and nobody with him all that time, which is a pity."

"He didn't like Hermon," Trent remarked. "He was very bitter in that tussle they had over vivisection."

"Yes, and he's got a naughty temper when he's crossed. Loses his self-control. He had to resign from the Hunter Club for knocking a man down in the smoking-room. Nobody would have anything to do with him if he wasn't such a wizard with the knife."

"And what about the servants in the building? Do they come into the picture at all?"

"All I can tell you is that none of their stories can be checked. Pimblett says he was in the basement all the afternoon until the Frenchman shouted for him; his wife was away calling on her sister in Highbury. The French manservant and Haggett's housekeeper say they never opened the doors of their flats until the police looked them up after the finding of the body. Maxwell's man says he had the afternoon off, went out after his master had gone, and sat through the cinema programme at the Byzantine, getting back a little before Anthony did. Well, what good's that? Like the other three, he can't prove anything at all about where he was for some hours before the police were called in."

"Any of them ever been in trouble?"

"Nothing known against any of them. Ex-Sergeant Pimblett—excellent record. Mrs. Hargreaves, the housekeeper—ditto. Weaver used to be employed at Harding's, the big barbershop in Duke Street, where old Hermon used to go when he was in town. He always had

Weaver to attend to him, and at last he took him on as his valet. Afterwards—"

"Yes, he told me; he was switched on to Anthony. Perfectly respectable. And the French domestic?"

"All I know about Aristide Recot is that he has a wooden face and side-whiskers, and doesn't mind being seen in an apron. What I'm told by his master is that he has been with him for some years, and given every satisfaction. But what's the use? We had to consider the servants, of course; but what motive could any of them have had? It's a different thing when you come to their employers. Haggett, for instance."

Trent looked the Inspector in the eyes. "You were talking about motive," he said gently. "Is Haggett's resentment really the strongest you can think of? I don't like being teased."

"All right; I was coming to it," Mr. Bligh responded with a faint grin. "Yes, I suppose the expectation of coming into the greater part of a very large fortune might operate as a motive. That is what Maxwell will do, according to our information. Unless something happens to him. His uncle made him a very generous allowance, and he lived rent-free, and Weaver's wages were paid by the old man. Maxwell ought to have been grateful, and perhaps he was; but there you are—he's a vicious young brute, and always in debt; and though Hermon wasn't strong, he might have lived to any old age. Now then! Will that do for you?"

"Something of the sort had crossed my mind," Trent admitted. "Certainly it will do—until something better comes along."

Mr. Bligh raised an impressive finger. "And now," he said, "I'll tell you something that hadn't crossed your mind. It's information received. If it's right, the coroner will hear it at a later stage, but at present we would rather the murderer didn't know about it. You remember I mentioned that Clayton Haggett left his flat at 2.30 that afternoon. Well, he had more to tell us than that. He went down by the lift, he said. It's rather a slow-motion lift. As it passed down by the floor below—Anthony's floor—Haggett heard some words spoken. He could see as he passed that the door of the flat was just being opened from inside, and as it opened he heard a loud, bullying voice call out, 'You do what I say, and look sharp about it. If you get on the wrong side of me, you know what to expect.' That is as near as Haggett can go to the actual words he heard—I asked him to be particular."

Trent stared at the Inspector with kindling eyes. "You do like saving up the best bit to the last, don't you? And you had this—this!—simply handed to you. On a plate."

"With parsley round it," added Mr. Bligh, unashamed.

"I have heard you use that phrase before," Trent said thoughtfully. "It meant, I think, that you were rather mistrustful of good things that came so easily. But now, what about this remarkable addition to the record? Did Haggett recognize the voice? Did he see anybody?"

"No. Haggett says it might have been Maxwell he heard talking; but he only knows Maxwell by sight, has never spoken to him, and has no idea what his voice would sound like if it was raised. And, of course, it might have been anybody else in the world. Then I asked him what class of voice it was—like a curate's, or a dustman's, or what. All he could tell me was that it was not a coarse voice, and not a refined one; just middling. Very useful! But that isn't all. As the lift got to the bottom, he heard a door above slam violently, which he assumed to be the one he had just seen being opened; and as he was getting into his car, Maxwell came out of the street door, with his hat on, looking furiously angry and very red in the face, and walked away rapidly."

Trent considered this. "So that is Haggett's information. And what does Maxwell say about it?"

"He hasn't been asked—yet. He is being given a little more time to make mistakes. But, of course, it may all be a lie. Yes, you may look surprised; but Haggett isn't out of it yet, as I told you. There's another piece of news I've got for you, which certainly isn't a lie. When Jackson did the post mortem, he found something that wants a lot of explaining."

"What! Another thing you are keeping dark?"

"For the present. He noticed that the finger nails of the right hand looked as if they had been scratching hard at something, and there was a very faint odour that he couldn't place; so he took some scrapings from the nails to be analysed. They found some tiny scraps of human skin; also traces of some things with hydrocarbo scientific names that don't seem to tell you much, and one thing that I have heard of quite often before."

"Yes. What?"

"Chloroform."

Thinking it over in his studio, Trent could make no more of this at first than Mr. Bligh and he had made between them. If there had been a struggle, and if chloroform had been used, it did seem to point to the one resident in the house who might be presumed to know all about chloroform and what could be done with it. And Haggett was known to be a hot-tempered man and a good hater, as well as a very able and successful professional man—not an unknown combination of qualities. But Trent found it hard to believe in such a character expressing its dislike in murder done by tricky and treacherous means. A quarrel; yes. An assault; possibly. An assault with a fatal result, legally a murder; such things did happen. But a planned and cold-blooded crime, with the murderer scheming to avoid detection by means of a trumped-up tale—Trent did not see it. In his experience, trained faculties, high responsibility, and professional distinction did not go with dirty actions and circumstantial lying.

But if Haggett's story of what he had heard and seen was true, how could it be fitted to the known facts? Maxwell's own statement about the time at which he had left the building agreed with Haggett's. Weaver's statement was that he had, as was natural, gone out a little later. Both of them had said nothing of this loud-voiced unknown who had used threatening language in Maxwell's flat. It might have been Maxwell himself. Could it have been Hermon? But Hermon had been fond, even foolishly fond, of his nephew. Unless—and here opened a new vista of ugliness—both Maxwell and his servant had been concealing the truth on that point, building up the fiction of a generous benefactor whom for worlds Maxwell would not have injured. There might be purpose enough in their doing so. The Inspector had not thought of that; at least (Trent reflected with a wry smile) he had not mentioned it. Hermon's visit, by the way, had been a surprise visit, according to Weaver.

Trent, at this point in his meditations, rose and began to pace the studio. Soon he went across to the model's dressing-room and examined his appearance in the mirror there. His hair had been cut fairly recently, but another trimming would not upset the balance of nature, he thought. Within the hour he was one of a dozen sheeted forms, sitting in a strange chair before a tall mirror, and had met the attendant's opening comment on the warmth of the day with the due rejoinder that it looked like rain later on.

Trent, like many other men, found his thoughts the clearer for being written down, and would often prepare for the drafting of a dispatch that could be published by a private memorandum including all that could not. That evening he sat at his bureau, and did not rise until the account of what he had discovered, and the conclusions drawn, was complete in black and white.

"Starting with the belief that Haggett's story was true (he wrote), I had to make out who the person in Maxwell's flat was who gave some order, in offensive words, coupled with a vague threat; and who the person ordered about and theatened was. As Bligh said, it might have been any one who used those words; some one who had not as yet come into view in the case. But it was as well to consider first those who were known to have been in the place; and one of these was Hermon. But the accounts we had of Hermon made this seem unlikely; and they were not only the accounts given by Maxwell and his valet. Hermon's general reputation was that of a man who would be the last in the world to bully and threaten.

As for the others who had been in the other flats, there was no visible shadow of a reason for suspecting any one of them.

"There remained Maxwell and his valet.

"Maxwell might be capable of bullying and threatening. He is not a nice young man. Could he have been the speaker, and either Hermon or Weaver the man spoken to?

"Well, is it likely? Maxwell is not a lunatic. No man in his senses would talk like that to his rich uncle, whose fortune he expected to inherit; nor to his valet unless he was prepared for the man leaving him on the spot, and for being obliged to do his own valeting and cooking and housework until he could get another servant. Unless, of course, he had got either of them under his thumb in some way. Has Hermon, or Weaver, a guilty past, known to Maxwell?

"I had got as far as this when a new point occurred to me. Weaver, when I saw him, had told me that Maxwell had not been expecting his uncle's visit. As this looked very much like a plain lie, I thought some attention paid to Weaver might be worth the trouble; and so I went and had my hair cut at Harding's.

"The man who cut it was as ready for conversation as barbers usually are. I spoke of the fatal accident to Mr. Hermon, and the barber, who may have been reading my own remarks on the subject, said that it was a funny sort of accident, giving his reasons for that view. Then I mentioned that I knew Mr. Hermon's former valet had once had a job at Harding's. The man remembered both of them very well. He only wished he had the chance of bettering himself as Weaver had done. He had not known that Weaver had become Mr. Maxwell's valet; but he had known that Weaver had done very well for himself. Besides that, Weaver had come into a bit of money of his own; he had mentioned it confidential. He was quite the gentleman now, especially in the last six months. He had taken to having his hair done at Harding's once a fortnight, probably just to show off a bit among his old pals. Gold wrist-watch, diamond tie-pin, quite the swell. Liked to do himself well, too, in his time off; and why not if you could run to it? Sometimes he would have my barber and other friends from Harding's to meet him after hours, and would stand drinks like a lord; and you could always see he had had a few beforehand.

"So far, my visit to Harding's had yielded more than I had any right to expect. But this was not all. My man came at length to that stage of the proceedings at which it is usual for the barber to hint delicately that the condition of one's scalp is not all that could be wished, and that this could be remedied by the use of some sort of hair-wash. With a flash of inspiration, I asked what Weaver was in the habit of buying for himself. The best hair-tonic there is, said my barber with enthusiasm; Harding's own preparation, Capillax—just the thing for me; and I would understand that Weaver knew, as a hair-dresser, how excellent it was. I thought, when I was told the price of it, that Weaver also knew how impressively costly it was. I was shown a bottle of Capillax; a green, fluted bottle, with NOT TO BE TAKEN stamped in the glass. Why, I asked my barber, should I be forbidden to take Capillax, if I should choose to buy Capillax?

"He turned the bottle over, and showed me on the back a tiny pasted label. It read:

This preparation, containing among other valuable ingredients a small amount of Chloroform, is in accordance with the Pharmacy Act hereby labelled POISON.

"I ordered a bottle, of course. I thought my barber had earned his commission on the sale. And I asked him if he could tell me why chloroform should be used in a tonic for the hair, because I had thought it was for putting people to sleep. He said, yes, but that was only the vapour of chloroform; in solution it acted as a stimulant to the skin, and had cleansing properties.

"My reconstruction of this crime is that Weaver planned the murder of Hermon. He had found out something that Maxwell did not dare have known about himself; he put the screw on him and bled him for every shilling he could raise. A servant who knows too much about his employer is a figure common enough in the odorous annals of blackmail. Weaver had 'come into money' indeed! Probably he got rid of a lot of it by betting. Anyhow, the more he got, the more he wanted. He had tasted easy money; he could not do without it; and there was no more in sight. But he knew that Maxwell, when his uncle died, would be a rich man. Weaver thought it over; and he formed a plan, to be carried out the first time that opportunity offered.

"On the morning of Hermon's death Maxwell heard, by letter or telephone, that his uncle intended to call that afternoon. Weaver's tale, that the old man had given no notice of his coming, was hardly credible. It was the height of summer, and it was utterly unlikely that Maxwell would be staying indoors that afternoon unless he was expecting a visitor. Hermon would certainly have let him know he was coming. This was what Weaver had been waiting for. After lunch he told Maxwell to leave the flat, go somewhere where he could mix with friends, and stay away until dinner-time. I do not believe Maxwell knew what was intended, because Haggett's story makes it plain that he protested against this. He did not see why he should deliberately absent himself when his uncle had asked him to be at home; why should he affront the old man? Weaver then went to the door of the flat, and as he opened it he raised his voice in the bullying words that Haggett caught as the lift went down. Maxwell, in a furious temper, did as he was told.

"When Hermon arrived, coming up by the lift, Weaver opened the door to him. He framed some lie to account for Maxwell's absence, and asked him to come in, perhaps for a rest and a cup of tea. Hermon did so; and while he was alone in the sitting-room, Weaver slipped out, took the lift to the floor above, and forced the lift-gate on Maxwell's floor. When the old man went, Weaver saw him to the lift, opened the gate, and thrust him into the empty shaft. He knew better than most people how bad Hermon's sight was, and how little strength he had for a struggle. And here the plan went wrong. Hermon realized at the last instant that the lift was not there, and grabbed at Weaver as he felt the push given him. His right hand clutched Weaver's hair, tearing some of it out as he fell to his death, and lacerating the man's scalp.

"Weaver had seen instantly that if hair was found in the dead man's hand there would be an end of the theory that he had met with an accident. The police would be looking for a man with black hair and a scratched head; and they would not have far to look. There was only one thing for it. Weaver ran down to the ground floor, forced the gate there, stepped into the well, and carefully removed the hair he found in the dead man's grasp. There was nothing else he could do. He must simply stick to the story he had already made up, and trust to luck. After all, as far as he knew, there had been no witness whatever to anything that had passed."

It was late by the time Trent had finished his memorandum. He read and re-read it; then slipped it into an envelope, addressed it to Mr. Bligh at Scotland Yard, went out and registered it at the district post office.

Trent was at work in his studio next morning when the telephone bell called him.

Mr. Bligh, not an effusive man by nature, said that Trent's report had reached him. "There's no doubt but what you're right," he went on. "It's a pity, though, that we shall never hear what it was Weaver knew about Maxwell. It might very well have been a job for us."

"Well, you called him a vicious young brute," Trent said. "With my morbid imagination and your fund of horrid experience, we ought to be able to guess a few of the things that it might have been. But why do you say you will never know? If you bring the murder home to Weaver, he will probably give Maxwell away, having no further use for his secret. It would be just like him."

"Weaver won't do that." There was a note of grimness in the Inspector's voice. "At 8.15 last night Weaver was on his way down Coventry Street. He had been drinking, and couldn't walk straight. A dozen people saw him stumble off the kerb and into the road, right under a passing bus. He was killed instantly. His injuries—"

"Thanks, I don't want to hear about his injuries." Trent wiped his brow. "They were fatal—that's enough for me."

"Yes, but there were some that weren't fatal. On the head, concealed by the hair, there were four deep scratches, not completely healed, and the signs of some hair having been torn out by the roots. I thought you'd like to know."

7

THE OLD-FASHIONED APACHE

When Dr. Francis Howland was attacked and left for dead in Stark Wood, near his house at Wargate, none of his many friends could imagine an explanation of the apparently motiveless crime. Among them was Sir James Molloy, editor of that powerful morning newspaper the *Record*, who often made one of the little company that welcomed Dr. Howland whenever he appeared at the Russell Club; and it was at Sir James's request that Philip Trent went down to Wargate next day "to see what he could make of the mystery" for Sir James's paper.

Trent, once on the spot, could make little enough of it at the outset; and the police, so far as he could discover, were equally at a loss. But he was able to add to the few bare facts reported in the first accounts of the crime, and to supply from his own knowledge, as Sir James had suggested, some details of the victim's unusual career. Sitting in his room at the Packhorse and Talbot Inn, he drew up a dispatch to reach London by train that evening.

"Dr. Howland (he wrote) has lived for some two years in this charming corner of Sussex at his little house Fairfield, his establishment consisting of a secretary, a housekeeper, and a domestic servant. Fairfield lies on the outskirts of Wargate village, and it has been his habit to take an hour's walk, usually alone, each evening before dinner in the surrounding country. Yesterday (Sunday) he went out as usual about 5.30.

"At about 6.15 Mr. Derek Scotson, walking on the main road from Wargate to Bridlemere with his spaniel, heard the dog barking excitedly behind him, and turning back he was guided by the sound to a spot, not far from the road, in Stark Wood, which lies to the left of it. He found the dog standing by a man's body, lying prone on the footpath, but with the right side of the face visible; and he at once recognized Dr. Howland, who was well known to him. He could see that the back of the head was terribly injured, and at first he believed that Dr. Howland was dead; but a movement of the features told him that it was not so, and Mr. Scotson, ordering his dog to stand guard over the victim, hurried off to the roadside telephone-box which he knew to be not far away.

"He rang up the police in Bridlemere, reporting the facts and asking them to send a doctor, as there is none living in Wargate; then rang up Dr. Howland's, intending to ask that Mr. Gemmell, the secretary, should bring first-aid equipment to Stark Wood immediately. Neither Mr. Gemmell nor the maid, however, was in the house at the time, and the housekeeper, who is very deaf, did not hear the bell. Mr. Scotson had therefore to leave the unconscious man still in charge of his dog while he stood at the roadside to halt the police car when it should arrive. Fortunately it was soon on the spot, accompanied by a motor ambulance. The doctor, after attending to the wounded man, removed him to the cottage hospital at Bridlemere, while the police, in the now failing light, made such beginning as they could in the search for traces.

"Dr. Howland's injuries were found to be serious enough, though probably not fatal. He had been struck more than once on the back of the head with some heavy weapon, possibly an iron bar, and at 4 p. m. to-day he was still unconscious. Detective-Inspector Clymer, continuing his investigation this morning, found a number of footprints in the damp soil of the path. He formed the opinion that Dr. Howland had been followed into the wood from the open field beyond it by his assailant, who had afterwards gone off at a run by the way he came. It seems likely that Dr. Howland owes his life to Mr. Scotson's dog, whose barking may well have frightened off the ruffian before his brutal work was done.

"From my own knowledge I may recall some leading facts about the career of Dr. Howland, which is better known to the French public than to his countrymen. Before his retirement, he had for many years a remarkable place in the legal world. He was born and brought up in Paris, where his father was the correspondent of an important newspaper. He was educated in England. At Oxford he studied law with brilliant success, and took, later, his doctorate in that school. After being called to the Bar, he returned to Paris, where he qualified as an advocate, and built up a practice among British subjects engaged in litigation, or faced with prosecution, in the French courts. This was soon extended to other foreigners in Paris; for Dr. Howland was a notable linguist, having mastered half a dozen continental tongues with extraordinary facility, and speaking them as readily as English and French. It was said of him (untruly) that if a client applied to him whose language he did not know, Dr. Howland would make an appointment with him for the following day, by which time he would be ready to discuss his case with him fluently and idiomatically in his own native speech.

"In this corner of his profession the Doctor made for himself a unique and very profitable place. He was best known to the public as a defender of accused persons, and as the deadliest cross-examiner of his day. At the same time he had won distinction among legal scholars with a few volumes on comparative jurisprudence. When I was living in Paris I met Dr. Howland more than once, and was struck by the gravely handsome presence and splendid voice which were so effective in the French tribunals.

"Dr. Howland had certainly made at least a moderate fortune at the French Bar, but much of it, according to rumour, had been sunk for ever in the financing of a new health resort in the Puy-de-Dôme which came to nothing. Then one day an aunt of the King of Annam, in French Indo-China, was accused by a mandarin, her enemy, of attempting to poison M. de Choiselle, the Resident-Superior, and Dr. Howland was offered an enormous fee by the King to leave his practice and go out to defend the lady. He spent six months in Hué, routed a dozen bought witnesses, saved his client, and at once decided to retire on his gains and settle down in England.

"So he came to Wargate, an elderly bachelor in easy circumstances. There he has lived in scholarly peace, working at another book, entertaining a few friends, and running up frequently to town for luncheon at the Russell Club, where his wit and his fund of curious experience have made him the centre of an admiring cirle. No man could be more liked and respected, and his being made the subject of a murderous attack has been heard of with no less amazement than concern."

At breakfast next morning Trent had the coffee-room to himself. As he was filling a pipe he heard a car draw up at the inn, and presently Inspector Clymer, whose acquaintance Trent had already made, ushered in to him a slim, hard-looking man who, Trent decided privately, would be at his best on horse-back in a weather-beaten scarlet coat. After this personage came young Mr. Gemmell, Dr. Howland's secretary, with whom also Trent had had some talk the day before.

"Can I have a word with you, Mr. Trent?" the slim man said. "My name's Hildebrand—Captain Hildebrand—Chief Constable in these parts."

Trent, who asked nothing better than this, said he would be glad if he could be of any use, and drew out chairs for Captain Hildebrand and the two others.

"Well, you may be of more use than any of us are, as it happens," the captain said, biting off the end of a cigar. "You understand our work, I know, and it seems you have lived in Paris and knew something of Dr. Howland. I read that article with your name at the top of it in the paper this morning."

"What is the news of the old gentleman?" Trent asked.

"Pretty good. They feel sure now that he'll get over it. I saw him last night. He was getting his wits back, and I think he knew me. Well now, I made this an early call, because I wanted to be sure of finding you, and I picked up Mr. Gemmell on my way, thinking he might be able to throw some light on the subject. I'll tell you what it is. When Inspector Clymer was going over the ground yesterday, he found two bits of paper, pieces of a torn-up letter, lying near the footpath through Stark Wood and close to where you come into it from the field—that's to say, about thirty yards from where the Doctor was found. Is that right, Clymer?"

"That's the measurement I made," said the inspector.

"Now, what is written on these pieces of paper seems to be in some sort of French. I can read French pretty well, and I've shown them to one of my superintendents who knows the language thoroughly, and neither of us can make head or tail of some of it. I've got them here, and I should like to hear what you think about it."

Captain Hildebrand produced from his pocket a letter-case, and extracted from it two battered scraps of note-paper which he handed to Trent. They bore a few lines written in a sprawling but sufficiently legible hand.

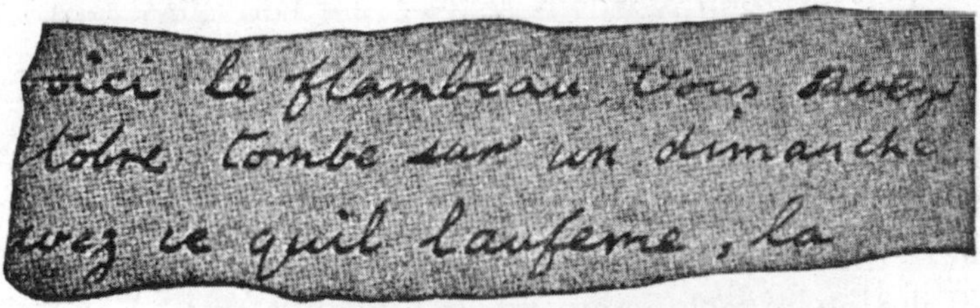

voici le flambeau. Vous avez
tobre tombe sur un dimanche
avez ce quil laufeme, la

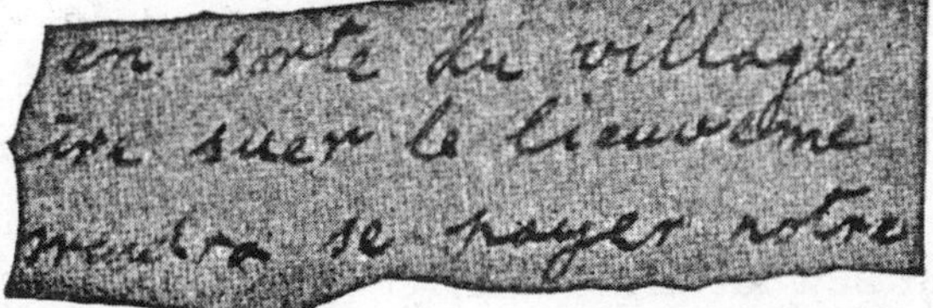

en sorte du village
ire suer le lieuveme
mentra se payer notre

Trent frowned over the sordid-looking scrawl for a few minutes. He held the bits of paper up to the light, while Captain Hildebrand and the inspector exchanged significant glances.

"There are some curious points about all this," Trent said at last. "Whoever wrote it knew French well enough—"

"Damned queer French too," the captain interjected.

"Almost too queer," Trent agreed. "But what I was saying is that he didn't know it thoroughly. You see this about some date in October falling on a Sunday—possibly that refers to the day of the crime, Sunday the fourteenth. Well, I can't see any Frenchman writing, or saying, 'tombe sur un dimanche.' He would write 'tombe un dimanche,'—that is the universal idiom, as far as I know. I doubt if this man is a Frenchman at all."

"Ha!" the captain exclaimed. "Now we're getting somewhere. What else?"

"The puzzling words here"—Trent laid the scraps on the table—"are queer French, as you say. They belong to a sort of thieves' patter, the same sort of thing as the old back-slang in the English underworld—only not so simple. You take a word, cut off the first letter and stick it on to the end, then put an L at the beginning, and finish off the job by tacking on the final syllable 'eme.' Louchébème, it's called—because the butchers of the Paris abattoirs invented it before the apaches took it up. You see: boucher—ouchéb—louchéb—louchébème."

"Golly, what a lingo!" Captain Hildebrand observed. He was keenly interested. The inspector's face expressed a certain bewilderment; Mr. Gemmell's nothing whatever. "Well then, what about 'laufème' and 'lieuvème'? I don't seem to get it."

"Why, that's another point, and an important one. You see, louchébème was a *spoken* secret language; it was meant to keep anybody guessing who heard you talking about your private affairs—not for letter-writing. That being so, any silent letters would be dropped out. Well then, 'laufème' gives you 'fau' and 'lieuvème' gives you 'vieu.' "

Captain Hildebrand bent over the writing. "Yes, of course—'vieu' is 'vieux,' the old man. We're getting on! But what do you make of 'fau,' then? Oh yes, I see! He must have written, 'Vous something-or-other ce qu'il faut.' It would be, 'You know what is necessary,' I dare say."

"Yes, probably. But what is odd about all this is that it's a good many years since I lived in Paris, and learnt about louchébème. Half my friends there knew about it too. We used to use louchébème words for fun. And of course that meant that the crooks had given it up; a slang that everybody understands is no good to them. I did hear, in fact, that they had got another called javanais; and the mere fact that I heard of it probably meant that it was already disused. So you see how strange it all is—a man apparently trying to write like a French crook, and not, I think, succeeding.

"You see the same thing in that word 'flambeau.' He seems to have written 'Voici le flambeau.' That used to be thieves' slang for 'This is the affair,' or 'the business'—I've come across it in novels as old as *Les Misérables*, as old as Dickens. It's like a modern English crook talking about 'cly-faking,' or calling the police 'slops.' And you can say the same about the word 'suer.' If he wrote 'faire suer le lieuvème'—make the old man sweat—it would mean in slang of the Bill Sikes vintage 'kill the old man.' Which somebody tried to do. There you are, Captain Hildebrand." Trent handed the pieces of paper to him. "I'm sure I hope you enjoy hearing lectures."

"Some lectures." The captain had a pleasant smile. "Then what it comes to is that this is just a blind, planted near the scene of the crime for us to pick up. Somebody being clever, in fact. And we had already come to the conclusion that it's in a disguised hand. Now, what about the watermark? I saw you spotted that. You can see on the long slip the end of a word, 'KOLAJ.'

"Or a name. Well, you know as much about that as I do. Words ending with a J don't belong at this end of Europe; at the other end they're as common as blackberries. Our friend couldn't have faked that, anyhow."

"Just so. It's another point for us to think about. Now, I told you I thought Mr. Gemmell here might be able to help us possibly, with you in support, as it were, Mr. Trent—knowing all you do about the Doctor's life abroad. You attended to his correspondence, Mr. Gemmell, I suppose?"

Mr. Gemmell's tight-lipped Scottish mouth opened for the first time since he had entered the room. "I made yesterday a full statement about myself and my recent movements to Inspector Clymer," he said. "Perhaps you have not seen it, Captain Hildebrand."

"Not yet."

"Well, I mentioned in it the fact that I have been only three weeks in Dr. Howland's employment. Until I came, he had done without a secretary. So it's not much that I can tell you about his correspondence."

"Hm! That's a pity," the captain said. "What I was going to ask is whether he had ever received anything in the nature of threatening letters, or ever answered anything of that kind."

"I cannot say what he may have received or what he may have answered personally," said Mr. Gemmell with caution. "From my brief experience I would say that his correspondence was not large. Since I came, he has dictated only a few letters to me, all of a business or formal character. My work was principally in connection with his legal studies and the book that he was writing." Mr. Gemmell produced a notebook from his breast-pocket. "I have here my shorthand notes of the letters I took. The addresses were E. L. Chambers & Son, booksellers, 92 Ermine Street, London; Mr. H. T. Saltwell, tailor, 143 Jermyn Street, London; the Manager, Henson's Bank, Bridlemere; Messrs. Quin & Barnard, stockbrokers, 54 Copthall Avenue, London; the Editor of *The Deipnosophist*, 11 Henrietta Street, London; the Secretary of the Cassowary Club, Singapore; Mr. L. G. Minks, antique dealer, 38 Godden Street, Maidstone. And the Bridlemere Gas Company, Bridlemere. That's all."

"None of them any use to us, I should think," Captain Hildebrand said. "Well, Clymer, you and I must be getting along. Sorry to have brought you here for nothing, Mr. Gemmell. We shan't be going by Fairfield again, or I'd offer you a lift back. Very many thanks for your help, Mr. Trent—your very valuable help. Good morning."

The captain and his satellite went briskly out. Mr. Gemmell rose and began to follow them at a more leisurely pace, paying no attention to Trent; but at a word from him the young Scotsman paused.

"I am thinking about one of those names you read out to us, Mr. Gemmell," Trent said. "Chambers & Son, of Ermine Street. You have your note of the letter. As it is only a business letter, would it be in order for you to tell me what was in it? It has just occurred to me that there might be something worth following up."

Mr. Gemmell regarded him with a wooden face for a few moments. "In my opinion," he then said, "it would be highly irregular. It is no part of my duty to give such information to any private individual. Good morning to you." And he walked out.

Trent, not at all discomposed by a snub which he had fully expected, set off for London in his car a little later. During the hour's run, he gave more thought to the question he had broached so unsuccessfully to the faithful Gemmell, and decided in favour of a little scouting. He had never had any dealings with the firm of Chambers & Son; but he happened to know—most people interested at all in the book world knew—that they specialized in foreign literature, stocking the books of the day in half a dozen languages, and would procure for a purchaser any foreign book that was still on sale. And was there not a foreign flavour about the whole business, about all of Dr. Howland's record, about the relic of French or pseudo-French script on which his advice had been sought? It was, he thought, a trail worth following. He would assist the police, and incidentally the *Record*, and satisfy his own inquisitive taste, by following it himself.

A little before noon he visited Chambers's establishment. The only shopman visible was attending to a customer, and Trent wandered among the neatly-kept shelves and tables, with their array of paper-covered volumes, until a little man wearing pince-nez, and radiating consciousness of his own importance, came down a staircase at the back and asked if there was anything he required. Trent, visited by an inspiration, wondered if a copy of Victor Hugo's *Quatre-Vingt-Treize* was to be had; the shopman, with the negligent air of a conjurer producing a rabbit from a hat, at once fished out the book from the recesses of a deep drawer.

Trent, showing himself properly impressed, talked with the little man, who seemed to have read, or to know all about, everything in the shop, and was very willing to display his erudition. When at length Trent asked if his friend Dr. Howland was a customer of Chambers's, the man shook his head. He did not know the name, he said; though any one, of course, could buy books without the person who served him knowing who he was.

Trent, presuming on his having made a purchase, next asked to see the manager, whose name, he was told, was Mr. Nauck, and whom he saw in a little office on the first floor. Mr. Nauck was a tall and bulky person, shaven-faced and crop-headed, whose correct and fluent English was marred only by a slight difficulty with the letters W and V. He knew Dr. Howland by name, but not as a client of Chambers's; he had been shocked to read of the brutal assault made upon him.

Had no letter been received from Dr. Howland? None, said Mr. Nauck. The firm dealt with a very large correspondence, both home and foreign; but Mr. Nauck had an excellent memory, and he was sure that there had been no such letter. In any case, if the letter had been received, it could easily be traced through the firm's files. Could Trent give the date of it?

Trent knew only that it had been dictated at some time during the past three weeks. Mr. Nauck, after a reference to his filing cabinet, declared positively that no letter from any one of the name of Howland had been received for a clear month past. It was clear that if the letter had been written, it had somehow gone astray. He was sorry to have been of no assistance to Trent, and took leave of him with a Nordic bow.

The little shopman was putting on his hat and overcoat, it being no doubt his time for lunch, as Trent passed through the shop on his way out. He returned to his house in Grove End Road, and passed an hour in mental review of the facts; then wrote and posted a letter to Inspector Clymer at Bridlemere.

The inspector met Trent the next morning, as he had suggested in his note, at a teashop in Ermine Street at the hour of noon. From a table by the window, Chambers' shop, on the other side of the way, was well in view; and they sat down to cups of coffee.

"I don't know what to make of your letter, Mr. Trent," Inspector Clymer began. "You say you think you may have got a line. You don't say much more and if it wasn't that you have a reputation, and the way you dealt with those bits of writing, I don't know that I should be justified in leaving my investigation on the spot. Not that it's led to anything yet. It isn't easy to trace a man that you know nothing about but the size of his foot. Nobody in the Wargate neighbourhood noticed any stranger about the place that evening. He could have got away by car, or cycle, or train from Bridlemere, or any of three coach-services that halt near the station. Nobody there could give me anything—why should they? There's plenty of traffic on Sunday evenings."

"And I suppose Dr. Howland has not been able to say anything yet. Is he doing as well as they expected?"

"Making a wonderful recovery, they say. He is conscious, and able to speak, but not much. The doctor allowed me to see him early this morning, and stood over me while I put a question or two on the main point—whether he saw anything of the man who attacked him. Nothing at all, the old man whispered—I could barely make out what he was saying. But he had heard the man talking to himself after he coshed him—something about 'smash you,' 'trying to smash me,' and then 'think nobody's a swell but yourself.' Which doesn't seem to make much sense. After that, he says, he heard Edward barking—that's the dog, we all know him in Bridlemere—and then he passed out. That was all I got; they wouldn't let me question him any further. But it does tell us something. If those bits of a letter were dropped by the criminal on purpose, which I think is a moral certainty, they were dropped by a man who spoke English, and what you might call colloquial English at that, when he thought he had knocked a man silly, and fully intended to finish him off properly."

Trent nodded. "And a man who talks to himself in English—"

"Is not a Frenchman, anyway; or any other kind of foreigner. It shows you we're right about those scraps being a blind, Mr. Trent, and that somebody was being clever, as the captain says. And now about that letter you wanted a copy of. I saw Gemmell this morning, and asked him to type it out for me from his shorthand note. He thought it over, and then said that in his opinion the proper procedure would be for me to take his carbon copy of the letter as sent. When I thanked him, he said it was his duty to assist the police, and that he would require a receipt. Well, I thought, Lord knows what will happen to the West Sussex Force if we lose this precious document; so I had it copied at the station, and here's one that you can keep—have it framed, if you like."

Trent took the envelope from him, and glanced over the contents. "You shouldn't let Gemmell annoy you. He is the slave of duty, and he isn't one of the glad hearts, without reproach or blot, who do its work and know it not. Well, Inspector, I am glad you got this. I think it is going to be helpful. Let me just go through it again."

The letter ran as follows:

FAIRFIELD,
WARGATE,
SUSSEX.
24th September, 19–

Messrs. E. L. Chambers & Sons,
92 Ermine Street,
London, W.1.

Dear Sirs,

Some weeks ago I asked your firm to procure for me the following books:

Darstellung der Leibnitzschen Philosophie
By Ludwig Feuerbach
Die Grundformen der Gesellschaft
By Eugen Eschscholz

When I visited your shop to give this order, I took the trouble, in order to prevent mistakes, to spell carefully the titles and the authors' names to the person who took the order.

After about a fortnight, having heard nothing from you, I wrote to a friend of mine in Leipzig, who sent me the books required. They arrived this morning.

I think that if it is not worth your while to make inquiry for books not published recently, and possibly seldom asked for, I should have been told so.

Yours faithfully,

Trent looked up at the inspector. "A very nasty letter indeed," he remarked approvingly. "Clear, precise, not a word wasted, and yet calculated to make Chambers & Son foam at their respective mouths. Did you ask, as I suggested, if it was quite certain the letter had been signed and posted?"

"Yes. Gemmell was quite sure of it."

"All right. Now, Inspector, I am going to explain to you what my notion is, but time presses, it's nearly 12.30. I want to confront Chambers' manager with this letter, and I want to do so while his chief assistant is not within call. The assistant goes out to lunch, unless I'm mistaken, just about now, and if you will take it on trust from me, you ought to have a look at him while I am interviewing the boss. If you will do that, and meet me here in half an hour, say, I'll tell you the whole thing." Trent paused, his eye on Chambers' doorway. "I may say it's possibly a chance for you, if you care about that."

"You bet I do!" said Inspector Clymer fervently. "Here! Is that him coming out now—the cocky little chap?"

"That's the man. Is it a cosmic law, d'you think, that conceited men's hats are always too small?" But the inspector, in no mood for probing the mysteries of the universe, was already at the door, bent on not losing sight of the little man.

"Vell, Mr. Trent," the manager said, as he took the copy from its envelope, "I shall be interested to see this letter. If it is as you say, I ought to see it, as I deal with the firm's correspondence, and it should haf been delivered here—" he glanced at the date—"nearly three weeks ago."

Mr. Nauck read; and as he did so his broad, bland face was transfigured to a mask of rage. As he finished the last paragraph, he struck the table with an enormous fist and exploded in a seven-syllable German oath; then, curbing his emotion with obvious difficulty, he turned to his visitor.

"I beg you to excuse me, Mr. Trent. Perhaps you don't see vot a bad business this is. It comes to this: that I am being deceived by a man I haf trusted. It is evident that my chief assistant, Mr. Votkin, took that order, and nefer passed it on to me, as he should haf done, for the sending of the necessary letters."

"But he might have mislaid it and then forgotten it," Trent suggested.

"Yes, that vas going to be his story," Mr. Nauck said grimly. "If Dr. Howland had inquired further about his order, that is vot Votkin could haf said, and he might expect to get off with a sharp reprimand and a caution. But he did not reckon on Dr. Howland doing vot he did, and then writing this—" here Mr. Nauck appeared to swallow something; probably, Trent thought, a vivid

German epithet—"this letter. Vot does this letter mean, Mr. Trent? It means that the firm has lost an order—a small matter, yes, but it also means that ve haf lost an important client, and that our reputation is compromised. Think vot Dr. Howland may haf been saying about us! If I had seen this letter, I should haf sacked Votkin on the spot and vell he knew it!"

Trent considered a moment. "But how could he know anything about it? You say the letter was never delivered."

"Oh yes, it vos! I know now vot happened. You see, Mr. Trent, my assistants come here in the morning a little earlier than I do, and it is Votkin's job to open the letters and sort them for my attention ven I arrive. He read that letter. He saw vot it meant for him, and he simply suppressed it."

"You think that was it? I see." Trent was, in fact, beginning to see somewhat further than did Mr. Nauck. "But what could have induced the man to act in this way? Why, I mean, should he have ignored that order in the first place?"

"Vy? Because Votkin is a puffed-up mass of conceit, Mr. Trent, and because he has a violent temper. I gif him his due; he is an excellent linguist and a valuable man for our business. His conceit is nothing to me, nor is his temper. He got nasty with me vonce, but he didn't do it again," said Mr. Nauck with significance. "But I vouldn't have his touchiness interfering with business, and more than vonce I haf censured him severely for being disrespectful to clients. Vell, you see vot Dr. Howland says here." He tapped the letter. "He took the trouble to spell the names carefully to the man who took his order.

He treated him like some commonplace, ignorant fellow, perhaps."

Trent called on his memories of the Doctor in past years. "He had rather a crushing manner at times. Eminent barristers often have."

"There you are!" Mr. Nauck exclaimed. "He must haf got Votkin into such a raving passion that he would do anything to spite him, and the only thing he *could* do was to keep him vaiting for his order. It vas an idiotic trick, of course; but it's just the sort of thing these irritable, vindictive fools do. Vell, I don't lose my temper often, but I am going to haf it out with Mr. Votkin as soon as I see him."

Trent took leave of the seething Mr. Nauck, and went out to wait for Inspector Clymer.

"He went to the St. Alban's buffet," the inspector reported, "having a drink at the bar first. I sat near him at the counter. He had a ham sandwich for lunch, which he didn't finish, and two more double whiskies, which he did. That's a badly frightened man if I ever saw one, his nerves are all to pieces. I left him there when I thought I had seen enough. And now, perhaps, Mr. Trent, you will let me know what all this means, and why you wanted me to join you here."

Trent let him know. He told how the name of a foreign bookseller, where half-sheets from foreign letters with foreign watermarks would be easily come by, had caught his attention. He told of Mr. Watkin's innocent display of his familiarity with French authors, and of his failure to remember Dr. Howland's name, although he had ordered books to be sent to him at his address. He told what Mr. Nauck had said of Watkin's disposition, and the story that Mr. Nauck had pieced together from the evidence. Finally, Trent told what he himself now guessed to be a later chapter of that story.

The inspector listened keenly, his face full of a restrained eagerness. "One thing's clear," he said. "It is my business to interrogate this Mr. Watkin, and the sooner the better. Look! There he comes now." And with Trent in attendance he left the teashop and hurried after his unconscious prey.

They entered the bookshop, and saw Mr. Watkin hanging up his hat and coat in a cupboard under the stairs at the back of the shop. He turned at the sound of their footsteps and came towards them; but the polite inquiry was checked on his lips, and his face turned white and frightened as he recognized Trent and took in the unmistakable appearance of Inspector Clymer.

"You are Mr. Watkin, I believe," the inspector said. The terrified man only stared at him in silence, putting a hand to his throat. "I am a police officer, and—" Here he broke off, for Watkin had turned and made as if to rush to the stairs. But coming down them at that moment appeared Mr. Nauck, wearing a tigerish scowl and holding out in a hand shaking with fury the paper which Trent had given him.

"Votkin!" roared the big man. "Vot does this mean? I hear this morning that you haf concealed from me a letter addressed to the firm, and not only that, but you haf—"

"Oh, let me alone, for God's sake!" Watkin staggered to a table and collapsed on to a chair beside it. For a moment he dropped his head on his arms; then looked up with a ghastly face at the inspector. "All right," he said. "You can take me. I shan't resist."

"Now, now! Pull yourself together!" Inspector Clymer snapped. "I haven't asked you anything yet, you know."

Again Watkin hid his head on his arms. "That be damned!" he said in a muffled voice. "I've had enough of it, I want to get it over, a little more of what I've been going through would drive me raving mad." He got to his feet. "If you won't take me in charge, I'm going round to the police-station to give myself up."

"I'm taking him down to Bridlemere this evening," Inspector Clymer said as they left the station in Chapman Row an hour later. "I'm sorry I had to ask you to wait, Mr. Trent, but I couldn't tell what sort of a statement he was going to make, and as it happens, there is a point I would like your opinion on. He has told all about how he went down there, and hung about watching for the old man, and followed him, and how he did it, and how he got away afterwards; but he never said a word about why he did it. As you know, we aren't allowed to put any questions about a voluntary statement. It seems a large order to try to murder a man because you didn't like his manner."

"It depends on how much insane vanity you have got crammed into your carcase," Trent said. "That wretched little fellow is stuffed to the gills with it, I should say, and when people like that take offence, they can hate to an extent that's impossible for nice men like you and me, Inspector. But Watkin had another motive, I think. The first time I talked to him it was plain that he was devoted to his job, revelled in it, and fancied himself hugely in it. When he read that letter of the Doctor's he saw it meant his being sacked without a character, and that even if he destroyed it he could never feel safe unless the writer was destroyed too."

"I see. That was what he meant when the old man heard him talking about 'trying to smash me.' Yes. But what about 'think nobody's a swell but yourself?' "

"The Doctor heard him imperfectly, I believe. The words were 'think nobody can spell but yourself.' That was the thing that rankled."

[8]

TRENT AND THE BAD DOG

AT THE very outset of Trent's investigation of the Headcorn murder he came to realize that no tears were being shed about the death of James Beadle Hoyt. Americans, as a rule, make themselves very well liked in England; but Hoyt was a marked exception. Plausible at first, he went off rapidly on further acquaintance. He drank too hard to be popular outside drinking circles. He was short-tempered, apt to turn sulky, and appeared to be really interested in nothing but whisky, gambling, and himself. Nothing whatever was known about him but his name, that he had been staying at a very expensive hotel in London, that he had had good clothes and plenty of money.

Hoyt had been one of two guests brought down by Gerald Shelley to his father's house, South Court, near Headcorn, in the depths of the garden of England. General Shelley, who in his latter years had suffered one domestic tragedy, could refuse nothing to his son and to Helena, his daughter. He had been delighted to receive Gerald's friends, the American Hoyt and a superbly-mannered Italian gentleman, Signor Giulio Capazza, who was understood to be engaged in some form of commerce —to judge from his appearance and style, a profitable form.

Gerald Shelley, as junior partner in a flourishing business, lived the life of the City and acquitted himself well in it. He had a weakness for high play at cards; but as he won—by his own account—more than he lost, it had led to no trouble hitherto.

Gerald had come down from London for a short holiday, with Hoyt and Capazza for company; and for the first time in his life he had looked seriously worried and depressed. There had been an interview with his father which had left the General in no better condition.

The three men had travelled down to Headcorn in Gerald's car on a Tuesday. The next Saturday afternoon had been fixed for a Garden Fête at a country house close by; one of those junketings to which District Nursing Associations, Women's Institutes, or Church Funds look for occasional support. After luncheon the servants at South Court, being given leave to attend the Fête, had all left the house. Miss Shelley and Signor Capazza had gone off soon afterwards with the same purpose. Gerald Shelley, before joining them at the Fête, had driven over to Maidstone to borrow an extra fishing-rod from a friend, for Capazza, whom every one liked, had begged to be instructed in the sport which was Gerald's favourite. General Shelley had retired as usual to his study for a rest, which meant as a rule a good two hours of refreshing slumber; and Hoyt had gone to sleep off his potations in a room on the ground floor, known as the gun-room, which Gerald Shelley and his friends used as a sitting-room of their own. The American and his host were thus the only persons left in the place that pleasant summer afternoon.

At six o'clock the servants had returned, and the parlour-maid had gone to put on a table in the gun-room some letters which had arrived for Gerald during their absence. She had been heard to shriek wildly; and the others, crowding into the room, had seen the dead body of Hoyt lying on its face in the middle of the floor, a knife driven into the back below the left shoulder-blade.

When, an hour later, the Shelleys and Capazza returned from the Fête, the police were already well advanced in the first stage of investigation. A statement had been taken from the General, who had seen or heard nothing unusual, and had not left his study until the house was roused by the parlour-maid's screams. No traces whatever appeared to have been left by the murderer. The weapon was of the hunting-knife type, bearing the mark of a Pittsburgh firm. Its blade, some ten inches long, was straight and single-edged, curving on the sharp side to a dangerously fine point; the handle was of coarsely cross-cut deerhorn, on which no finger-marks could show.

As for the means by which the murderer could have gained admission to the house, the matter was simple enough. The doors at the front and back were locked only at night, and could be opened by turning a handle. Any prowling thief who had seen the servants and the others leave, and might have assumed that the place was deserted, could have got in without any difficulty. But nothing had been taken from any room; Hoyt's watch and well-filled note-case were in his pockets. The mystery was complete, and the Italian's suggestion of a murder for hatred or revenge—he called it a vendetazzia —seemed as reasonable a guess as any.

These facts, which appeared in an expurgated form in Trent's first dispatch to the *Record*, were gathered by him partly from the police, largely from Miss Shelley, who was very ready to give information, as she said, where it was likely to do any good. She was a handsome, self-possessed brunette, who had just been, in her own words, "having a shot at her Mus. Bac." at Oxford, and was now at home waiting to learn her fate at the examiners' hands. She had talked to Trent as they paced a narrow lawn at the back of the house, separated from it by a gravel path and a flower-bed that skirted the wall. Miss Shelley was escorted by a recently barbered black poodle.

"It's no use to pretend," she said, "that any of us liked Mr. Hoyt. I couldn't stand him myself. He began by paying me offensive compliments; and when I let him see I didn't like it, and especially after I took Signor Capazza for a run in the car without asking him to join us, he was like a bear with a sore head. He drank more whisky in a day than father gets through in a month. He was insolent to the servants; and once when he wanted to go out in Gerald's car by himself, and our chauffeur told him plainly he wasn't in a fit state to drive, he shouted at him in the most disgusting language I have ever heard. Then again, I knew he had been ill-treating my dog Harlequin, beating him or kicking him on the sly; because after the first day Hoyt was here, Harlequin was scared to death of him—you know, dumb and shivering whenever he was about, though Harlequin is naturally a spirited and friendly sort of dog.

"Another thing—Hoyt was often rude to my brother; and when I spoke to Gerald about it he confessed that he had lost much more than he could pay to Mr. Hoyt, playing poker with him and Signor Capazza. Gerald said Hoyt had won a lot from Capazza too, but he had paid up, being quite well-off, apparently. Gerald admitted, too, that he had asked father to help him; and that must have been a dreadful shock to father, because he can only just make ends meet keeping up this place. You see," Miss Shelley went on with the candour of her generation, "my poor mother went out of her mind two years ago, and keeping her in a home over at Smeeth costs more than you would believe. Father has never been the same man since that disaster, because he was devoted to her; and now this new trouble over Gerald, with a man murdered in the house to follow it up, has simply broken him, poor dear."

Trent hoped he did not look his embarrassment at being so frankly taken behind the family scenes. He had suggested that Helena Shelley should tell him all the details she could think of about the crime; and she was taking him at his word. He spoke some words of the sympathy that he felt; then added, "I believe you and Signor Capazza were the last members of the household to see Hoyt alive."

"I was going to tell you about that. About an hour after lunch, Capazza and I came out into the garden, because I was going to take him over to the Garden Fête in Sir Gilbert Tregelles's meadow, which is just next to father's land—only two minutes' walk from here. Capazza was interested, because I had entered Harlequin for the Bun Race at the Fête, and it was a new idea to him."

"So it is," Trent said, "to me."

"It's rather fun. The owners run with their dogs on the lead, and when they get to a point a hundred yards away each owner and each dog has to eat a bun, and when both buns are finished—not before—run back to the starting-place. The first couple to get back wins the prize. As Harlequin is the greediest dog I know, and I can bolt my food when I like, I hoped we should win; and so we did, by a short head, amidst fearful excitement. It was a great day for Harlequin, because he also won the prize in the Dog-with-the-Most-Pathetic-Eyes class at the Comic Dog Show. You can see if you look at him . . . Now where," Miss Shelley broke off, perching a pair of thick-lensed spectacles on her pretty nose, "has that animal got to?"

Trent pointed. "There he is, straight in front of you, in the middle of that flower-bed, looking at you—very pathetically indeed."

"Come here, sir!" his owner called. "How dare you go in that bed? Well, as I was saying—bad dog!—we came out through the drawing-room, and were walking over this lawn to get to the other end of the garden, where there is a gate leading towards the Tregelles' place."

She took a few steps and paused before a small circular bed of rose trees in the midst of the lawn.

"That window just opposite us now is the window of the room where Hoyt was at the time. It was open, and as we came near it, Capazza asked if he might have a flower for his coat. I said yes, of course, and at that moment Hoyt appeared at the window. He gave a sneering sort of laugh and said, 'That's right, Miss Shelley, the white flower of a blameless life for him, he surely has it coming to him,' or something like that; and he added, looking at Capazza, 'I'm going to keep my promise.' His manner was most offensive, and I was so disgusted I turned my back on him and began cutting a rose with the scissors out of my bag. After I had pinned it in Capazza's buttonhole we went on our way."

"And that was the last you saw of Hoyt?"

"Well, very nearly. When we got to the gate—you can see it down there, in the holly hedge—he shouted after us, and as I glanced back he waved his arm. Harlequin began barking and dragging at the lead, trying to run back, and I thought the noise might wake my father, so I said something peevish about the way Hoyt was behaving, and Capazza said in his quaint accent, 'I think he wish us to return. Poor fellow, he dooes not know what he doos. Do you wish to return, Miss Shelley?' I said, certainly not, that I shouldn't dream of it; and we went on to the Fête.

"That was actually the last that any of us saw of Hoyt before he was murdered. The police asked us if it sounded as if he was shouting for help—hoping to fix the time of the murder, I suppose. Well, it didn't sound like that. He certainly didn't shout 'Help!' It was just a 'Hi!' as if he was trying to attract our attention; and I believe that's all it was."

Trent looked down to the gate in the hedge, some seventy yards. "Yes; if he had shouted anything articulate I suppose you must have heard it. And your father, I understand, heard nothing at all."

"No; he wouldn't—what with being rather deaf, and asleep too, as he would be at the time, and the study being on the other side of the house. But he is terribly distressed that he did not—I think he persuades himself that he is to blame in a way. The whole thing has been quite shattering for him."

Trent considered for a few moments of silence. "And at the Fête you met your brother?"

"Yes; he came there straight from Maidstone. It is only a twenty-minutes' run, and he probably got there before we did. He had been there some time, he said, when we ran into him in the crowd. After that the three of us were together until we returned here, and heard what had happened."

Trent found Gerald Shelley and Signor Capazza in the middle of a meadow that sloped down to a stream bounding the General's property on one side. They had rods in their hands, and it was evident that the Italian was being given a dry-land initiation in the art of casting a fly. "There! You've got the trick of it," Trent heard Shelley say. "I've never known a beginner so quick at picking it up." "Aha! Sono molto pescatore!" the other laughed. "Watch out, you feesh, when I get-a going!"

Shelley, a slight, fair young man with a distraught and worn-out look, made a striking contrast with his friend, a tall, swarthy and solidly built man of about thirty, with health and vigour in every athletic line of him.

Shelley had quite agreed with his sister, he said, that Trent should be told all they could tell him, because he and his paper had a name for not printing anything the family wouldn't like. He supposed she had already told him what she and Signor Capazza knew about it, which was more than any one else knew, as no one else had seen Hoyt between lunch-time and the time when he was found murdered.

Shelley dwelt upon this point, and volunteered a particular account of his own doings on the afternoon of the crime, mentioning several persons who had seen him in Maidstone, and appealing to the Italian to bear out his statement that the two of them and Miss Shelley had not been out of each other's sight during the time spent at the Fête. Trent, who could think of one period when, by the girl's account, she had not been with the other two, turned to Signor Capazza.

"Eet ees true," Capazza said. His voice was deep and soft. "Togezzer all-a time, and so he tell-a da police. But my friend ees afraid they suspect-a heem," he added with a dazzling smile. "Ees all-a bunk, eh? Ees-a not likely he keel a man een hees own house, and among hees own-a famiglia, and for no reason. You theenk?"

Trent agreed that it did not seem probable.

"Oh, they suspect everybody, of course," Shelley said gloomily. "They suspect my father, for instance, just because he happened to be in the house when this murderer got in—which only shows you, because the governor would as soon shoot himself as do violence to a guest under his roof, to say nothing of stabbing him in the back."

"Well, they have to work to their system, you know," Trent said. "Will you tell me, Signor, about that time when you and Miss Shelley saw Hoyt at the window. He said something, did he, about keeping his promise? What could he have meant by that?"

A shade of embarrassment passed over Capazza's expressive face. "I do not like to speak of eet, Mr. Trent; but of course everything must be explain, I know eet. What you ask, I tell-a da police-inspector already. You see, Hoyt would make-a fun of me often, because I drink always water. That day when he was keel he had drink-a much whisky, and after lunch he start on me again, why I not get souse once in a while and enjoy myself. Then I say to heem, 'These friend of ours do not enjoy themself when you are souse, you know. They ought to be consider, when you are guest. Why do you not go easy on da liquor while you are here, so they like you better?' And Hoyt say, 'I believe you give-a me good advice, and I show you I can lay off da booze when I want. After thees I am on the water-cart while I am here, and that ees a promise.' So you see what he mean when he tell-a Mees Shelley about my blameless life, and that he will keep-a da promise."

Trent nodded. "Yes, I see. And a little later he shouted after you, when you and Miss Shelley were at the gate. Why was that, I wonder?"

Capazza shrugged lightly. "How can I tell? I think he weesh us to return, but Mees Shelley say no, he is not sober, let us go on. And that ees the last time we see him alive."

"And when you heard of the murder, you could not form any idea of who did it, or why? I suppose you have not thought of anything since then, Signor Capazza. I mean, Hoyt was a friend of yours, and you knew something of his life and his circumstances, no doubt."

Capazza wagged a forefinger in a Latin gesture of emphatic denial. "No, no, Mr. Trent; make-a no mistake. I know no more of heem than Mr. Shelley knows. We all meet for da first time at da Greville Hotel, where Hoyt and I are both staying to visit your wonderful London. We sit in a bridge game a few times after dinner, and so we become acquaint. One evening Hoyt came to me in da smoke-room, and Mr. Shelley with heem, and Hoyt say, 'Thees gentleman and I have meet in da cocktail bar and got-a talking, and we think we would like to have a spot of poker. Will you join us?' I say, I will be very please indeed; so we play in Hoyt's sitting-room, and we are all pretty good players, and we have a good time. After that we meet some more times; and then we are so friendly that Mr. Shelley invite the two of us here to thees charming house. And now eet is all come to thees terrible end." Signor Capazza, sighing deeply, rolled his fine eyes heavenward.

At the inquest next day, before the customary adjournment at the request of Chief-Inspector Jewell, in charge of the inquiry, the medical evidence was taken. Describing the wound, the witness said the knife had penetrated the left lung and the left ventricle of the heart. Such an injury must have been instantly fatal, and the victim had probably died without uttering a cry. The blow could not possibly have been self-inflicted. It would not have required any great strength, because the point of the weapon was as sharp as a knife-point could be.

Trent, after hearing this evidence, was seen no more that day. He had driven back to London, and had spent an afternoon hour at the office of a friend of his, in the neighbourhood of Leicester Square. He had then written a carefully considered letter to Inspector Jewell, who received it duly the next morning.

"I have (Trent wrote) a few suggestions to make which you may think it worth while to follow up. Some of the points, perhaps all of them, will have occurred to you already, but for the sake of clearness I will put down all that I think, and something that I know.

"Gerald Shelley believes that he is under suspicion of having committed the crime; and so no doubt he is. Everything points to his having lost more money than he could pay to Hoyt and having applied to his father for help, probably at Hoyt's suggestion. It may well be that General Shelley's financial position was already not an easy one, and that Gerald was told so by him. If Hoyt's antecedents could be traced, it might turn out that he was a professional sharper and swindler. In any case, if he had got Gerald in a desperate difficulty, Hoyt's death would be very convenient for Gerald—and for his father also, who therefore falls under suspicion too, the more so as he was admittedly in the house when the murder was done. That is not the case with Gerald; but his alibi is no good. He could easily have called at the house, without being seen by any one, on returning from Maidstone; and then proceeded at once to the Fête.

"You will have considered that, of course; but you may not be as confident as I am that that is precisely what Gerald did do. What happened was, I believe, that he drove back to South Lodge for some purpose, went to the gun-room, and there found Hoyt lying dead with the knife in his back. At the same time he saw through the open window Miss Shelley and Signor Capazza walking towards the gate in the hedge. He ran to the window, shouted to them, and waved his arms, before he knew what he was doing. He saw them turn and glance towards him, while the poodle barked, recognizing him, and leapt about in sympathy with his excitement, as dogs will. When they went on without paying any further attention to him, he was naturally astonished, for although he knew his sister was too short-sighted, even with glasses, to recognize him at that distance, he had no reason to suppose that Capazza was short-sighted too. Still, he could only think that neither of them, in fact, had recognized him; and when he began to realize his position, he was glad indeed to think so.

"He saw that if he was known to have been in the room where the murdered man lay, before the body was found by any other person, he would be in the gravest danger. He knew what motive would be imputed to him, and he could not imagine, then or afterwards, who else could possibly have murdered Hoyt. He was in the position of an innocent man who fears to tell the truth because it points directly at his own guilt.

"He determined to do his best to fabricate an alibi, weak though he must have seen it to be; and his statement to you was the result.

"I was led to this conclusion by noting some curious details in the account given to me by Miss Shelley of what happened on that same occasion. In the first place, she said that when she heard Hoyt shouting, she glanced back and saw him waving his arm. Now I knew from my own observation that Miss Shelley could not see well enough to have made out, at a glance and at that distance, who it was at the window. What she actually did was to assume that it was Hoyt; and quite naturally, having really seen him at that window a minute before. She said, too, that she was annoyed by the dog trying to run back, and making a noise that might disturb her father's siesta. I was struck by that, because she had already told me that the dog was terrified of Hoyt, and could only shiver and cringe when he was about. But if she had had the least uncertainty about its being Hoyt at the window, it must have been banished by Signor Capazza recognizing him as Hoyt, and asking her if she wished to go back at the invitation of a tipsy man.

"That was quick and clever of Capazza, for if it was really Gerald at the window, as I believe, Capazza would have recognized him instantly. His sight is exceptionally keen. I know that now; and I had got that impression before, when I heard how quickly he had mastered the art of throwing a fly, which is a difficult combination of the work of wrist and eye.

"There was another thing which struck me about Miss Shelley's story of what had happened when Hoyt spoke from the window to herself and Capazza. She said that his manner had been offensive and sneering—and she is, I think, a perfectly honest witness. But Capazza, telling me of the same facts, put an entirely different colour on them. He represented Hoyt as being in a rather chastened temper, after having sworn off drink at Capazza's suggestion, and as having merely repeated his promise made a short time before. That would have been quite a plausible explanation of the words Hoyt had said, but for Miss Shelley's description of the way he had said them. And she was very sure about that, because she had been so much offended that she turned her back on him and gave her attention to cutting a rose.

"It was that final detail which put an idea into my head. It was an idea which might be wild, but which provided an answer, at least, to some curious questions.

"Why had the dog behaved in that way, if the man who shouted from the window had been Hoyt?

"If the man was not Hoyt, why had Capazza pretended to Miss Shelley that he was Hoyt? And why had he reminded her that Hoyt had been drinking, if he believed Hoyt to be at that time in a penitent mood, and anxious not to make himself objectionable?

"Lastly, had something happened, unseen by Miss Shelley, while her back was turned; while she was taking the scissors from her bag and cutting a rose?

"Perhaps you see the direction that my ideas were taking. I waited for the inquest, to hear what the doctor would say about the cause of death; and it did not dispose of my suspicion. A few hours later I paid a visit to Mr. Hyman Weingott, of 247 Green Street, who has a theatrical and vaudeville agency, and knows all there is to know about the business. I described Signor Capazza to him, and I asked him a question. Mr. Weingott went to a book-case filled with cardboard folders, arranged alphabetically, and took down one from among the B's. The name on the cover was Briccione. He took out some papers and three photographs, which he handed to me. They were excellent likenesses of Signor Giulio Capazza.

"Then I told Mr. Weingott the whole story, and my guess as to how Hoyt had met his death. He was keenly interested. He said there were many people in London who could identify Briccione, but he would like to do it himself. He will travel to Headcorn to-morrow afternoon by the train which gets in at 3.28, and will report to you when he arrives.

"Tito Briccione was born at Calascibetta in Sicily. He is an American citizen, his parents having emigrated when he was an infant; and he was brought up amongst the poor Italians in New York. Briccione is the most eminent knife-thrower in that small and highly-paid profession, having learnt his art from the celebrated Leo Latti. He can hit the ace of spades at 20 feet, and has never been known to miss. He has toured all over Europe and America for years, and in England his minimum fee has been £50 for a ten-minute turn. He is said to have made a good deal of money, in spite of his career having been interrupted by two terms of imprisonment in New York State. In both cases his offence was aggravated assault as the result of a quarrel. Owing to his ferocious temper and readiness to use the knife he always carried (under his left arm), he is reputed a dangerous man, and credited with several murders and stabbings that were never brought home to him. He is rigidly abstemious, because knife-throwers have to be; but he is a confirmed gambler, and associates a good deal with professional card-sharks.

"So there you have a brief history of Signor Capazza. I don't know what you thought about his story of how he became acquainted with Hoyt, and afterwards with Gerald Shelley. It sounded to me at the time just like a card-sharping variation of the confidence trick, and I think it fits in—as also does the sort of English Capazza talks—with what Mr. Weingott told me. Probably the two of them had conspired to fleece Gerald, and Capazza would not leave Hoyt until the money had been collected and divided.

"I suggest that Capazza murdered Hoyt by throwing his knife at a moment when Hoyt turned away from the gun-room window, Miss Shelley having her back to it; that he did so while standing close to Miss Shelley, but between her and the window, and at a distance from it of about 16 feet. Gerald Shelley entered the room while they were walking to the gate in the hedge, and as they reached it he shouted after them. Briccione-Capazza is a man who can think and act very swiftly. He saw instantly that Miss Shelley took the man at the window to be Hoyt, and that if they both gave evidence to that effect his alibi would take a lot of breaking; so he played up to her belief.

"Why he killed Hoyt can be matter of guess-work only. My own guess is that Hoyt, who resented Miss Shelley's preferring Capazza's company to his own, had threatened to tell the Shelley family the story of Capazza's 'blameless life' unless he gave up cultivating Miss Shelley's society; that when Hoyt heard him asking for a rose he determined to 'keep his promise,' and he said so; that this was too much for Briccione's fiendish temper, and that when Hoyt turned from the window he seized his chance with a gambler's boldness."

On the afternoon of the day on which Inspector Jewell received this letter, Trent was at home in his studio. He had plenty to do there, and on the scene of the murder there was no more, he thought, to be discovered. A representative of the *Record*, who remained on the spot, was to telephone him the result of Mr. Weingott's visit; and Trent had already drafted, in advance of the facts, a message announcing the latest action taken by the police, and revealing the true identity of Giulio Capazza. At 4.15 the call came through, and Trent had little to add to his story before dispatching it to Fleet Street.

An official version of what had happened came to Trent by the first post next morning. The letter ran as follows:

Dear Sir,

I have to acknowledge your favour of the 22nd inst., and to thank you for the contents of same.

Mr. Weingott arrived here this afternoon as per your letter, and we then proceeded to South Court. In view of your information *re* the criminal record of Briccione, alias Capazza, I thought it best that we should be accompanied by a uniformed constable. We found Briccione with Mr. Gerald Shelley fishing in the stream, and they did not observe our approach until Mr. Weingott said to me, "That is the man. I should know him anywhere." Briccione looked up and appeared to recognize Mr. Weingott, to whom he applied an obscene epithet. Acting with such rapidity that for a moment we were unable to intervene, Briccione then flung himself upon Mr. Weingott, seized him by the hair with both hands and attempted to bite him in the throat. Mr. Weingott struck Briccione a heavy blow over the ear, and another below the belt, while we were pinioning him from behind, so that the arrest was effected without further difficulty. Subsequently Briccione was charged before the magistrate in Maidstone, and committed for trial at the next assizes.

Mr. Gerald Shelley has confessed that his statement made to us on the day of the crime was an incomplete account of his movements, which were substantially as suggested in your letter. As he appears to have had no knowledge of the identity of the murderer of Mr. Hoyt, and no motive but to avoid being implicated in the crime, we have decided as at present advised to bring no charge against him.

I am,

Yours faithfully,

C. M. Jewell

(CHIEF-INSPECTOR).

[9]

THE PUBLIC BENEFACTOR

Colonel White drifted gently out from the enormous portal of the Hotel Artemare, and relapsed into a chair on the veranda overlooking the sunlit picture of Monte Carlo, with the wall of mountain majesty that made a sublimely unconscious background for its trivial charm. With his long, slim fingers he lighted a long, slim cigar, and his heavy-lidded eyes roamed slowly over the scene. Presently he rose to his feet as a tall, fair young woman came from the hotel and took a chair near his.

"You are looking fine this morning, Mrs. Ashley," the Colonel said. He knew that an allusion to her appearance was what this lady expected from every man, and he wanted to get it over, for the subject bored him.

Mrs. Ashley blinked her sandy eye-lashes at him, taking no notice of what she regarded as an observation forced from him by the spectacle of herself. She was fully satisfied with the two hours' work which she and her maid had lately completed at her toilet; and she believed that insolent manners were a mark of social distinction.

"How is your father this morning?" the Colonel asked.

"Bad," Mrs. Ashley said briefly. "Something has upset him again—I don't know what. He is more shaky and depressed than ever, and I have phoned for Dr. Cole to see him again. He may be here any minute."

Colonel White fingered his neat black moustache. "I suppose," he said, "I ought not to butt in, but as a friend of your father's I may perhaps ask if you are quite satisfied with Dr. Cole."

"Well, I ought to be," Mrs. Ashley said a little sharply. "I've known him for years, and he is wonderful with nervous cases. It was great luck his being here when father had this trouble. Oh! Here he is."

A robustly handsome man, who looked as if his study of nervous disorder had been entirely unassisted by personal experience, came up the steps and joined them on the veranda. "I was sorry to get your message, Mrs. Ashley," he said. "Morning, Colonel. Mrs. Ashley has told you, I suppose, that she thinks her father is not so well to-day."

"She didn't tell me that," Colonel White answered. "She told me he was worse than ever." Something in his tone brought a flush to the doctor's face, but he turned to Mrs. Ashley coolly enough.

"I met some one you know on my way here," he said. "Philip Trent—he's staying with friends at the Cluny. He knew you were here, and he was going to call, but he hadn't heard of Mr. Somerton being ill, of course. I told him it would do your father nothing but good to see him, and the sooner the better—he wants taking out of himself as much as anything. So Trent is coming this afternoon. Shall I go up to Mr. Somerton now? He is in your sitting-room, I suppose."

Mrs. Ashley rose, and the doctor followed her to the hotel entrance. As they reached it, Colonel White heard

Dr. Cole say, in a tone of contempt obviously intended to reach his ears, "Your American friend is very polite this morning."

The Colonel smiled. "Like hell he is!" he murmured to the landscape.

When Trent was shown up to Mr. Somerton's suite that afternoon, he was astonished at the change in his appearance. Somerton, a few months ago, had been carrying his sixty-odd years lightly. With his short, thick-set figure and square, snub-nosed countenance, he had never been a beauty; but he had been the picture of health and vitality. Now he looked an old man and a sick one. His face was white and drawn, his eyes were tragic, he was stoop-shouldered, his whole being bespoke distress and haunting fear.

"I am devilish glad to see you, Trent," he said. "You may be able to help me—this breakdown of my health has come at an awkward time. I am in a fix, my boy. Here, have a cigar." He pushed over a box. "I've had to give them up myself, but even the smell of a good cigar will be something."

Trent helped himself, and through the blue haze looked thoughtfully at Somerton. "What do you mean by being in a fix?" he asked. "You aren't being hunted by mad cannibals in an African jungle. There are doctors enough in Monte Carlo to sink a battleship. You've got your daughter here to look after you. And that American Colonel I met just now would be a useful friend, I should think."

"Yes, White is a good fellow," Somerton said. "I don't know what I should have done without him. I met him here last year, and we got very friendly then; but since this trouble of mine began he has been kindness itself."

"He is young for a colonel," Trent observed.

"Oh, he's not a soldier; it's only an honorary title, he told me. He is immensely rich, and when he began life he hadn't a shilling. As for Jo being here to look after me—well, I'm sorry to say that is why the position is so bad. You see, when my—my nerves began to go wrong, a week ago, she sent for this man Cole. She knew he was staying here, and she believes in him. Well, I think he's a fool, and I know he has done me no good at all."

"Then why not get rid of him? You've never been afraid of telling people what you thought of them."

"It isn't that, it's Jo. Look here, Trent, if I want you to help me I must tell you the truth. Jo is an only child and a spoilt one, she is hard and selfish, but I'm devoted to her and can't bear to give her any cause for resentment. I couldn't, even if she was sweet-tempered, but the fact is she gets furious if she is crossed in anything, and in the state I am in now I simply dare not face one of her scenes. I can't suggest going home before she wants to. I can't tell her Cole is no use to me. On the contrary, I'm expected to like him." Somerton wiped his forehead with a shaking hand, then resumed, "You may as well know it all. I believe she's in love with him. They are always about together. It was Cole who attended Hugh Ashley when he went to pieces; and since his death she and Cole have been bosom friends."

Trent reflected over his cigar. "You don't think Cole is a wrong 'un, do you?" he asked at length.

"Oh no, nothing of the sort. After being a beak for nearly twenty years, and having had half the rascals in

London up before me, I know dishonesty when I see it. Cole doesn't understand me, that's all, and he won't realize it. Now, Trent, can't you do something for me? You see how it is. You might say a word to Jo about getting another opinion, perhaps. She might listen to you; and anyhow she can't make you suffer as she can make me. White has dropped a hint or two, he tells me, but she pays no attention."

"I will do anything I can, of course," Trent said. "But, Somerton, what exactly is the matter with you? You speak of your nerves going wrong; that might mean anything. You certainly don't look well; but how does it take you?"

Somerton held up a weary hand. "For God's sake, don't tell me I don't look well! I'm sick of hearing that. People I've never met come up to me in the street and tell me I look ill, and ask if they can do anything. How does it take me?" Somerton leaned forward in his chair and stared miserably into Trent's eyes. "I'll tell you. I believe I'm going out of my mind—dying at the top."

Trent showed nothing of the shock he felt. "Oh, come!" he said with a smile. "You're as sane as I am, Somerton. You haven't said a word yet that wasn't perfectly rational."

"All the same, there's something desperately wrong. I'll tell you how it began. One evening, about a week ago, Jo suggested we might run over to Mentone and take the mountain railway to Sospel, which we'd never seen, and come back by Nice. We made up a small party in the hotel, to go next day. Well, next morning I was down before the others, and Gaston, the head porter, came up to me and said he had got the time-table I asked for, with the service to Sospel. I was astounded, because I could have taken my dying oath I had never asked him for any time-table, or even thought of doing so.

"I said nothing about this to the others, because, of course, they would have thought I had simply forgotten asking for the time-table; but it kept coming back into my mind all day. Then in the evening, when I was dressing in my room here, there was a knock at the door, and a man came in saying he was the valet. I said I hadn't rung for the valet, or for anybody. The fellow looked surprised. He said the bell had rung in the valets' room; and the little blue light over the bedroom door, which goes on when you ring, had been showing when he knocked, and he had only that moment switched it off. I said there must be something wrong with the electrical arrangements, and he went off, looking at me queerly. After what had happened that morning, I didn't like this. I hadn't rung, or wanted anything to ring for—but could I have rung all the same? I felt worried; and at dinner Jo asked me what I had got on my mind. Of course, I said there was nothing; and I worried all the more, and slept badly afterwards.

"The next morning, when I was shaving, exactly the same thing happened. The valet knocked, asked what monsieur desired; and do you know, Trent, rather than have him look at me again as if I was crazy, I told him I wanted some cigarettes. That shows you how shaken I was; for I hadn't the faintest recollection of having rung, and I felt by now that there must be something wrong mentally.

"The following day some of us went down to the front to watch a regatta, and I had a bet with a man on a crew I fancied in a boat race. I lost, and found I was short of money to pay him; so I went on to the Lyonnais where I have a credit, and drew ten *milles* and some smaller notes. I rejoined our party, and we had a few more bets. When I took out my case to settle what I owed, I found I had twenty *milles* in it.

"I said nothing about it, I was too much upset. I went back to the bank and asked how much I had drawn. The cashier showed me my cheque—10,500 francs. I said they had given me twenty *milles*, and produced my case to show him. There were only ten *milles* in it. The man looked at me exactly as the valet had done. I could have screamed.

"The next day White and I were out for a stroll, and we stopped at Madame Joubin's stall, as we often did, to buy papers. I got the *Times* of the day before—Tuesday, February 2nd; it was too early for that day's issue. When we sat down to look at our papers, I caught sight of the date on the front page of mine, which I hadn't unfolded. It was the *Times* for Monday, February 2nd—of last year!

"I said to White, 'Here's a curious thing. Look at the date on my paper.' He took it and said, 'Why, what's wrong with it?' I said, 'Can't you see? It's a year old.' White stared at me, with that look I had got to dread so much. He only said, 'No, it's yesterday's paper all right'; and when I looked again, it was so.

"As soon as we got back to the hotel, I told Jo I must see a doctor at once, that for the first time in my life my nerves had gone wrong. I didn't say anything about mental trouble. She said she was sure it would be wise, that I had been looking queer for some days past; and she sent off for this fellow Cole. Well, you know what I think of him. I told him all that I've told you—I've never told any one else until now. He wagged his head and thought a little, then he asked me if I hadn't been in Monte Carlo about this time last year. I said I always came here at this time. Then Cole said that probably I had done last year all these things which I had done again unconsciously this year, or imagined myself doing this year; that I had got a kink in my memory, or something like that; that I had drawn 20,000 francs one day a year ago, and bought a *Times* on February 2nd a year ago, and so on. Well, I couldn't say it wasn't so; but you can imagine that it didn't altogether relieve my mind. It's not a good sign when your memory takes to turning somersaults. Besides, it didn't explain the time-table incident. Well, Cole said I must take a sedative, which he prescribed, and on no account let myself get tired, and give up smoking and stimulants."

Trent, who had listened in silence while Somerton set out all these strange facts, or fancies, in their due order, now crushed out his cigar-butt and spoke. "I don't know anything about it, but I agree it looks as if nerve trouble, in the ordinary sense, hardly covers the facts. And yet, you know, Somerton, you're not a bit like a mental case, as far as my small experience goes."

Somerton uttered an impatient exclamation. "That's just it! I feel absolutely sane—and all the same there's the fact that I don't know what I'm doing sometimes. And you haven't heard the worst, either—the thing that bowled me over this morning. You see, a week ago I sent my wife a birthday present. She is at our flat in Brook Street just now; she hates Monte Carlo. I sent her a small

Chinese statuette in white jade—got it at Grangette's little shop in the Rue de la Scala, and wrote down the name and address for him to send it to.

"This morning I had a letter from Mary thanking me warmly for the present, but at the same time asking whether the address I had sent it to was some sort of joke. Fortunately the people at that address knew where we live now, but even so it had taken three days to reach her. She enclosed the label with the address written on it. Have a look at it, will you?"

Trent took the paper from Somerton's quivering hand, and read what follows:

Mrs. J. L. Somerton,
23, Talford Street,
London, S.W.7.
Angleterre.

"I don't wonder she was puzzled," Trent observed, looking up at the other. "What is this address?"

"23 Talfourd Street—there ought to be a U after the O—is the house where we lived from the time we were married. We left it in 1912—fourteen years ago." Somerton lay back in his chair with closed eyes. "I've never seen it since, or given it a thought during most of that time. So there you are. A nice thing to be faced with when I was already afraid—" he left the sentence unfinished and covered his face with his hands.

Trent looked at him in silence a few moments; then stared again at the label. He rose and took it to the window, where he studied it with his back to the stricken figure in the chair. Then, looking out over the sunlit Escalier des Fleurs, he began to whistle almost inaudibly.

"And you had no thought of this address in your mind when you were giving Grangette his instructions."

Somerton looked up irritably. "I told you. Why, I had almost forgotten I had ever lived there until I read that label this morning. You see how it fits in with the rest. But to my mind going back to a year ago, without my being conscious of it, is one thing; fourteen years is another."

Trent left the window and laid a hand on Somerton's shoulder. "Don't you lose heart," he said. "It seems bad, I know, but I believe I may be able to help you. In fact, I am quite confident you can be put right if you'll leave it to me." And Trent, slipping the label into his pocket, took a hasty leave of his friend.

An hour later Trent found Colonel White in his favourite seat on the veranda, turning the lively pages of *The New Yorker.*

"I have just been having an interesting talk, Colonel," he said without preliminary, leaning back on the railing as he faced the other. "I have been to Grangette's little antique shop—you know the place."

Colonel White laid aside his paper. "Sure I know it," he said. "I have done business with Grangette a few times."

"Yes, I know you have done business with him," Trent said with an acrid smile. He drew from a pocket the label which he had taken away from Somerton's room, and tossed it on the small table at the Colonel's elbow.

"That is a pretty good address, as they go," Trent went on. "There are only two things wrong with it. The name of the street is spelt the way an American would spell it.

It ought to be T-A-L-F-O-U-R-D."

The Colonel, inspecting the label with languid interest, nodded. "Pronounced T-A-L-F-O-R-D," he remarked. "Yes, I see."

"Also," Trent continued, "that postal direction, 'S.W.7.', is a little too modern. The Post Office didn't begin putting a numeral after the district letters until long after Somerton had left that address. I am not sure when they started doing so, but I know it was during the war."

Colonel White sighed. "Now isn't that just too bad?" he commented.

"I took that label to Grangette," Trent went on, "and I told him I was making inquiries on behalf of Somerton, and I wanted to know how his packet came to be sent to that address. I said that it was a *situation grave*. Grangette is not a reliable tool, Colonel. He began to go to pieces at once. He swore Somerton had given him the address; but the next moment he was declaring that he hadn't meant any harm, and that anyhow there was nothing illegal. So I said that was a matter for the Correctional Court to decide. I think Grangette must have been in trouble before, because as soon as I mentioned the Court he broke down and began to beg to be let off, and told me the whole thing. He even told me how much you paid him to address the packet wrongly. What I should like to know is how you got hold of that address."

The Colonel smiled amiably. "Anything else you would like to know?" he inquired.

"I can imagine," Trent said, "how some of this malicious persecution was carried out. It was easy to bribe the porter and the floor-valet to pretend that Somerton had asked for a time-table and that he had rung his bedroom bell. It was easy to pay people to speak sympathetically to him in the street about how ill he was looking. But I don't see how the trick with the newspaper was done; and that business of changing the bank-notes in Somerton's note-case puzzles me. Not that it matters very much; because the thing is going to stop now, and Somerton is going to be told that all this trouble of his was due to a heartless fraud. What he will do about it is for him to say. Probably he will prosecute you, for Somerton can be a very hard man when he likes."

Colonel White rose from his chair and approached Trent. "I know he can. I know he can." He stared into Trent's eyes and tapped him lightly on the chest. "You don't have to tell me that. And I can be hard too, when I like. Now, Mr. Trent, I am not sorry you have found all this out. I wanted it to be known; it was part of my plan that it should be known. You have speeded matters up by a day or two, that's all. I had very nearly finished with Somerton, and my intention was to go away suddenly, without a word to him, leaving a letter for him in which I reminded him of certain matters between ourselves. What I am now going to do is this. I shall write *you* a letter about this heartless fraud of mine—I have no objection to that way of putting it—because since you have found out so much, I should prefer you to know just why I did it. You shall have the letter to-day and you can show it to Somerton when you've read it. But I will tell you one thing now—the way the bank-note trick was worked." The Colonel paused a moment, then asked, "Have you got a cigarette?"

Trent put his hand mechanically to his handkerchief pocket, looked surprised, then searched several other pockets in vain. "I'm sorry. I must have mislaid my case somewhere."

"No," Colonel White said. "It was in that outside pocket of yours all right. I noticed this afternoon that you carry it there. I've got it now. Here it is." He held out the case to Trent, who took it with a slightly bewildered air. "I took it when I faced right up to you a minute ago, and emphasized my remarks by poking you in the upper vest. That was how I attended to Somerton's note-case—only with him it was much easier, because he has the reckless habit of carrying his money in his hip-pocket. Now that is all I'm going to say before I leave you, and I don't suppose we shall meet again."

"I hope not, most sincerely," Trent said. "I look forward to reading the explanation of your proceedings; but on the facts, as far as I know them, you seem to be a dangerous and unscrupulous rascal. Do you make a living out of that little accomplishment you were giving me a display of just now?"

Colonel White shook his head. "On the contrary," he said, "playing off that little accomplishment on our friend Somerton has cost me some thousands of dollars, one way and another. And don't try to make me lose my temper, Mr. Trent—you can't do it. I am feeling perfectly satisfied. I have done what I came to Monte Carlo to do and I leave for Paris to-night. The Hotel Meurice will find me for the next ten days, in case Somerton should want to start anything; but he won't. You will receive my letter in the course of the evening." The Colonel turned away with a slight bend of the head, and, looking more distinguished than ever, faded away into the hotel.

While Trent was dressing for dinner at his own hotel, two hours later, Colonel White's letter was brought to him. The neat, clear handwriting covered a number of sheets of Artemare notepaper. There was neither date nor signature, and the document began without preliminary as follows:

"I was born in Islington, London, 38 years ago. My mother, who was an Italian, was a good woman, and brought me up well; but my father was an English pickpocket, as his father was before him, and I took after him, especially in having the right sort of hands. It is not highly thought of as a profession, but my father was at the top of it and made a decent living out of it. He was very seldom caught, I believe; never in the ten years that I remembered him. Before he died I had learnt all he could show me, and he said I was better than he was, but probably that was parental pride.

"I always worked alone, as he did. It is much more difficult than when you work with stalls, and as regards class there is all the difference in the world. I had had a fair education; I could pass anywhere as far as appearance and dress and speaking good English went. I spoke as my father did, it was natural to me; how he got his quiet, unaffected upper-class way of talking I don't know, I never met another man who could do it without being born to it.

"When I was seventeen I was caught in the act, by a piece of bad luck. I came up before the North London magistrate, Mr. Somerton. He was a recent appointment, and he wasn't popular with the crooks. I knew that, but I was surprised at the way he treated me. As it was my first appearance, I thought I might be bound over, or get off with a month at the very worst. But it was clear from the start that he had taken a dislike to me. When the police had told him that I associated with criminals and was a bad influence, and I said it was a lie, he kept a vicious eye on me, and finally said he could not take a lenient view of this case, and gave me three months.

"Not long after I came out, I came before Somerton again. There had been a jewellers' window smashed and a lot of stuff taken, and a policeman, a man with whom I had had some unpleasantness, gave evidence. There were three men in it, and he had come up just as they were making off. He gave chase, and they got away, but he swore that he recognized one of them, and that I was that one. Actually I had been nowhere near the place at the time, but I couldn't prove it, and when I said the cop was trying to frame me because we were not on good terms, the magistrate got to drumming with his fingers and looking more and more sour. He gave me six months. I didn't like being punished harshly, on insufficient evidence, for something I never did—a spite sentence—and being treated as if my word against the cop's wasn't worth a damn, but the worst was what he said before passing sentence. He need not have said it, it was simply meant to hurt, you could see that by the way he glared at me as he said it. He told me I thought I looked like a gentleman, but what was I but a common thief, who could never enter a decent house or mix with decent people. There was more, but those words were what I never forgot. What I decided Somerton should pay for one day, and what he has paid for, was using his position to insult and browbeat me.

"Every day while I was serving that sentence I was thinking about Mr. James Lingard Somerton, and what I would do to him one day. I'm not what you would call a vindictive man in the ordinary way, I think; but all my life when I have got set on a thing I have kept that thing before me and fixed my will on it, and I was very much set on making Somerton pay.

"I knew it was going to be a very long job. I meant it to be. I meant to make good, in the first place. I didn't mind his telling me I was a thief, because I was, but I objected to his saying I thought I looked like a gentleman, because I knew I looked like a gentleman, and a lot more like a gentleman than Somerton did, or does now. In my business it was necessary to look that way—all first-class dips do. And I wasn't going to be told I could never mix with decent people, either. That was telling me I didn't have character enough to become a good citizen—and the consequence was that I got set on becoming just that thing; which was very far from what Somerton intended.

"When I came out of prison I knew just what I meant to do. I went to my mother's brother, who was a fruit merchant, and told him I was going to go straight for the future. I asked him if he would pay my passage to America, so I could begin life again. He agreed to do that, and I emigrated. There was no difficulty about getting into the United States in those days. I soon found employment clerking. To make a short story of it, in five years' time I had a good position with a firm in Harrison, Colorado, and was saving money. When I was twenty-eight, some land I had bought near the town for a speculation turned out to be mostly copper-ore under the surface, and the first thing I knew I was a millionaire.

"After that I engaged in all kinds of business, and prospered still more. I donated a library and a hospital to Harrison, founded professorships at Denver and Boulder, subscribed liberally to charities. I was a prominent citizen and a public benefactor. The Governor of the State appointed me a member of his personal staff with the rank of Colonel. That was just an honour, I didn't have to do a thing for it. I liked being a Colonel, for I thought it might be useful when I got after Somerton. I had plenty else to think about, but I never forgot him.

"Three years ago I put a private inquiry agency on to Somerton. I had reports of his position, his health, his way of life. I got the addresses he had lived at during the years since I last saw him. I found he had come into a lot of money and resigned from the bench; and among other things I heard he had the habit of spending a month in Monte Carlo after Christmas, staying at the Artemare.

"Well, the next time he went there, last year—I went there too. We became acquainted, we got on well together. When I left to attend to my business interests at home, we both hoped we should meet again next year—that is to say, this year. During those few weeks I learnt a lot more about him than I knew before, I had spied out the land for my enterprise, and I had my little scheme ready for a year ahead. The hotel staff knew me as a man who tipped extravagantly. I was on the best of terms with Madame Joubin at the paper-stand and I had wasted a lot of money with old Grangette.

"When Somerton arrived at the Artemere a fortnight ago I was already here. He was delighted to see me, and I spent all my time with him and his daughter and their friends. After a few days I started on him, in the way you know. The hotel servants, who disliked him, entered thoroughly into the spirit of the thing. The people who spoke to him in the street would have done a lot more than that for a 100-franc bill.

"I have told you, in part, how I managed the matter of Somerton's bill-fold. I expected he would be going to the bank for money some time, and I had been practising for months till my hands had got the old dexterity. I was with him when he went to the Crédit Lyonnais, saw him draw his ten bills, returned with him to the crowd watching the regatta. Lifting a wallet from a hip-pocket is one of the easiest things an expert dip ever does. I put in ten more *milles*, returned the case, watched him turn white when he made the discovery. That was good! A minute later I had the case out again, removed my own ten, put it back. It all went over very smoothly.

"The newspaper trick was done in this way. Passing through London I had obtained from the *Times* back-date department copies of the paper covering a fortnight of this time last year. Madame Joubin willingly agreed, for a consideration, to help me work a practical joke on Somerton. She was to hand him a year-old paper the first time we both came to her stand together. I timed that for the day after the bill-fold incident. I already had in my coat pocket a *Times* of the right date, which I had provided myself with an hour before. When he took his paper from Madame Joubin I bought a copy of *Esquire*, which is a large-size American magazine, and I held my own *Times* ready underneath it. When he did notice the date on his paper, and exclaimed about it, I very naturally held out my hand for it. Looking him in the eyes—as I did with you, you may remember—I changed the papers in an instant, and then remarked that the date was all right. His ghastly face as I handed it to him was well worth all my trouble and expense, believe me.

"What I had in mind when I got Somerton's old address was this. The year before, he had sent his wife a birthday present, which I had helped him choose, from Grangette's. I gambled on his doing the same again, and he did; but if he didn't, I thought I would be able to make a good use of that address some way. As it happened, he actually asked me to go with him to Grangette's again, for the same purpose; he had confidence in my judgment. As you know, I didn't make the mistake of offering Grangette too little; he would probably have done it for much less, but I wanted that thing done.

"Of course, it went wrong because the inquiry agent made a couple of errors in giving me that old address. I do not blame him, at that. No man could have thought of the slight change in the postal direction since Somerton lived there, and the mis-spelling of Talfourd was a very natural slip. I am not worrying, anyway. I got the effect I wanted. And I have found it quite a pleasure telling this story to an intelligent person who can appreciate it.

"I believe that is all. I have had a very interesting and happy time. Somerton will miss me, I am afraid. He can put in the time thinking about all the pleasant little talks we have had together, beginning in his own police court twenty years ago."

"A very interesting and happy time!" Trent repeated to himself. "Monte Cristo in miniature!" He turned back a few sheets. "A prominent citizen and a public benefactor, was he? And a private malefactor in his spare time.

Well, Somerton won't like this; but I dare say he will like it better than being driven out of his mind. All the same, I don't think I'll deliver it by hand."

He telephoned to the porter's office for a *chasseur*.

10

THE LITTLE MYSTERY

IT WAS early on a Saturday afternoon that Philip Trent, passing through Cadogan Place, caught sight of a trim figure in the portico of one of the tall old houses. The girl came down the steps as he stopped his car.

"How goes it, Marion?" he said. "It must be all of a year since I saw you last."

"Why, Phil! What a surprise!" She glanced back at the door she had just left. "Have you come to see the doctor? But no, you can't do that without an appointment—and besides, he's just going out himself."

Trent got out of the driving seat and shook hands with Marion Silvester, whom he had known for most of her twenty-two years. "So this is the doctor's. Ah yes, I see—brass plate so tiny you don't notice it's there. A great man, evidently—the smaller the plate the bigger the doctor. Still, I don't want to see him. I have just been lunching in Chelsea, but it wasn't as bad as all that."

"Well, you will see him, whether you want to or not," she said in a low tone as the door opened, and a tall, gaunt man, black-bearded, came out. He took off his hat to Marion, with a swift glance at Trent as he returned the salutation, and passed on his way.

"He's not a doctor, really, he's a surgeon," Marion explained. "But he is a Pole, and it seems that whatever degree you take in his country, you're called a doctor."

Trent examined the brass plate. "Dr. W. Kozicki. There is something very tragic about the look of your Dr. W. Kozicki, Marion. An interesting, cultured face. And he has very small ears, with hardly any lobes. Beautiful hands; and he has had the left one badly bitten by a dog, or possibly a patient—some years ago by the look of the scar. No baldness, though he must be over fifty. Short nose, long upper lip—he wouldn't look nearly so handsome if he was clean-shaved."

She laughed. "Isn't that just like you! You see a person for a split second, and you've got him photographed. Well, I'm his secretary, and as Saturday's a short day, I get off after lunch."

"Is there anywhere I can take you? I am free for the next hour."

She thought for a moment. "You know, Phil, meeting you like this is really rather lucky. Several times I've wished I could tell you about something that's been annoying me, because I can't understand it, and perhaps you could, though it's not one of your crime problems. If you could take me home, I could explain it best there. I suppose you don't know Reville Place."

"I know where it is."

"Then you know it's where a quite nice neighbourhood shades off into a dingy one. I've got a cheap top floor at number 43." Trent opened the door of the car, and she took her place. "It's not a very cheery spot, but my flatlet is all right once you're inside the door. Mother let me have some decent furniture and things, and it's airy and comfortable."

The car started, and Marion continued, "Yes, I am on my own now. Of course, we haven't met since father died. We weren't left any too well off, as you may imagine, knowing him as you did."

Trent nodded. He had indeed known Colin Silvester well enough to be surprised that he had left anything at all. Probably, he reflected, Mrs. Silvester had her own income. Silvester had made money easily and abundantly, but he had loved entertaining on a generous scale, and loved yet more anything in the nature of a gamble for high stakes. He had been well known and popular in the social world, though a malicious wit had made him not every one's friend; which had added a spice to the news that, at his death, he had left behind him the material for a volume of memoirs, to be published in due time.

"Mother has the house in Wallingford," Marion said, "and not too much to run it on, when Fred's school bills have been paid. I had a little capital of my own, enough to keep me while I was learning to make a living, so I decided to come to London and train for a secretary's job. I took this place we're going to, and started a course at Needham's."

Trent asked when she had finished her course.

"Why, I never did finish it," Marion said. "I hadn't been at it three months when Paula Kozicki looked me up. You wouldn't know her—she's my boss's daughter, of course, and she was my greatest friend at school. She had all her education in England, and you would never know she was a Pole. She's lived with her father since he came to London. He had a son who went to the devil, Paula told me, and since then the old man has been entirely devoted to her. Well, when she called on me, she told me her father wanted a new secretary, and nothing would do but that he must have me for the job.

"I was astonished. I had only seen him once in my life, when Paula brought him to tea in Reville Place. I had heard about him sometimes from father, who for some reason didn't like him, and I had always imagined he was very disagreeable; but when he came I quite took to the old chap, he so evidently doted on Paula. But of course I hadn't ever dreamed of an offer like this. Well, she made me come round and see him; and he was most charming—said he had been so much touched by Paula's story of me and my doings—he laid it on rather thick, really. You know the sort of thing men say when a girl doesn't merely curl up and collapse when things get difficult."

"Yes, I do know," Trent said with feeling. "Your pluck, your self-reliance, your—"

"All right, I see you've got it by heart," interrupted the girl of the period. "So when we had got over that part, he asked if I could come to him, as his secretary was leaving him for a better position—which I knew from Paula; only she also told me the doctor had got her another post because he wanted to have me. I said how gratified I was, but that I had had very little training and no experience; and he said any fool could do the work—though he didn't put it quite that way—as it was just keeping a list of appointments with patients, and receiving them when they came, and taking some correspondence, and noting up the fees. And then he offered me about double what I should have expected for my first job.

"Well, I took it. There was absolutely nothing wrong with it; and there still isn't, after a month of it. The work's not hard, and in fact there's often not much to do, so that I can get a little work done on father's book. Oh! I didn't tell you that I was putting his rough notes for his memoirs into shape for the publishers. They're very rough ones, and I have to write the whole thing out myself. I take some of the stuff to the doctor's every day. There's quite a lot of it—I haven't read it all yet, in fact; but a good deal of what I have read is pretty scandalous, believe me."

Trent, with a vivid memory of Silvester's vein of unexpurgated anecdote about people of importance, said that this was easy to believe. "But you say there's still nothing wrong with this heaven-sent job of yours. Marion, you blast my hopes. I thought I was going to hear that Kozicki had made dishonourable proposals to you, or that he drinks laudanum, or that he has a private delusion that he is a weasel. Well, it's all very capital for you, and I am gladder than I can say—and here we are at 43 Reville Place."

This was an old-fashioned, high-roofed, stucco-fronted house with a basement and three other floors; like all its neighbours, slightly dingy in appearance, though not dilapidated. They mounted the steps, and Marion opened the door with a latchkey. It could be seen, as they went up the stairs, that each floor had been partitioned off to form a self-contained flat; and Marion's own door, like the front door, was fitted with a Yale lock.

"Well, here's my top floor," she said as they entered.

There were four rooms opening off the landing, all fairly lofty and well lighted.

"And a very good top floor," Trent observed when he had been shown the living-room, bedroom, bathroom and kitchen. "Much better than the top floor in my own place; and furnished, as I think you said, with faultless taste. If ever you want to get rid of that little tallboy you might let me know. And that mahogany writing-table—it was a spinet when it was young, wasn't it? You want to keep that, I suppose."

Marion laughed. "Are you setting up an antique shop? But now, let me tell you what it was I wanted your advice about. To begin with, look at the top of that table."

He bent over it. "You mean these faint scratches here and there—as if something hard and heavy had been shifted about on it. Curious? The scratches are in four lots—making the four corners of a square. Was it done when the furniture was moved here from Wallingford?"

"No, it was done fairly lately—three weeks ago, say; perhaps more. That table was as smooth as glass till then. I rub it over with a duster every day, so I noticed it at once. And it wasn't done by the charlady who comes in two mornings a week. She is a very careful, neat-handed woman; and besides, I first saw the scratches on a Thursday, and her days are Tuesday and Friday. Of course, I don't like having my table scratched, but what I like much less is not knowing who did it, and how any one could have been here to do it. The entrance door is locked when I'm out, of course; and the street door always is. And don't look as if you thought I was worrying about a trifle. There are other things that tell me plainly some one comes into this place when I'm not here.

"You see the velvet cushion in that armchair? It's embroidered a prettier pattern on one side than on the other, and I always leave it showing that side, as it is now. But several times I have come in and found it turned the other way round. Any one who had been sitting in that chair, and had punched the cushion into shape again before going away, would be as likely as not to leave it wrong way round. Then again there is that old writing-table you covet so much. There is nothing of value in either of the drawers—I keep father's notes for his memoirs in the left-hand one, and as much as I have done of the fair copy in the other—but three times some one has been at them."

"They are not locked?" Trent asked.

"No—nothing in the place is locked except the door of the flat. Now, look at these drawers. You see"—she opened both and shut them again—"they both push in a little too far when you close them, and I always pull them back so as to be just level with the woodwork round them. I'm fussily particular, perhaps you think; anyhow, I am absolutely certain I have never left those drawers pushed right in as I found them three days running not long ago. And now here"—she led the way into the kitchen—"I'll show you the thing that makes me quite certain, and that is this sink. When I've washed up after breakfast I leave it not only perfectly clean, but quite dry, bottom and sides as well."

"Why?" Trent wondered.

"Because I've been well brought up," Marion said conclusively. "Well, every day for some time past I have come home and found it perfectly clean, but not dry—drops of water on the sides, which you get from the splashes when you're running the tap. Look! You see those drops? A man wouldn't, I suppose, unless they were pointed out to him. They weren't here when I left this morning."

Marion and her guest looked at one another in silence for some moments; then Trent remarked, "You say nothing about having missed anything—jewellery, or any other sort of portable property."

"No," she said. "Absolutely nothing has ever been stolen, I am sure. I often leave money in my dressing-table drawer, and my jewellery, such as it is, is kept there, too, and nothing has been taken. What food I have had in the place has never been touched, nor any of the household things—unless you count those matches, which I suppose came from my box."

Trent rose and paced the floor. "It all sounds pretty mad, I must say," he observed. "And it doesn't make it seem any saner to suggest that one of the people on the lower floors may be your visitor, as they haven't got your private key."

"Yes, and besides, why should they? As for my keys, they are always in my handbag, which is with me all the time. The only duplicates are a pair I keep in the dressing-table drawer, and a pair the charwoman has; and if you ever saw Mrs. Kinch you would know she was incapable of doing anything eccentric or not respectable. She worships the Vicar of St. Mark's, just round the corner, and she sings hymns while she is doing out the place, as she calls it; and she has a son in a solicitor's office, and likes to let you know it. There have been other things, too, which you can't possibly connect with Mrs. Kinch. There's that window you saw me shut when we came in. She knows I always leave it open, to air the room. Well, several times I have come home and found it shut. You see?"

Trent went to the window and opened it for a moment. "Yes, there might be a draught that any one sitting in this armchair would feel. I agree; it does look as if somebody has been coming in here while you were away—in particular, sitting in your armchair, and plumping up the cushion when he leaves the place."

An exclamation of disgust came from Marion Silvester. "And that's a nice thing to think of, isn't it? I prefer to know something about people who visit my flat and sprawl in my armchair. And it's no use going to the police about it, as you can see. What have I got to tell them? The place hasn't been broken into, nothing has been stolen. I've no actual proof that any one has been making themselves at home here. They'd only grin, and say—or think—I was fancying things."

Trent considered. "Yes, I suppose they would. By the way, what time do you leave here in the morning?"

"Nine-fifteen; and get back about seven, usually."

"Much at home during the week-ends?"

"No, not a lot. I spend a good deal of the time with friends—Paula Kozicki and other people I know in London. On Sundays I get out into the country if the weather's decent, and have a day in the open air, with or without a companion. I don't have at all a dull life, Phil. The one bad spot is this silly little mystery."

"Perhaps," Trent said, "the best thing you can do, Marion, is to leave it to me. I must be on my way now, but I will let my giant intellect play round the subject, and make a few inquiries and see you again very soon."

She jumped up. "Heaven bless you, Phil! That's what I hoped you would say."

"And before I go, would you like to trust me with those spare keys of yours?"

She fetched them from the bedroom. "If you use them, you must promise not to pilfer anything, or smash up the furniture."

Trent expressed the hope that he would be able to overcome his lower nature. Before he left the house, he tried each of the keys in its lock, and found that they fitted easily.

In the Cactus Club most ways of life are represented, and there are few subjects on which some information cannot be gleaned from fellow-members whenever there is a large muster. Lunching there next day, Trent was able to draw upon more than one source for facts about Dr. Kozicki. He was an orthopædic specialist with certain methods of his own devising and a fancy for making his own surgical appliances. He had built up a large practice in his native city of Posen, and made a European reputation. The afflicted grandson of Jason B. Rhodes, the sulphur magnate, had been brought across the ocean to him for treatment, and had been cured.

An ex-patient of the doctor, who had attended him at his own house, gave some more intimate details. Kozicki was a widower. His son and daughter had been sent to school in England, so as to escape the influence of German culture, of which the doctor disapproved, for he had been an ardent Polish patriot under the German rule. This had not been a success in the case of the son, who had turned out a hopeless waster.

Some ten years ago Dr. Kozicki had, it was vaguely known, "got into trouble" with the German authorities, and had found it advisable to transfer himself to London, where he had resumed his practice, and was doing more than well. The son, going from bad to worse, had turned his attention to forgery, and had been sent to penal servitude. The doctor was entirely wrapped up in his daughter, who was a Slade art student. He had not succeeded in spoiling her, and every one thought her charming.

Beside his liking for Marion Silvester, Trent had another motive for taking up her "little mystery." He thought there might be something more in the affair than she imagined, and his curiosity was awake. It might be worth while to look further into the affairs of Dr. Kozicki; and there was one line, at least, that could be followed up. After leaving the Cactus Club, he spent a fruitless hour searching the files in the offices of the *Record* for a report of the trial of the younger Kozicki; and he was still at this task when Homan, the paper's regular crime expert, came into the library.

"If you're hunting for the name Kozicki," Homan said, "you won't find it. I remember the case. He was prosecuted under the name of Jackson, by which he was known to the police as being mixed up with a bad lot. He had forged a stolen cheque and collected the money. It didn't come out till afterwards that he was the doctor's son, and the fact was never made public. He was informed on by a man he had quarrelled with, and his evidence got Jackson five years."

Thus put on the right track, Trent soon turned up the report of the case. It was colourless enough; but Trent noted that the name of the informer was given as Whimster, that he had been on intimate terms with Jackson before their quarrel, and that his going to the police had the air of an act of treachery rather than of dauntless public spirit. A public house called the Cat and Fiddle, in the Harrow Road, had figured in the evidence as a rendezvous of Jackson, Whimster, and their associates. A comparison of dates showed that Jackson-Kozicki's sentence had still six months to run; but as Homan pointed out, it might be shortened considerably as the reward of good conduct.

The landlord of the Cat and Fiddle, whose beer Trent found to be in excellent condition, had known Whimster very well. Jackson had been before his time. When the landlord first came to the place, three years ago, Whimster had been using the Cat and Fiddle regularly. He was a racing tipster, and seemed to do pretty well out of it, taking good times with bad. Last year Whimster had left the district, saying nothing to nobody; but Joe Chittle, being over in Woolwich not long ago, had seen him in the street. Joe could swear it was Whimster; but when he spoke to him he said that wasn't his name, and he had never seen Joe in his life—quite nasty about it he was, Joe said. Well, what could you make of it?

Funny, but Trent was not the first to be asking after Whimster, the landlord said. There had been a gent in not long ago wanting to get in touch with the same party, and the landlord had told him the same as he had told Trent.

"Would you know that man again?" asked Trent.

Yes, the landlord would; it was a face that gave you a funny feeling, you couldn't easily forget it. But what, the landlord wondered, was the reason for all this interest in Whimster?

Trent could only tell him that he thought Whimster might have some information that would be useful to him. What was the landlord having? The landlord's was a toothful of old Jamaica—good stuff this chilly weather. Happy days, sir!

Chief Inspector Bligh, receiving Trent in his little office at Scotland Yard, pushed the cigarette-box across the table.

"Yes, I can tell you something more about Ladislas Kozicki, alias George Jackson," Mr. Bligh said, when Trent had set forth the extent of his own information. "I'm glad you got the landlord of the Cat to talk; his evidence will be useful. We hadn't got on to that line, because, you see, the man you know as Whimster has called himself Barling since he went to live in Woolwich. They must be the same man; I can see that. We have got plenty on Jackson as it is, but you can't have too much."

"Why, is he in trouble again?"

"You might call it that," the inspector said grimly. "He came out of prison five weeks ago. He's wanted now for attempted murder. Last Tuesday night Barling passed two men who knew him walking up Foxhill Street, where he lives. There was nobody else about. They exchanged greetings as they passed; and then the two chaps met another, whose face they say they didn't like. This fellow was staring after Barling, and looked as if he was following him. Well, out of curiosity they turned and followed too.

"Just as Barling was approaching a pub called the Red Cow, which he was probably on his way to, they saw the follower catch him up and take him by the arm. They were too far behind to hear what was said, but the other man seemed to steer Barling into the entry of a builder's yard at the side of the pub. Then they heard Barling yelling for help, and as they ran up, the other man came bolting out of the entry and made off in the opposite direction, towards the main road.

"They found Barling lying in his blood, apparently dead; he had been stabbed twice. His injuries were serious, but not fatal. Next day he was able to state that the man who had knifed him was George Jackson, who had done time for forgery. We looked him up in the Rogue's Gallery, and showed the two witnesses his picture, which they recognized at once. Barling refuses to say anything more."

Trent, his elbows on the table, had followed this terse narrative with kindling eyes. "And Jackson is still on the run?"

"He is. He probably slowed down when he got to the main road, seeing he wasn't being pursued; and he could have boarded any one of a dozen buses or trams. It was easy for him to vanish. His description has gone out, of course, with his prison photo; but there's no trace of him as yet. As we knew his real name and history, Dr. Kozicki was called on and interrogated; but he could tell us nothing—didn't even know his son was at liberty, he says. He had had six months knocked off his sentence, you see, for being a good boy. He shed his virtue with his convict's uniform—they often do—"

Trent eyed the inspector thoughtfully for a few moments, then looked away. "It all fits in," he said as if to himself. "I don't like it, but it can't be helped."

"What's on your mind?" Mr. Bligh demanded. "Is it another of your bright ideas? They are usually worth something, so let's have it."

"Well, I have an idea—I don't know if you'll call it a bright one—about where you can lay hands on your man. But it means more tragedy for some one, if I'm right."

"It'll mean tragedy for you, my lad, if you connive at the escape of a dangerous criminal," the inspector said briskly, drawing his chair up to the table. "Come on; let's hear it."

Trent let him hear it.

At the corner of Reville Place next morning Trent met Mr. Bligh, who was followed at some distance by another plain-clothes officer, already known to Trent as Sergeant Borrett. A closed car was waiting there, and as they passed it the inspector and its driver exchanged almost imperceptible nods.

"You've told her what to do?" Mr. Bligh asked.

"She will have got my letter this morning," Trent said. "As we arranged, I didn't tell her anything—only asked her to leave at her usual time, not to take any notice of us when she sees us at the door, and to go straight off to her job as if nothing was happening."

"Right."

They came to the door of No. 43, and Trent opened it with Marion's latch-key. When the sergeant had joined them in the entry, they went quickly up to the top floor and waited before the entrance to the flat. "Probably nothing will happen until she's been gone some time," the inspector remarked, "but we don't want to have this door opening and shutting more than it usually does."

At nine-fifteen precisely Marion, equipped with hat and handbag, opened the entrance door and came out. She was flushed and bright-eyed as she took in the sight of the three tall figures waiting on the stair-head. "I got your note," she murmured to Trent; then hurried down below.

The three men entered quietly, shutting the door behind them, however, not so quietly. Mr. Bligh, after a glance into each of the four rooms that opened upon the landing, led the way into the largest, the living-room in which Trent had listened to Marion's story; and there they waited in silence with the room door open, for what seemed to Trent the longest half-hour his watch had ever told.

At last a sharp, slight noise came from without, and the inspector motioned the others to stand farther back from the door. Other faint sounds followed; and then there came into view through the doorway an object which was slowly descending from the ceiling outside the room. It was a small suitcase, dangling from a cord fastened to its handle. This came noiselessly to rest on the landing; the cord dropped beside it; and then with a dry rattle, a rope-ladder with rungs of cane unrolled itself swiftly from above until its end just cleared the floor.

The ladder began to thresh about and to creak, and two feet appeared. A man was feeling his way down by this awkward means; a short, strongly-made man with disproportionately broad shoulders. But just before the head on the shoulders came into the watchers' field of vision the two officers were out of the room with a rush.

The man was instantly dragged from the ladder. There followed a furious and wordless struggle, during which a small hall-table and the bowl of flowers upon it were smashed to pieces, and a panel of the entrance-door was cracked by a boot-heel. At last the handcuffs snapped, and George Jackson was formally acquainted with the reason for his arrest as he stood glowering and panting in the secure grasp of Sergeant Borrett.

Jackson's broad, high forehead and over-developed jaws made his face almost square; his lips were thin, his chin was short, his narrow-lidded eyes were much too far apart, and he was villainously unshaven.

Mr. Bligh jerked an automatic pistol from the captive's breast-pocket.

"You see," he remarked to Trent, "there couldn't have been a better way of getting him. If he'd had his hands free, somebody might have been hurt with this Betsy before he could be stopped. If we had tried to get him in that loft, somebody would have been killed pretty certainly, and he could have stood the whole Force off up there, so long as he had food and ammunition. But if he was making use of the flat, there had to be a rope or a ladder of some kind; and while he was coming down he was helpless."

He went to the window opening on the street, put his head out and waved a hand. The car at the corner rolled gently up to No. 43.

"Take him along, Borrett," Mr. Bligh said, opening the entrance door. "I'll be over when I have had a look round up above."

The sergeant twined one fist scientifically into Jackson's collar, the other into a sleeve, and propelled him at arm's length through the doorway and down the stairs. From first to last he had not spoken a word.

"First we'll have a look at his travelling outfit," Mr. Bligh said, as he slipped the catches of the suitcase on the floor. "Good idea, that—saved a lot of climbing up and down. What have we here? Toothbrush, soap, and towel, brush and comb—he has nice, clean habits, anyhow, and didn't like to use anything of Miss Silvester's more than he had to. He was able to wash regularly and leave no traces—have a bath, too. No shaving tackle—as you might expect from the look of him."

"That was the notion, I think," Trent said. "To lie low—or rather high—until the hunt for him had cooled off, and meanwhile grow a beard and moustache that would be a better disguise than anything else. What's that you've got there?"

The inspector held it up, eyeing it appreciatively. "Boned chicken in glass—none of your vulgar tins. Tomato soup in bottle. Biscuits, butter—his old man was doing him well, I must say. Salt and pepper, packet of tea. Two cloths—for washing up, I suppose, so as not to use Miss Silvester's. He must have made free with her plates and knives and forks and kitchen things, though; there's none of them here. By the way, she may notice a rise in her gas-bill, if Jackson has been using the cooker as well as the kitchen and bathroom geysers, and the gas-fire in the sitting-room. I should say he was very comfortable here, making himself quite at home for eight hours or so a day."

"And at intervals the doctor would look in with fresh supplies," Trent remarked. "That would be when he was supposed to be attending patients at their own homes, no doubt."

The inspector closed the suitcase and rose from his knees. "I'm glad his old man supplied a ladder. It will be easier than a rope for anybody my size."

"It will certainly be easier than the way Jackson first got up into the loft," Trent remarked, "if I am right in thinking they dragged the living-room table on to the landing and put a chair on top of it. Johnson would only just be able to push up the trap-door with his fingers, and hauling himself up required some strength. The scratches made by the feet of the chair gave me an idea almost at the start."

"But that wasn't all you had to go on?" suggested the inspector.

"No. Before that I thought the doctor must have some reason for manufacturing a job for a girl he didn't know, and keeping her safe in his own house all day. What he did know was that she lived in a top-floor flatlet; and he visited her once to see if the usual loft and trap-door were where they could be made use of. When she started work with him, he borrowed the keys from her bag at the first opportunity, took a squeeze of them, and filed duplicates from a couple of Yale blanks—he's quite a craftsman, I'm told. Then he laid in the necessary stores, and one evening when Miss Silvester was at the theatre with his daughter he met Ladislas, brought him here, and left him settled in under the roof. That's my story, anyhow. I've thought over it a lot since yesterday, and that's how I fill in the outlines."

Mr. Bligh grunted. "It must have been something like that. Of course he knew his son was released as soon as it happened. Probably he got the doctor on the phone and arranged a meeting somewhere. He may have told him what he meant to do to Whimster. He must have told him he was going to be wanted by the police again, and must have a safe hide-out. Then the doctor was struck by a notion, and he began working on the plan for making a hide-out of the loft over his daughter's friend's place. A good plan, too."

"Perhaps he didn't need to be told what a lad like that was going to do to the man who put him away," Trent suggested. "If you're a Pole, as well as a wrong 'un, you are not apt to have a forgiving nature. If it was a question of saving his son from a hanging, I suppose he was ready for anything."

"Well, he'll get plenty, I daresay—though there'll be sympathy for him, too. Now will you hold on to the foot of this ladder while I go up? If you want to come, you'll have to manage by yourself, as Jackson did."

"If I want to come?"

By the light of the inspector's big electric torch they surveyed the sleeping quarters of the *soi-disant* George Jackson. Between two of the roof-beams a light canvas hammock was slung, folded blankets within it. Some sheets of pasteboard had been laid over the ceiling-joists in one corner, and on them stood an array of preserved foods, a tin of biscuits, a carton of eggs, a packet of candles, and other household necessaries. In another corner was a pile of newspapers.

"Nothing to sit on," Trent observed. "You can't carry a chair about the streets without exciting remark—besides, there's nowhere for a chair to stand. No wonder he had a fondness for that armchair below."

"It must have taken the doctor several visits to get this place furnished," the inspector said. "Well, I've seen enough. I'll have all this removed before Miss Silvester comes home. I wonder how she'll like it when you tell her the story. It'll be something for her to talk about for the rest of her life—how she had a young man staying in her flat for a fortnight without knowing it."

When they had made the descent, Trent turned to gathering up the wreckage on the floor and stowing it in a corner of the kitchen.

"I shall have to get Marion a new table and bowl," he remarked. "I promised her I wouldn't smash up the furniture." He laughed suddenly.

Mr. Bligh inquired what the joke was.

"Why, I just remembered," Trent said, "that she told me this wasn't one of my crime problems."

11

THE UNKNOWN PEER

WHEN Philip Trent went down to Lackington, with the mission of throwing some light upon the affair of Lord Southrop's disappearance, it was without much hope of adding anything to the simple facts already known to the police and made public in the newspapers. Those facts were plain enough, pointing to but one sad conclusion.

In the early morning of Friday, the 23rd of September, a small touring car was found abandoned by the shore at Merwin Cove, some three miles along the coast from the flourishing Devonian resort of Brademouth. It had been driven off the road over turf to the edge of the pebble-beach.

Examined by the police, it was found to contain a heavy overcoat, a folding stool, and a case of sketching materials with a sketching-block on the back seat; a copy of Anatole France's *Mannequin d'Osier*, two pipes, some chocolate, a flask of brandy, and a pair of binoculars in the shelves before the driving-seat; and in the pockets a number of maps and the motoring papers of Lord Southrop, of Hingham Blewitt, near Wymondham, in Norfolk. Inquiries in the neighbourhood led to the discovery that a similar car and its driver were missing from the Crown

Inn at Lackington, a small place a few miles inland; and later the car was definitely recognized.

In the hotel register, however, the owner had signed his name as L. G. Coxe; and it was in that name that a room had been booked by telephone early in the day. A letter, too, addressed to Coxe, had been delivered at the Crown, and had been opened by him on his arrival about 6.30. A large suit-case had been taken up to his room, where it still lay, and the mysterious Coxe had deposited an envelope containing £35 in bank-notes in the hotel safe. He had dined in the coffee-room, smoked in the lounge for a time, then gone out again in his car, saying nothing of his destination. No more had been seen or heard of him.

Some needed light had been cast on the affair when Lord Southrop was looked up in *Who's Who*—for no one in the local force had ever heard of such a peer. It appeared that his family name was Coxe, and that he had been christened Lancelot Graham; that he was the ninth baron, was thirty-three years old, and had succeeded to the title at the age of twenty-six; that he had been educated at Harrow and Trinity, Cambridge; that he was unmarried, and that his heir was a first cousin, Lambert Reeves Coxe. No public record of any kind, nor even any "recreation" was noted in this unusually brief biography, which, indeed, bore the marks of having been compiled in the office, without any assistance from its subject.

Trent, however, had heard something more than this about Lord Southrop. Sir James Molloy, the owner of the *Record*, who had sent Trent to Lackington, had met everybody, including even the missing peer, who was quite unknown in society. Society, according to Molloy, was heartily detested and despised by Lord Southrop. His interests were exclusively literary and artistic, apart from his taste in the matter of wine, which he understood better than most men. He greatly preferred Continental to English ways of life, and spent much of his time abroad. He had a very large income, for most of which he seemed to have no use. He had good health and a kindly disposition; but he had a passion for keeping himself to himself, and had indulged it with remarkable success. One of his favourite amusements was wandering about the country alone in his car, halting here and there to make a sketch, and staying always at out-of-the-way inns under the name he had used at Lackington.

Lord Southrop had been, however, sufficiently like other men to fall in love, and Molloy had heard that his engagement to Adela Tindal was on the point of being announced at the time of his disappearance. His choice had come as a surprise to his friends; for though Miss Tindal took art and letters as seriously as himself, she was, as an authoress, not at all averse to publicity. She enjoyed being talked about, Molloy declared; and talked about she had certainly been—especially in connection with Lucius Kelly, the playwright. Their relationship had not been disguised; but a time came when Kelly's quarrelsome temper was no longer to be endured, and she refused to see any more of him.

All this was quite well known to Lord Southrop, for he and Kelly had been friends from boyhood; and the knowledge was a signal proof of the force of his infatuation. On all accounts, in Molloy's judgment, the match would have been a complete disaster; and Trent, as he thought the matter over in the coffee-room of the Crown, was disposed to agree with him.

Shortly before his arrival that day, a new fact for his first dispatch to the *Record* had turned up. A tweed cap had been found washed up by the waves on the beach between Brademouth and Merwin Cove; and the people at the Crown were sure that it was Lord Southrop's. He had worn a suit of unusually rough, very light-grey homespun tweed, the sort of tweed that, as the head waiter at the Crown vividly put it, you could smell half a mile away; and his cap had been noted because it was made of the same stuff as the suit. After a day and a half in salt water, it had still an aroma of Highland sheep. Apart from this and its colour, or absence of colour, there was nothing by which it could be identified; not even a maker's name; but there was no reasonable doubt about its being Lord Southrop's, and it seemed to settle the question, if question there were, of what had happened to him. It was, Trent reflected, just like an eccentric intellectual—with money—to have his caps made for him, and from the same material as his clothes.

It was these garments, together with the very large horn-rimmed spectacles which Lord Southrop affected, which had made most impression on the head waiter. Otherwise, he told Trent, there was nothing unusual about the poor gentleman, except that he seemed a bit absent-minded-like. He had brought a letter to the table with him—the waiter supposed it would be the one that came to the hotel for him—and it had seemed to worry him. He had read and re-read it all through his dinner, what there was of it; he didn't have only some soup and a bit of fish. Yes, sir; consommé and a nice fillet of sole, like there is this evening. There was roast fowl, but he wouldn't have that, nor nothing else. Would Trent be ordering his own dinner now?

"Yes, I want to—but the fish is just what I won't have," Trent decided, looking at the menu. "I will take the rest of the hotel dinner." An idea occurred to him. "Do you remember what Lord Southrop had to drink? I might profit by his example."

The waiter produced a fly-blown wine-list. "I can tell you that, sir. He had a bottle of this claret here, Château Margaux 1922.

"You're quite sure? And did he like it?"

"Well, he didn't leave much," the waiter answered. Possibly, Trent thought, he took a personal interest in unfinished wine. "Were you thinking of trying some of it yourself, sir? It's our best claret."

"I don't think I will have your best claret," Trent said, thoughtfully scanning the list. "There's a Beychevelle 1924 here, costing eighteen-pence less, which is good enough for me. I'll have that." The waiter hurried away, leaving Trent to his reflections in the deserted coffee-room.

Trent had learned from the police that the numbers of the notes left in the charge of the hotel had been communicated by telephone to Lord Southrop's bank in Norwich, the reply being that these notes had been issued to him in person ten days before. Trent had also been allowed to inspect the objects, including the maps, found in the abandoned car. Lackington he found marked in pencil with a cross; and working backwards across the country he found similar crosses at the small towns of

Hawbridge, Wringham, and Candley. The police, acting on these indications, had already established that "L. G. Coxe" had passed the Thursday, Wednesday and Tuesday nights respectively at inns in these places; and they had learned already of his having started from Hingham Blewitt on the Monday.

Trent, finding no more to be done at Lackington, decided to follow this designated trail in his own car. On the morning after his talk with the waiter at the Crown he set out for Hawbridge. The distances in Lord Southrop's progress, as marked, were not great by the most direct roads; but it could be guessed that he had been straying about to this and that point of interest—not, Trent imagined, to sketch, for there had been no sketches found among his belongings. Hawbridge was reached in time for lunch; and at the Three Bells Inn Trent again found matter for thought in a conversation—much like chat which he had already enjoyed at the Crown Inn—with the head waiter. So it was again at the Green Man in Wringham that evening. The next day, however, when Trent dined at the Running Stag in Candley, the remembered record of Lord Southrop's potations took a different turn. What Trent was told convinced him that he was on the right track.

The butler and housekeeper at Hingham Blewitt, when Trent spoke with them the following day, were dismally confident that Lord Southrop would never be seen again. The butler had already given to the police investigator from Devon what little information he could. He admitted that none of it lent the smallest support to the idea that Lord Southrop had been contemplating suicide; that he had, in fact, been unusually cheerful, if anything, on the day of his departure. But what, the butler asked, could a person think? Especially, the housekeeper observed, after the cap was found. Lord Southrop was, of course, eccentric in his views; and you never knew—here the housekeeper, with a despondent head-shake, paused, leaving unspoken the suggestion that a man who did not think or behave like other people might go mad at any moment.

Lord Southrop, they told Trent, never left any address when he went on one of these motoring tours. What he used to say was, he never knew where he was going till he got there. But this time he did have one object in mind, though what it was or where it was the butler did not know; and the police officer, when he was informed, did not seem to make any more of it. What had happened was that, a few days before Lord Southrop started out, he had been rung up by some one on the 'phone in his study; and as the door of the room was open, the butler, in passing through the hall, had happened to catch a few words of what he said.

He had told this person he was going next Tuesday to visit the old moor; and that if the weather was right he was going to make a sketch. He had said, "You remember the church and chapel"—the butler heard that distinctly; and he had said that it must be over twenty years. "What must be over twenty years?" Trent wanted to know. Impossible to tell: Lord Southrop had said just that.

The butler had heard nothing further. He thought the old moor might perhaps be Dartmoor or Exmoor, seeing where it was that Lord Southrop had disappeared. Trent thought otherwise, but he did not discuss the point.

"There's one thing you can perhaps tell me," he said. "Lord Southrop was at Harrow and Cambridge, I believe. Do you know if he went to a preparatory school before Harrow?"

"I can tell you that, sir," the houskeeper said. "I have been with the family since I was a girl. It was Marsham House he went to, near Sharnsley in Derbyshire. The school was founded by his lordship's grandfather's tutor, and all the Coxe boys have gone there for two generations. It stands very high as a school, sir; the best families send their sons there."

"Yes, I've heard of it," Trent said. "Should you say, Mrs. Pillow, that Lord Southrop was happy as a schoolboy—popular, I mean, and fond of games, and so forth?"

Mrs. Pillow shook her head decisively. "He always hated school, sir; and as for games, he had to play them, of course, but he couldn't abide them. And he didn't get on with the other boys—he used to say he wouldn't be a sheep, just like all the other something sheep—he learned bad language at school, if he didn't learn anything else. But at Cambridge—that was very different. He came alive there for the first time—so he used to say."

In Norwich, that same afternoon, Trent furnished himself with a one-inch Ordnance Survey map of a certain section of Derbyshire. He spent the evening at his hotel with this and a small-scale map of England, on which he marked the line of small towns which he had already visited; and he drew up, not for publication, a brief and clear report of his investigation so far.

The next morning's run was long. He had lunch at Sharnsley, where he made a last and very gratifying addition to his string of coffee-room interviews. Marsham

House, he learnt, stood well outside Sharnsley on the verge of the Town Moor; which, as the map had already told him, stretched its many miles away to the south and west. He learnt, too, what and where were "the Church and Chapel," and was thankful that his inquiring mind had not taken those simple terms at their face value.

An hour later he halted his car at a spot on the deserted road that crossed the moor; a spot whence, looking up the purple slope, he could see its bareness broken by a huge rock, and another less huge, whose summits pierced the skyline. They looked, Trent told himself, not more unlike what they were called than rocks with names usually do. Away to the right of them was a small clump of trees, the only ones in sight, to which a rough cart-track led from the road; and from that point, he thought an artist might well consider that the Church and Chapel and their background made the best effect. He left his car and took the path through the heather.

Arrived at the clump, which stood well above the road, he looked over a desolate scene. If any one had met Lord Southrop there, they would have had the world to themselves. Not a house or hut was in sight, and no live thing but the birds. He looked about for traces of any human visitor; and he had just decided that nothing of the sort could reasonably be expected, after the lapse of a week, when something white, lodged in the root of a fir-tree, caught his eye.

It was a small piece of torn paper, pencilled on one side with lines and shading the look of which he knew well. A rapid search discovered another piece near by among the heather. It was all that the wind had left undispersed of an artist's work; but for Trent, as he scanned the remnants closely, it was enough.

His eyes turned now over a wider range; for this, though to him it spelt certainty, was not what he had been looking for. Slowly following the track over the moor, he came at length to the reason for its existence—a small quarry, to all appearance long abandoned. A roughly circular pond of muddy water, some fifty yards across, filled the lower part of it; and about the margin was a confusion of stony fragments, broken and rusted implements, bits of rotting wood and smashed earthenware—a typical scene of industrial litter. With his arm bare to the shoulder Trent could feel no bottom to the pond. If it held any secret, that opaque yellow water kept it well.

There was no soil to take a footprint near the pond. For some time he raked among the débris in which the track ended, finding nothing. Then, as he turned over a broken fire-bucket, something flashed in the sunlight. It was a small, flat fragment of glass, about as large as a threepenny piece, with one smooth and two fractured edges. Trent examined it thoughtfully. It had no place in his theory; it might mean nothing. On the other hand . . . he stowed it carefully in his note-case along with the remnants of paper.

Two hours later, at the police headquarters in Derby, he was laying his report and maps, with the objects found on the moor, before Superintendent Allison, a sharp-faced, energetic officer, to whom Trent's name was well known.

It was well known also to Mr. Gurney Bradshaw, head of the firm of Bradshaw & Co., legal advisers to Lord Southrop and to his father before him. He had at Trent's telephoned request, given him an appointment at three o'clock; and he appeared at that hour on the day after his researches in Derbyshire. Mr. Bradshaw, a courteous but authoritative old gentleman, wore a dubious expression as they shook hands.

"I cannot guess," he said, "what it is that you wish to put before me. It seems to me a case in which we should get the Court to presume death with the minimum of difficulty; and I wish I thought otherwise, for I had known Lord Southrop all his life, and I was much attached to him. Now I must tell you that I have asked a third party to join us here—Mr. Lambert Coxe, who perhaps you know is the heir to the title and to a very large estate. He wrote me yesterday that he had just returned from France, and wanted to know what the position was; and I thought he had better hear what you have to say, so I asked him for the same time as yourself."

"I know of him as a racing man," Trent said, "I had no idea he was what you say until I saw it in the papers."

The buzzer on the desk-telephone sounded, and Bradshaw put it to his ear. "Show him in," he said.

Lambert Coxe was a tall, spare, hard-looking man with a tanned, clean-shaven face, and a cordless monocle screwed into his left eye. As they were introduced he looked at the other with a keen and curious scrutiny.

"And now," Bradshaw said, "let us hear your statement, Mr. Trent."

Trent put his folded hands on the table. "I will begin by making a suggestion which may strike you gentlemen as an absurd one. It's this. The man who drove that car to Lackington, and afterwards down to the seashore, was not Lord Southrop."

Both men stared at him blankly; then Bradshaw, composing his features, said impassively, "I shall be interested to hear your reasons for thinking so. You have not a name for making absurd suggestions, Mr. Trent, but I may call this an astonishing one."

"I should damned well think so," observed Coxe.

"I got the idea originally," Trent said, "from the wine which this man chose to drink with his dinner at the Crown Inn before the disappearance. Do you think that absurd?"

"There is nothing absurd about wine," Mr. Bradshaw replied with gravity. "I take it very seriously myself. Twice a day, as a rule," he added.

"Lord Southrop, I am told, also took it seriously. He had the reputation of a first-rate connoisseur. Now this man I'm speaking of had little appetite that evening, it seems. The dinner they offered him consisted mainly of soup, fillet of sole, and roast fowl."

"I am sure it did," Bradshaw said grimly. "It's what you get nine times out of ten in English hotels. Well?"

"This man took only the soup and the fish. And with it he had a bottle of claret."

The solicitor's composure deserted him abruptly.

"Claret!" he exclaimed.

"Yes, claret, and a curious claret too. You see, mine host of the Crown kept a perfectly good Beychevelle 1924—I had some myself. But he had also a Margaux 1922; and I suppose because it was an older wine he thought it ought to be dearer, so he marked it in his list eighteen-pence more than the other. That was the wine which was chosen by our traveller that evening. What do you think of it? With a fish dinner he had claret, and he chose a wine of a bad year, when he could have had a wine of 1924 for less money."

While Coxe looked his bewilderment, Mr. Bradshaw got up and began to pace the room slowly. "I will admit so much," he said. "I cannot conceive of Lord Southrop doing such a thing if he was in his right mind."

"If you still think it was he, and that he was out of his senses," Trent rejoined, "there was a method in his madness. Because the night before, at Hawbridge, he chose one of those wines bearing the name of a château which doesn't exist, and is merely a label that sounds well; and the night before that, at Wringham, he had two whiskies and soda just before dinner, and another inferior claret at an excessive price on top of them. I have been to both the inns and got these facts. But when I worked back to Candley, the first place where Lord Southrop stayed after leaving home, it was another story. I found he had picked out about the best thing on the list, a Rhine wine, which hardly anybody ever asked for. The man who ordered that, I think, was really Lord Southrop."

Bradshaw pursed up his mouth. "You are suggesting that some one in Lord Southrop's car was impersonating him at the other three places, and that, knowing his standing as a connoisseur, this man did his ignorant best to act up to it. Very well; but Lord Southrop signed the register in his usual way at those places. He received and read a letter addressed to him at Lackington. The motor tour as a whole was just such a haphazard tour as he had often made before. The description given of him at Lackington was exact—the clothes, the glasses, the abstracted manner. The cap that was washed up was certainly his. No, no, Mr. Trent. We are bound to assume that it was Lord Southrop; and the presumption is that he drove down to the sea and drowned himself. The alternative is that he was staging a sham suicide, so as to be able to disappear, and there is no sense in that."

"Just so," observed Lambert Coxe. "What you say about the wine may be all right as far as it goes, Mr. Trent, but I agree with Mr. Bradshaw. Southrop committed suicide; and if he was insane enough to do that, he was insane enough to go wrong about his drinks."

Trent shook his head. "There are other things to be accounted for. I'm coming to them. And the clothes and the cap and the rest are all part of my argument. This man was wearing Lord Southrop's tweed suit just because it was so easily identifiable. He knew all about Lord Southrop and his ways. He had letters from Lord Southrop in his possession, and had learnt to imitate his writing. It was he who wrote and posted that letter addressed to L. G. Coxe; and he made a pretence of being worried by it. He knew that Lord Southrop's notes could be traced; so he left them at the bureau to clinch the thing. And, of course, he did not drown himself. He only threw the cap into the sea. What he may have done is to change out of those conspicuous clothes, put them in a bag which he had in the car, and which contained another suit in which he proceeded to dress himself. He may then have walked, with his bag, the few miles into Brademouth, and travelled to London by the 12.15—quite a popular train, in which you can get a comfortable sleeping-berth."

"So he may," Bradshaw agreed with some acidity,

while Lambert Coxe laughed shortly. "But what I am interested in is facts, Mr. Trent."

"Well, here are some. A few days before Lord Southrop set out from his place in Norfolk, some one rang him up in his library. The door was ajar, and the butler heard a little of what he said to the caller. He said he was going on the following Tuesday to visit a place he called the old moor, as if it was a place as well known to the other as to himself. He said, 'You remember the church and the chapel,' and that it must be over twenty years; and that he was going to make a sketch."

Coxe's face darkened. "If Southrop was alive," he sneered, "I am sure he would appreciate your attention to his private affairs. What are we supposed to gather from all this keyhole business?"

"I think we can gather," Trent said gently, "that some person, ringing Lord Southrop up about another matter, was told incidentally where Lord Southrop expected to be on that Tuesday—the day, you remember, when he suddenly developed a taste for bad wine in the evening. Possibly the information gave this person an idea, and he had a few days to think it over. Also we can gather that Lord Southrop was talking to some one who shared his recollection of a moor which they had known over twenty years ago—that's to say, when he was at the prep. school age, as he was thirty-three this year. And then I found that he had been at a school called Marsham House, on the edge of Sharnsley Town Moor in Derbyshire. So I went off there to explore; and I discovered that the Church and Chapel were a couple of great rocks on the top of the moor, about two miles from the school. If you were there with your cousin, Mr. Coxe, you may remember them."

Coxe was drumming on the table with his fingers. "Of course I do," he said aggressively. "So do hundreds of others who were at Marsham House. What about it?"

Bradshaw, who was now fixing him with an attentive eye, held up a hand. "Come, come, Mr. Coxe," he said. "Don't let us lose our tempers. Mr. Trent is helping to clear up what begins to look like an even worse business than I thought. Let us hear him out peaceably, if you please."

"I am in the sketching business myself," Trent continued, "so I looked about for what might seem the best view-point for Lord Southrop's purpose. When I went to the spot, I found two pieces of torn-up paper, the remains of a pencil sketch; and that paper is of precisely the same quality as the paper of Lord Southrop's sketching-block, which I was able to examine at Lackington. The sketch was torn from the block and destroyed, I think, because it was evidence of his having been to Sharnsley. That part of the moor is a wild, desolate place. If some one went to meet Lord Southrop there, as I believe, he could hardly have had more favourable circumstances for what he meant to do. I think it was he who appeared in the car at Wringham that evening; and I think it was on Sharnsley Moor, not at Lackington, that Lord Southrop—disappeared."

Bradshaw half-rose from his chair. "Are you not well, Mr. Coxe?" he asked.

"Perfectly well, thanks," Coxe answered. He drew a deep breath, then turned to Trent. "And so that's all you have to tell us. I can't say that—"

"Oh no, not nearly all," Trent interrupted him. "But let me tell you now what I believe it was that really happened. If the man who left the moor in Lord Southrop's car was not Lord Southrop, I wanted an explanation of the masquerade that ended at Lackington. What would explain it was the idea that the man who drove the car down to Devonshire had murdered him, and then staged a sham suicide for him three hundred miles away. That would have been an ingenious plan. It would have depended on every one making the natural assumption that the man in the car was Lord Southrop, and how was any one to imagine that he wasn't?

"Lord Southrop was the very reverse of a public character. He lived quite out of the world; he had never been in the news; very few people knew what he looked like. He depended on all this for maintaining his privacy in the way he did when touring in his car—staying always at small places where there was no chance of his being recognized, and pretending not to be a peer. The murderer knew all about that, and it was the essence of his plan. The people at the inns would note what was conspicuous about the traveller; all that they could say about his face would be more vague, and would fit Lord Southrop well enough, so long as there was no striking difference in looks between the two men. Those big horn-rims are a disguise in themselves."

Bradshaw rubbed his hands slowly together. "I suppose it could happen so," he said. "What do you think, Mr. Coxe?"

"It's just a lot of ridiculous guesswork," Coxe said impatiently. "I've heard enough of it, for one." He rose from his chair.

"No, no, don't go, Mr. Coxe," Trent advised him. "I have some more of what you prefer—facts, you know. They are important, and you ought to hear them. Thinking as I did, I looked about for any places where a body could be concealed. In that bare and featureless expanse I could find only one: an old, abandoned quarry in the hillside, with a great pond of muddy water at the bottom of it. And by the edge of it I picked up a small piece of broken glass.

"Yesterday evening this piece of glass was shown by a police officer and myself to an optician in Derby. He stated that it was a fragment of a monocle, what they call a spherical lens, so that he could tell us all about it from one small bit. Its formula was not a common one —minus 5; so that it had been worn by a man very short-sighted in one eye. The police think that as very few people wear monocles, and hardly any of them would wear one of that power, an official inquiry should establish the names of those who had been supplied with such a glass in recent years. You see," Trent went on, "this man had dropped and broken his glass on the stones while busy about something at the edge of the pond. Being a tidy man, he picked up all the pieces that he could see; but he missed this one."

Lambert Coxe put a hand to his throat. "It's infernally stuffy in here," he muttered. "I'll open a window, if you don't mind." Again he got to his feet; but the lawyer's movement was quicker. "I'll see to that," he said; and stayed by the window when he had opened it.

Trent drew a folded paper from his pocket. "This is a telegram I received just before lunch from Superintendent Allison, of the Derbyshire police. I have told him all I am telling you." He unfolded the paper with deliberation. "He says that the pond was dragged this morning, and they recovered the body of a man who had been shot in the head from behind. It was stripped to the underclothing and secured by a chain to a pedal bicycle.

"That, you see, clears up the question how the murderer got to the remote spot where Lord Southrop was. He couldn't go there in a car, because he would have had to leave it there. He used a cycle, because there was to be a very practical use for the machine afterwards. The police believe they can trace the seller of the cycle, because it is in perfectly new condition, and he may give them a line on the buyer."

Bradshaw, his hands thrust into his pockets, stared at Coxe's ghastly face as he inquired, "Has the body been identified?"

"The Superintendent says the inquest will be the day after to-morrow. He knows whose body I believe it is, so he will already be sending down to Hingham Blewitt about evidence of identity. He says my own evidence will probably not be required until a later stage of the inquest, after a charge has been—"

A sobbing sound came from Lambert Coxe. He sprang to his feet, pressing his hands to his temples; then crashed unconscious to the floor.

While Trent loosened his collar, the lawyer splashed water from the bottle on his table upon the upturned face. The eyelids began to flicker. "He'll do," Bradshaw said coolly. "My congratulations, Mr. Trent. This man is not a client of mine, so I may say that I don't think he will enjoy the title for long—or the money, which was what really mattered, I have reason to believe. He's dropped his monocle again, you see. I happen to know, by the way, that he has been half-blind of that eye since it was injured by a cricket ball at Marsham."

12

THE ORDINARY HAIRPINS

A SMALL committee of friends had persuaded Lord Aviemore to sit for a presentation portrait, and the painter to whom they gave the commission was Philip Trent. It was a task that fascinated him, for he had often seen and admired, in public places, the high, half-bald skull, vulture nose, and grim mouth of the peer who was said to be deeper in theology than any other layman, and all but a few of the clergy; whose devotion to charitable work had made him nationally honoured. It was not until the third sitting that Lord Aviemore's sombre taciturnity was laid aside.

"I believe, Mr. Trent," he said abruptly, "you used to have a portrait of my late sister-in-law here. I was told that it hung in the studio."

Trent continued his work quietly. "It was just a rough drawing I made after seeing her in *Carmen*—before her marriage. It has been hung in here ever since. Before your first visit I removed it."

The sitter nodded slowly. "Very thoughtful of you. Nevertheless, I should like very much to see it, if I may."

"Of course." Trent drew the framed sketch from behind a curtain. Lord Aviemore gazed long in silence at

Trent's very spirited likeness of the famous singer, while the artist worked busily to capture the first expression of feeling that he had so far seen on that impassive face. Lighted and softened by melancholy, it looked for the first time noble.

At last the sitter turned to him. "I would give a good deal," he said simply, "to possess this drawing."

Trent shook his head. "I don't want to part with it." He laid a few strokes carefully on the canvas. "If you care to know why, I'll tell you. It is my personal memory of a woman whom I found more admirable than any other I ever saw. Lillemor Wergeland's beauty and physical perfection were unforgettable. Her voice was a marvel; her spirit matched them; her fearlessness, her kindness, her vigour of mind and character, her feeling for beauty, were what I heard talked about even by people not given to enthusiasm. She had weaknesses, I dare say—I never spoke to her. I heard her sing very many times, but I knew no more about her than many other strangers. A number of my friends knew her, though, and all I ever gathered about her made me inclined to place her on a pedestal. I was ten years younger then; it did me good."

Lord Aviemore said nothing for a few minutes. Then he spoke slowly. "I am not of your temperament or your circle, Mr. Trent. I do not worship anything of this world. But I do not think you were far wrong about Lady Aviemore. Once I thought differently. When I heard that my eldest brother was about to marry a prima donna, a woman whose portrait was sold all over the world, who was famous for extravagance in dress and what seemed to me self-advertising conduct—I was appalled when I heard from him of this engagement. I will not deny that I was shocked, too, at the idea of a marriage with the daughter of Norwegian peasants."

"She was country-bred, then," Trent observed. "One never heard much about her childhood."

"Yes. She was an orphan of ten years old when Colonel Stamer and his wife went to lodge at her brother's farm for the fishing. They fell in love with the child, and having none of their own, they adopted her. All this my brother told me. He knew, he said, just what I would think; he only asked me to meet her, and then to judge if he had done well or ill. Of course I asked him to introduce me at the first opportunity."

Lord Aviemore paused and stared thoughtfully at the portrait. "She charmed every one who came near her," he went on presently. "I resisted the spell; but before they had been long married she had conquered all my prejudice. It was like a child, I saw, that she delighted in the popularity and the great income her gifts had brought her. But she was not really childish. It was not that she was what is called intellectual; but she had a singular spaciousness of mind in which nothing little or mean could live—it had, I used to fancy, some kinship with her Norwegian landscapes of mountain and sea. She was, as you say, extremely beautiful, with the vigorous purity of the fair-haired northern race. Her marriage with my brother was the happiest I have ever known."

He paused again, while Trent worked on in silence; and soon the low, meditative voice resumed. "It was about this time six years ago—the middle of March—that I had the terrible news from Taormina, the day after my return from Canada. I went out to her at once. When I saw her I was aghast. She showed no emotion; but there was in her calmness the most unearthly sense of desolation that I have ever received. From time to time she would say, as if she spoke to herself, 'It was all my fault.' "

At Trent's exclamation of surprise Lord Aviemore looked up. "Few people," he said, "know the whole of the tragedy. You have heard that a slight shock of earthquake caused the collapse of the villa, and that my brother and his child were found dead in the ruins; you have heard, I suppose, that Lady Aviemore was not in the house at the time. You have heard that she drowned herself afterwards. But you have evidently not heard that my brother had a presentiment that this visit to Sicily would end in death, and wished to abandon it at the last moment; that his wife laughed away his forebodings with her strong common-sense. But we belong to the Highlands, Mr. Trent; we are of that blood and tradition, and such interior warnings as my brother had are no trifles to us. However, she charmed his fears away; he had, she told me, entirely lost all sense of uneasiness. On the tenth day of their stay her husband and only child were killed. She did not think, as you may think, that there was coincidence here. The shock had changed her whole mental being; she believed then, as I believed, that my brother inwardly foreknew that death awaited him if he went to that place." He relapsed into silence.

"I know slightly," Trent remarked, "a man called Selby, a solicitor, who was with Lady Aviemore just after her husband's death."

Lord Aviemore said that he remembered Mr. Selby. He said it with such a total absence of expression of any kind that the subject of Selby was killed instantly; and he did not resume that of the tragedy of the woman whom the world remembered still as Lillemor Wergeland.

It was a few months later, when the portrait of Lord Aviemore was to be seen at the show of the N.S.P.P., that Trent received a friendly letter from Arthur Selby. After praising the picture, Selby went on to ask if Trent would do him the favour of calling at his office by appointment for a private talk. "I should like," he wrote, "to put a certain story before you, a story with a problem in it. I gave it up as a bad job long ago, myself, but seeing your portrait of A. reminded me of your reputation as an unraveller."

Thus it happened that, a few days later, Trent found himself alone with Selby in the offices of the firm in which that very capable, somewhat dandified lawyer was a partner. They spoke of the portrait, and Trent told of the strange exaltation with which his sitter had spoken of the dead lady. Selby listened rather grimly.

"The story I referred to," he said, "is the Aviemore story. I acted for the Countess when she was alive. I was with her at the time of her suicide. I am an executor of her will. In the strictest confidence, I should like to tell you that story as I know it, and hear what you think about it."

Trent was all attention; he was deeply interested, and said so. Selby, with gloomy eyes, folded his arms on the broad writing-table between them, and began.

"You know all about the accident," he said. "I will start with the 15th of March, when Lord Aviemore and his son were buried in the cemetery at Taormina. That was before I came on the scene. Lady Aviemore had already discharged all the servants except her own maid, with whom she was living at the Hotel Cavour. There, as I gathered afterwards, she seldom left her rooms. She was undoubtedly overwhelmed by what had happened, though she seems never to have lost her grip on herself. Her brother-in-law, the present Lord Aviemore, had come out to join her. He had only just returned from Canada"—Selby raised a finger and repeated slowly—"from Canada, you will remember. He had gone out to get ideas about the emigration prospect, I understand. He remained at the hotel, meaning to accompany Lady Aviemore home when she should feel equal to the journey.

"It was not until the 18th that we received a long telegram from her, asking us to send some one representing the firm to her at Taormina. She stated that she wished to discuss business matters without delay, but did not yet feel able to travel. At the cost of some inconvenience, I went out myself, as I happen to speak Italian pretty well. You understand that Lady Aviemore, who already possessed considerable means of her own, came into a large income under her husband's will."

"She was a client who could afford to indulge her whims," Trent observed. "If you were already her adviser, she probably expected you to come."

"Just so. Well, I went out to Taormina, as I say. On my arrival Lady Aviemore saw me, and told me quite calmly that she was acquainted with the provisions of her late husband's will, and that she now wished to make her own. I took her instructions, and prepared the will at once. The next day, the British Consul and I witnessed her signature. You may remember, Trent, that when the contents of her will became public after her death, they attracted a good deal of attention."

"I don't think I heard of it," Trent said. "If I was giving myself a holiday at the time, I wouldn't know much about what was going on."

"Well, there were some bequests of jewellery and things to intimate friends. She left £2,000 to her brother, Knut Wergeland, of Myklebostad in Norway, and £100 to her maid, Maria Krogh, also a Norwegian, who had been with her a long time. The whole of the rest of her property she left to her brother, the new Lord Aviemore, unconditionally. That surprised me, because I had been told that he had disapproved bitterly of the marriage, and hadn't concealed his opinion from her or any one else. But she never bore malice, I knew; and what she said to me at Taormina was that she could think of nobody who would do so much good with the money as her brother-in-law. From that point of view she was justified. He is said to spend nine-tenths of his income on charities of all sorts, and I shouldn't wonder if it was true. Anyhow, she made him her heir."

"And what did he say to it?"

Selby coughed. "There is no evidence that he knew anything about it before her death. No evidence," he repeated slowly. "And when told of it afterwards he showed precious little feeling of any kind. Of course, that's his way. But now let me get on with the story. Lady Aviemore asked me to remain to transact business for her until she should leave Taormina. She did so on the 27th of March, accompanied by Lord Aviemore, myself, and her maid. To shorten the railway journey, as she told us, she had planned to go by boat first to Brindisi, then to Venice, and so home by rail. The boats from Brindisi to Venice all go in the daytime, except once a week, when a boat from Corfu arrives in the evening and goes on about eleven. She decided to get to Brindisi in time to catch that boat. So that was what we did; had a few hours in Brindisi, dined there, and went on board about ten o'clock. Lady Aviemore complained of a bad headache. She went at once to her cabin, which was a deck-cabin, asking me to send some one to collect her ticket at once, as she wanted to sleep as soon as possible and not be awakened again. That was soon done. Shortly before the boat left, the maid came to me on her way to her own quarters and told me her mistress had retired. Soon after we were out of the harbour, I turned in myself. At that time Lord Aviemore was leaning over the rail on the deck on to which Lady Aviemore's cabin opened, and some distance from the cabin. There was nobody else about that I could see. It was just beginning to blow, but it didn't trouble me, and I slept very well.

"It was a quarter to eight next morning when Lord Aviemore came into my cabin. He was fearfully pale and agitated. He told me that the Countess could not be found; that the maid had gone to her cabin to call her at seven-thirty and found it empty.

"I got up in a hurry, and went with him to the cabin. The dressing-case she had taken with her was there, and her fur coat and her hat and her jewellery-case and her hand-bag lay on the berth, which had not been slept in. The only other thing was a note, unaddressed, lying open on the table. Lord Aviemore and I read it together. After the inquiry at Venice, I kept the note. Here it is."

Selby unfolded and handed over a sheet of thin ruled paper, torn from a block. Trent read the following words, written in a large, firm, rounded hand:

"Such an ending to such a marriage is far worse than death. It was all my fault. This is not sorrow, it is complete destruction. I have been kept up till now only by the resolution I took on the day when I lost them, by the thought of what I am going to do now. I take my leave of a world I cannot bear any more."

There followed the initials "L.A." Trent read and re-read the pitiful message, so full of the awful egotism of grief, then he looked up in silence at Selby.

"The Italian authorities found that she had met her death by drowning. They could not suppose anything else—nor could I. But now listen, Trent. Soon after her death I got an idea into my head, and I have puzzled over the affair a lot without much result. I did find out a fact or two, though; and it struck me the other day that if I could discover something, you could probably do much better."

Trent, still studying the paper, ignored this tribute. "Well," he said, "what is your idea, Selby?"

Selby, evading the direct question, said, "I'll tell you the facts I referred to. That sheet, you see, is torn from an ordinary ruled writing-pad. Now I have shown it to a friend of mine who is in the paper business. He has told me that it is a make of paper never sold in Europe, but sold very largely in Canada. Next, Lady Aviemore never was in Canada. And there was no paper-pad in her dressing-case or anywhere in the cabin. Neither was there any pen or ink, or any fountain pen. The ink, you see, is a pale sort of grey ink."

Trent nodded. "Continental hotel ink, in fact. This was written in a hotel, then—probably the one where you had dinner in Brindisi. You could identify her writing, of course."

"Except that it seems to have been written with a bad pen—a hotel pen, no doubt—it is her usual handwriting."

"Any other exhibits?" Trent asked after a brief silence.

"Only this." Selby took from a drawer a woman's hand-bag of elaborate bead-work. "Later on, when I saw Lord Aviemore about the disposal of her valuables and personal effects, I mentioned that there was this bag, with a few trifles in it. 'Give it away,' he said. 'Do what you like with it.' Well," Selby went on, smoothing the back of his head with an air of slight embarrassment, "I kept it. As a sort of memento—what? The things in it don't mean anything to me, but you have a look at them." He turned the bag out upon the writing-table. "Here you are—handkerchief, notes and change, nail-file, keys, powder-thing, lipstick, comb, hairpins—"

"Four hairpins." Trent took them in his hand. "Quite new ones, I should say. Have they anything to tell us, Selby?"

"I don't see how. They're just ordinary black hairpins—as you say, they look too fresh and bright to have been used."

Trent looked at the small heap of objects on the table. "And what's that last thing—the little box?"

"That's a box of Ixtil, the anti-sea-sick stuff. Two doses are gone. It's quite good, I believe."

Trent opened the box and stared at the pink capsules. "So you can buy it abroad?"

"I was with her when she bought it in Brindisi, just before we went on board."

Again Trent was silent a few moments. "Then all you discovered that was odd was this about the Canadian paper, and the note having obviously been prepared in advance. Queer enough, certainly. But going back before that last day or two—all through the time you were with Lady Aviemore, did nothing come under your notice that seemed strange?"

Selby fingered his chin. "If you put it like that, I do remember a thing that I thought curious at the time, though I never dreamed of its having anything to do—"

"Yes, I know, but you asked me here to go over the thing properly, didn't you? That question of mine is one of the routine inquiries."

"Well, it was simply this. A day or two before we left Sicily I was standing in the hotel lobby when the mail arrived. As I was waiting to see if there was anything for me, the porter put down on the counter a rather smart-looking package that had just come—done up the way they do it at a really first-class shop, if you know what I mean. It looked like a biggish book, or box of chocolates, or something; and it had French stamps on it, but the postmark I didn't notice. And this was addressed to Mlle. Maria Krogh—you remember, the Countess's maid. Well, she was there waiting, and presently the man handed it to her. Maria went off with it, and just then her mistress came down the big stairs. She saw the parcel, and just held out her hand for it, and Maria passed it over as if it was a matter of course, and Lady Aviemore went upstairs with it. I thought it was quaint if she was ordering goods in her maid's name; but I thought no more of it, because Lady Aviemore decided that evening about leaving the place, and I had plenty to attend to. And if you want to know," Selby went on, as Trent opened his lips to speak, "where Maria Krogh is, all I can tell you is that I took her ticket in London for Christiansand, where she lives, and where I sent her legacy to her, which she acknowledged. Now then!"

Trent laughed at the solicitor's tone, and Selby laughed too. His friend walked to the fireplace, and pensively adjusted his tie. "Well, I must be off," he announced. "How about dining with me on Friday at the Cactus? If by that time I've anything to suggest about all this, I'll tell you. You will? All right, make it eight o'clock." And he hastened away.

But on the Friday he seemed to have nothing to suggest. He was so reluctant to approach the subject that Selby supposed him to be chagrined at his failure to achieve anything, and did not press the matter.

It was six months later, on a sunny afternoon in September, that Trent walked up the valley road at Myklebostad, looking farewell at the mountain far ahead, the white-capped mother of the torrent that roared down a twenty-foot fall beside him. He had been a week in this remote backwater of Europe, seven hours by motor-boat from the nearest place that ranked as a town. The savage beauty of that watery landscape, where sun and rain worked together daily to achieve an unearthly purity in the scene, had justified far better than he had hoped his story that he had come there in search of matter for his brush. He had worked and he had explored, and had learnt as much as he could of his neighbours. It was little enough, for the postmaster, in whose house he had a room, spoke only a trifle of German, and no one else, as far as he could discover, had anything but Norwegian, of which Trent knew no more than what could be got from a traveller's phrase-book. But he had seen every dweller in the valley, and he had paid close attention to the household of Knut Wergeland, the rich man of the valley, who had the largest farm. He and his wife, elderly and grim-faced peasants, lived with one servant in an old turf-roofed steading not far from the post office. Not another person, Trent was sure, inhabited the house.

He had decided at last that his voyage of curiosity to Myklebostad had been ill-inspired. Knut and his wife were no more than a thrifty peasant pair. They had given him a meal one day when he was sketching near the place, and they had refused with gentle firmness to take any payment. Both had made on him an impression of complete trustworthiness and competency in the life they led so utterly out of the world.

That day, as Trent gazed up to the mountain, his eye was caught by a flash of sunlight against the dense growth of birches running from top to bottom of the steep cliff that walled the valley to his left. It was a bright blink, about half-a-mile from where he stood; it remained steady, and at several points above and below he saw the same bright appearance. He perceived that there must be a wire, and a well-used wire, led up the precipitous hill-face among the trees. Trent went on towards the spot on the road whence the wire seemed to be taken upwards. He had never been so far in this direction until now. In a few minutes he came to the opening among the trees of a rough track leading upwards among rocks and roots, at such an angle that only a vigorous climber could attempt it. Close by, in the edge of the thicket, stood a tall post, from the top of which a wire stretched upwards through the branches in the same direction as the path.

Trent slapped the post with a resounding blow. "Heavens and earth!" he exclaimed. "I had forgotten the *saeter*!"

And at once he began to climb.

A thick carpet of rich pasture began where the deep birch-belt ended at the top of the height. It stretched away for miles over a gently-sloping upland. As Trent came into the open, panting after a strenuous forty-minute climb, the heads of a score of browsing cattle were sleepily turned towards him. Beyond them wandered many more; and two hundred yards away stood a tiny hut, turf-roofed.

This plateau was the *saeter;* the high grass-land, attached to some valley farm. Trent had heard long ago, and never thought since, of this feature of Norway's rural life. At the appointed time, the cattle would be driven up by an easier detour to the mountain pastures for their summer holiday, to be attended there by some peasant—usually a young girl—who lived solitary with the herd. Such wires as that he had seen were kept bright by the daily descent of milk-churns, let down by a line from above, received by a farm-hand at the road below.

And there, at the side of the hut, a woman stood. Trent, as he approached, noted her short, rough skirt and coarse, sack-like upper garment, her thick grey stockings and clumsy clogs. About her bare head her pale-gold hair was fastened in tight plaits. As she looked up on hearing Trent's footfall, two heavy silver earrings dangled about the tanned and careworn face of this very type of the middle-aged peasant women of the region.

She ceased her task of scraping a large cake of chocolate into a bowl, and straightened her tall body. Smiling, with lean hands on her hips, she spoke in Norwegian, greeting him.

Trent made the proper reply. "And that," he added in his own tongue, "is a large part of all the Norwegian I know. Perhaps, madam, you speak English." Her light blue eyes looked puzzlement, and she spoke again, pointing down to the valley. He nodded; and she began to talk pleasantly in her unknown speech. From within the hut she brought two thick mugs; she pointed rapidly to the chocolate in the bowl, to himself and herself.

"I should like it of all things," he said. "You are most kind and hospitable, like all your people. What a pity it is we have no language in common!" She brought him a stool and gave him the chocolate-cake and a knife, making signs that he should continue the scraping; then within the hut she kindled a fire of twigs and began to boil water in a black pot. Plainly this was her dwelling, the roughest Trent had ever seen. He could discern that on two small shelves were ranged a few pieces of chipped earthenware. A wooden bed-place, with straw and two neatly-folded blankets, filled a third of the space in the hut. All the carpentering was of the rudest. From a small chest in a corner she drew a biscuit-tin, half full of flat cakes of stale rye bread. There seemed to be nothing else in the tiny place but a heap of twigs for fuel.

She made chocolate in the two mugs, and then, at Trent's insistence in dumb show, she sat on the only stool at a rude table outside the hut, while her guest made a seat of an upturned milking-pail. She continued to talk amiably and unintelligibly, while he finished with difficulty the half of a bread-cake.

"I believe, madam," he said at last, setting down his

empty mug, "you are talking simply to hear the sound of your own voice. In your case, that is excusable. You don't understand English, so I will tell you to your face that it is a most wonderful voice. I should say," he went on thoughtfully, "that you ought to have been one of the greatest sopranos that ever lived."

She heard him calmly, and shook her head as not understanding.

"Well, don't say I didn't break it gently," Trent protested. He rose to his feet. "Madam, I know that you are Lady Aviemore. I have broken in on your solitude, and I ask pardon for that; but I could not be sure unless I saw you. I give you my word that no one else knows or ever shall know from me, what I have discovered." He made as if to return by the way he had come.

But the woman held up a hand. A singular change had come over her brown face. A lively spirit now looked out of her desolate blue eyes; she smiled another and a much more intelligent smile. After a few moments she spoke in English, fluent but with a slight accent of her country.

"Sir," she said, "you have behaved very nicely up till now. It has been an amusement for me; there is not much comedy on the *saeter*. Now, will you have the goodness to explain?"

He told her in a few words that he had suspected she was still alive, that he had thought over such facts as had come to his knowledge, and had been led to think she was probably in that place. "I thought you might guess I had recognized you," he added, "so it seemed best to assure you that your secret was safe. Was it wrong to speak?"

She shook her head, gazing at him with her chin on a

hand. Presently she said, "I think you are not against me. I can feel that, though I do not understand why you wanted to search out my secret, and why you kept it when you had dragged it into the light."

"I dragged it because I am curious," he answered. "I have kept it and will keep it because—oh well, because it is your own, and because to me Lillemor Wergeland is a sort of divinity."

She laughed suddenly. "Incense! And I in these rags, in this hovel, with what unpleasantness I can see in this little spotty piece of cheap mirror! . . . Ah well! You have come a long way, curious man, and it would be cruel not to gratify your curiosity a little more. Shall I tell you? After all, it was simple.

"It was very soon after the disaster that the resolve came to me. I never hesitated. It was my fault that we had gone to Sicily—you have heard that? Yes, I see it in your face. I felt I must leave the world I knew, and that knew me. I never really thought of suicide. As for a convent, unhappily there is none for people with minds like mine. I meant simply to disappear, and the only way to succeed was to get the reputation of being dead. I thought it out for some days and nights. Then I wrote, in the name of my maid, to an establishment in Paris where I used to buy things for the stage."

"Ha!" Trent exclaimed. "I heard of that, and I guessed."

"I sent money," she went on, "and I ordered a dark-brown transformation—that is a lady's word for wig—some stuff for darkening the skin, various pigments, pencils, *et tout le bazar*. My maid did not know what I had sent for; she only handed the parcel to me when it came. She would have thrown herself in the fire for me, I think, my maid Maria. When the things arrived, I announced that I would return to England by the route you have heard of, perhaps."

He nodded. "The route that gave you a night passage to Venice. And you disguised yourself in your cabin at Brindisi, and slipped off in the dark before the boat started."

"Indeed, I was not such a fool!" she returned. "What if my absence had been discovered somehow before the boat left Brindisi? That could easily happen, and then good-bye to the fiction of my suicide. No; when we reached Brindisi, we had, as I knew, some hours there. We left our things at a hotel, where we were to dine, and then I put on a thick veil and went out alone. At the office near the harbour I took a second-class passage to Venice for myself, in the name of Miss Julia Simmons, in the same boat I had planned to take. It would be at the quay, they told me, in an hour. Then I went into the poorer streets of the town, and bought some clothes, very ugly ones, some shoes, toilet things—"

"Some black hairpins," Trent murmured.

"Naturally, black," she assented. "My own gilt pins would have looked queer in a dark-brown wig, and I had to have pins to fasten it properly. I bought also a little cheap portmanteau-thing, and put my purchases in it. Then I took a cab to the quay, found the boat had arrived, and gave one of the stewards a tip to show me the berth named on my ticket, and to carry my baggage there. After that I went shopping again on shore. I bought a long mackintosh coat and a funny little cap, the very things for Miss Simmons; took them to the hotel and pushed them under the things my maid had already packed in my big case.

"On the steamer, when Maria had left me and I had locked the cabin-door, I arranged a dark, rather catty sort of face for myself, and fitted on Miss Simmons's hair. I put on her mackintosh coat and cap. When the boat began to move away from the quay, I opened my door an inch and peeped out. As I expected, every one was looking over the rail, and so—the sooner the better—I just slipped out, shut the cabin door, and walked straight to Miss Simmons's berth at the other end of the ship. . . . There is not much more to say. At Venice, I did not look for the others, and never saw them. I went on to Paris, and wrote to my brother Knut that I was alive, telling him what I meant to do if he would help me. Such things do not seem so mad to a true child of Norway."

"What things?" Trent asked.

"Things of deep sorrow, malady of the soul, escape from the world. . . . He and his wife have been true and good to me. I am supposed to be her cousin, Hilda Bjoernstad. In my will I left them money, more than enough to pay for me, but they did not know that when they welcomed me here."

She ceased, and smiled vaguely at Trent, who was considering her story with eyes that gazed fixedly at the skyline.

"Yes, of course," he remarked presently in an abstracted manner. "That was it. As you say, so simple. And now let me tell you," he went on with a change of tone, "one or two little details you have forgotten.

"At Brindisi you bought, just before going on board with the others, a box of the stuff called Ixtil, because it looked as if there might be bad weather. You took a dose at once, and another a little later, as the directions told you. You might have needed more of it before reaching Venice, but as Mr. Selby was with you when you bought it, you thought it wiser to leave it behind when you vanished. Also, you left behind you four new black hairpins, which had somehow, I suppose, got loose inside your hand-bag, and were found there by Selby. You see, Lady Aviemore, it was Selby who brought me into this. He told me all the facts he knew, and he showed me your bag and its contents. But he didn't attach any importance to the two things I have just mentioned."

She raised her eyebrows just perceptibly. "I cannot see why he should. And I cannot see why he should bring in you or anybody."

"Because he had some vague notion of your brother-in-law having either caused your death, or at least having known of your intention to commit suicide. He never told me so outright, but it was plain that that was in his mind. Selby wanted me to clear that up, if I could. You see, your brother-in-law stood to benefit enormously by your death, and then there was the matter of the note announcing your suicide."

"It announced," she remarked, "the truth; that I was leaving a world I could not bear any longer. The words might mean one thing or another. But what about the note?"

"The perfectly truthful note was written with pen and ink, of which there was none in your cabin. It was written on paper which had been torn from a writing-pad, and no pad was found. Also that make of paper is sold in Canada, never in Europe. You had never been in Canada.

Your brother-in-law had just come back from Canada. You see?"

"But did not Selby perceive that Charles is a saint?" inquired the lady with a touch of impatience. "Surely that was plain! More Dominic than Francis, no doubt; but an evident saint."

"In my slight knowledge of him," Trent admitted, "he did strike me in that way. But Selby is a lawyer, you see, and lawyers don't understand saints. Besides, your brother-in-law had taken a dislike to him, I think, and so perhaps he felt critical about your brother-in-law."

"It is true," she said, "he did not care about Mr. Selby, because he disliked all men who were foppish and worldly. But now I will tell you. That evening in the hotel at Brindisi I wanted to write that note, and I asked Charles for a sheet from the block he had in his hand and was just going to write on. That is all. I wrote it in the hotel writing-room, and took it afterwards in my bag to the cabin."

"We supposed you had written it beforehand," Trent said, "and that was one of the things that led me to feel morally certain you were still alive. I'll explain. If, as we thought, you had written the note in the hotel, your suicide was a premeditated act. Yet it was afterwards that Selby saw you buying that Ixtil stuff, and it was plain that you had taken two doses. And it struck me, though it didn't seem to have struck Selby, that it was unlikely any one already resolved to drown herself at sea would begin treating herself against sea-sickness.

"Then there were those new black hairpins. The sight of them was a revelation to me. For I knew, of course, that with that hair of yours you had probably never used a black hairpin in your life."

The Countess felt at her pale-gold plaits, and gravely held out to him a black hairpin. "In the valley we use nothing else."

"It is very different in the valley, I know," he said gently. "I was speaking of my world—the world that you have left. I was led by those hairpins to think of your having changed your appearance, and I even guessed at what was in the parcel that came for your maid, which Selby had told me about."

She regarded her guest with something of respect. "It still remains," she said, "to explain how you knew it was in Norway, and here, as a poor farm servant, that I should hide myself. It seemed to me the last thing in the world—your world—that a woman who had lived my life would be expected to do."

"All the same, I thought it was a strong possibility," he answered. "Your problem, you see, was just what you say—to hide yourself. And you had another—you had to make a living somehow. Everything you possessed—except some small amount in cash, I suppose—you left behind when you disappeared. And a woman can't go on acting and disguising herself for ever. A man can grow hair on his face, or shave it off; for a woman, disguise must be a perpetual anxiety. If she has to get employment, and especially if she has no references, it's something very like an impossibility."

She nodded gravely. "That was how I saw it."

"So," he pursued, "it came to this: that the world-famous Lillemor Wergeland had to come to the surface again somewhere, and in no long time—Lillemor Wergeland, whose type of beauty and general appearance were so marked and unmistakable, whose photographs were known everywhere. The fact is that for some time I couldn't see for the life of me how it could possibly have been done. There were only a few countries, I supposed, of which you knew enough of the language to attempt to live in any of them; and if you did, you would always be conspicuous by your physical type and your accent. If you attracted attention, discovery might follow at any moment. The more I thought of it, the more marvellous it seemed that you had not been recognized—assuming you were still alive—during the six years or so that had passed before I heard the full story and guessed at the truth.

"And then an idea came. There was one country in which your looks and speech would not betray you as a foreigner—your own country. And if there were any corners of the world where you could go with a fair certainty of being unrecognized, the remoter villages of Norway would be among them. And at Myklebostad, on the Langfjord, which the map told me was one of the remotest, you had a brother, who was two thousand pounds richer by your supposed death. You see how it was, then, that I came to this place on a sketching holiday."

Trent stood up and gazed across the valley to the sunlit white peaks beyond. "I have visited Norway before, but never had such an interesting time. And now, before I return to the haunts of men, let me say again that I shall forget at once all that has happened to-day. Don't think it was merely a vulgar curiosity that brought me here. There was once a supreme artist, whose gifts made me her debtor and servant. Anything that happened to her touched me; I had a sort of right to go seeking what it really was that had happened."

She stood before him in her coarse and stained clothes, her hands clasped behind her, with a face and attitude of perfect dignity. "Very well—you stand on your right, and I on mine—to arrange my own life, since I am alone in it. I will spend it here, where it began. My soul was born here before it went out to have adventures, and it has crept home again for comfort. Believe me, it is not only that, as you say, I am safe from discovery here. That counts for very much; but also I felt I must go and live out my life in my own place, this far-away, lonely valley, where everything is humble and unspoilt, and the hills and the fjords are as God made them before there were any men. It is all my own, own land!

"And now," she ended suddenly, "we understand one another, and we can part friends." She extended her hand, saying, "I do not know your name."

"Why should you?" he asked. He bent over the hand, then went quickly from her. At the beginning of the descent he glanced back once; she waved to him.

Half-way down the rugged track he stopped. Far above a wonderful voice was singing to the glory of the Norse land.

> "*Ja, herligt er mit Fodeland*
> *Der ewig trodser Tidens Tand*"

sang the voice.

Trent looked out upon the wild landscape. "Her fatherland!" he soliloquised. "Well, well! They say the strictest parents have the most devoted children."

A CATALOGUE OF SELECTED DOVER BOOKS IN ALL FIELDS OF INTEREST

A CATALOGUE OF SELECTED DOVER BOOKS IN ALL FIELDS OF INTEREST

RACKHAM'S COLOR ILLUSTRATIONS FOR WAGNER'S RING. Rackham's finest mature work—all 64 full-color watercolors in a faithful and lush interpretation of the *Ring.* Full-sized plates on coated stock of the paintings used by opera companies for authentic staging of Wagner. Captions aid in following complete Ring cycle. Introduction. 64 illustrations plus vignettes. 72pp. 8⅝ x 11¼. 23779-6 Pa. $6.00

CONTEMPORARY POLISH POSTERS IN FULL COLOR, edited by Joseph Czestochowski. 46 full-color examples of brilliant school of Polish graphic design, selected from world's first museum (near Warsaw) dedicated to poster art. Posters on circuses, films, plays, concerts all show cosmopolitan influences, free imagination. Introduction. 48pp. 9⅜ x 12¼. 23780-X Pa. $6.00

GRAPHIC WORKS OF EDVARD MUNCH, Edvard Munch. 90 haunting, evocative prints by first major Expressionist artist and one of the greatest graphic artists of his time: *The Scream, Anxiety, Death Chamber, The Kiss, Madonna,* etc. Introduction by Alfred Werner. 90pp. 9 x 12. 23765-6 Pa. $5.00

THE GOLDEN AGE OF THE POSTER, Hayward and Blanche Cirker. 70 extraordinary posters in full colors, from Maitres de l'Affiche, Mucha, Lautrec, Bradley, Cheret, Beardsley, many others. Total of 78pp. 9⅜ x 12¼. 22753-7 Pa. $5.95

THE NOTEBOOKS OF LEONARDO DA VINCI, edited by J. P. Richter. Extracts from manuscripts reveal great genius; on painting, sculpture, anatomy, sciences, geography, etc. Both Italian and English. 186 ms. pages reproduced, plus 500 additional drawings, including studies for *Last Supper,* Sforza monument, etc. 860pp. 7⅞ x 10¾. (Available in U.S. only) 22572-0, 22573-9 Pa., Two-vol. set $15.90

THE CODEX NUTTALL, as first edited by Zelia Nuttall. Only inexpensive edition, in full color, of a pre-Columbian Mexican (Mixtec) book. 88 color plates show kings, gods, heroes, temples, sacrifices. New explanatory, historical introduction by Arthur G. Miller. 96pp. 11⅜ x 8½. (Available in U.S. only) 23168-2 Pa. $7.50

UNE SEMAINE DE BONTÉ, A SURREALISTIC NOVEL IN COLLAGE, Max Ernst. Masterpiece created out of 19th-century periodical illustrations, explores worlds of terror and surprise. Some consider this Ernst's greatest work. 208pp. 8⅛ x 11. 23252-2 Pa. $5.00

UNCLE SILAS, J. Sheridan LeFanu. Victorian Gothic mystery novel, considered by many best of period, even better than Collins or Dickens. Wonderful psychological terror. Introduction by Frederick Shroyer. 436pp. 5⅜ x 8½. 21715-9 Pa. $4.00

JURGEN, James Branch Cabell. The great erotic fantasy of the 1920's that delighted thousands, shocked thousands more. Full final text, Lane edition with 13 plates by Frank Pape. 346pp. 5⅜ x 8½. 23507-6 Pa. $4.00

THE CLAVERINGS, Anthony Trollope. Major novel, chronicling aspects of British Victorian society, personalities. Reprint of Cornhill serialization, 16 plates by M. Edwards; first reprint of full text. Introduction by Norman Donaldson. 412pp. 5⅜ x 8½. 23464-9 Pa. $5.00

KEPT IN THE DARK, Anthony Trollope. Unusual short novel about Victorian morality and abnormal psychology by the great English author. Probably the first American publication. Frontispiece by Sir John Millais. 92pp. 6½ x 9¼. 23609-9 Pa. $2.50

RALPH THE HEIR, Anthony Trollope. Forgotten tale of illegitimacy, inheritance. Master novel of Trollope's later years. Victorian country estates, clubs, Parliament, fox hunting, world of fully realized characters. Reprint of 1871 edition. 12 illustrations by F. A. Faser. 434pp. of text. 5⅜ x 8½. 23642-0 Pa. $4.50

YEKL and THE IMPORTED BRIDEGROOM AND OTHER STORIES OF THE NEW YORK GHETTO, Abraham Cahan. Film *Hester Street* based on *Yekl* (1896). Novel, other stories among first about Jewish immigrants of N.Y.'s East Side. Highly praised by W. D. Howells—Cahan "a new star of realism." New introduction by Bernard G. Richards. 240pp. 5⅜ x 8½. 22427-9 Pa. $3.50

THE HIGH PLACE, James Branch Cabell. Great fantasy writer's enchanting comedy of disenchantment set in 18th-century France. Considered by some critics to be even better than his famous *Jurgen*. 10 illustrations and numerous vignettes by noted fantasy artist Frank C. Pape. 320pp. 5⅜ x 8½. 23670-6 Pa. $4.00

ALICE'S ADVENTURES UNDER GROUND, Lewis Carroll. Facsimile of ms. Carroll gave Alice Liddell in 1864. Different in many ways from final Alice. Handlettered, illustrated by Carroll. Introduction by Martin Gardner. 128pp. 5⅜ x 8½. 21482-6 Pa. $2.00

FAVORITE ANDREW LANG FAIRY TALE BOOKS IN MANY COLORS, Andrew Lang. The four Lang favorites in a boxed set—the complete *Red, Green, Yellow* and *Blue* Fairy Books. 164 stories; 439 illustrations by Lancelot Speed, Henry Ford and G. P. Jacomb Hood. Total of about 1500pp. 5⅜ x 8½. 23407-X Boxed set, Pa. $14.00

THE AMERICAN SENATOR, Anthony Trollope. Little known, long unavailable Trollope novel on a grand scale. Here are humorous comment on American vs. English culture, and stunning portrayal of a heroine/villainess. Superb evocation of Victorian village life. 561pp. 5⅜ x 8½.
23801-6 Pa. $6.00

WAS IT MURDER? James Hilton. The author of *Lost Horizon* and *Goodbye, Mr. Chips* wrote one detective novel (under a pen-name) which was quickly forgotten and virtually lost, even at the height of Hilton's fame. This edition brings it back—a finely crafted public school puzzle resplendent with Hilton's stylish atmosphere. A thoroughly English thriller by the creator of Shangri-la. 252pp. 5⅜ x 8. (Available in U.S. only)
23774-5 Pa. $3.00

CENTRAL PARK: A PHOTOGRAPHIC GUIDE, Victor Laredo and Henry Hope Reed. 121 superb photographs show dramatic views of Central Park: Bethesda Fountain, Cleopatra's Needle, Sheep Meadow, the Blockhouse, plus people engaged in many park activities: ice skating, bike riding, etc. Captions by former Curator of Central Park, Henry Hope Reed, provide historical view, changes, etc. Also photos of N.Y. landmarks on park's periphery. 96pp. 8½ x 11. 23750-8 Pa. $4.50

NANTUCKET IN THE NINETEENTH CENTURY, Clay Lancaster. 180 rare photographs, stereographs, maps, drawings and floor plans recreate unique American island society. Authentic scenes of shipwreck, lighthouses, streets, homes are arranged in geographic sequence to provide walking-tour guide to old Nantucket existing today. Introduction, captions. 160pp. 8⅞ x 11¾. 23747-8 Pa. $6.95

STONE AND MAN: A PHOTOGRAPHIC EXPLORATION, Andreas Feininger. 106 photographs by *Life* photographer Feininger portray man's deep passion for stone through the ages. Stonehenge-like megaliths, fortified towns, sculpted marble and crumbling tenements show textures, beauties, fascination. 128pp. 9¼ x 10¾. 23756-7 Pa. $5.95

CIRCLES, A MATHEMATICAL VIEW, D. Pedoe. Fundamental aspects of college geometry, non-Euclidean geometry, and other branches of mathematics: representing circle by point. Poincare model, isoperimetric property, etc. Stimulating recreational reading. 66 figures. 96pp. 5⅝ x 8¼.
63698-4 Pa. $2.75

THE DISCOVERY OF NEPTUNE, Morton Grosser. Dramatic scientific history of the investigations leading up to the actual discovery of the eighth planet of our solar system. Lucid, well-researched book by well-known historian of science. 172pp. 5⅜ x 8½. 23726-5 Pa. $3.00

THE DEVIL'S DICTIONARY. Ambrose Bierce. Barbed, bitter, brilliant witticisms in the form of a dictionary. Best, most ferocious satire America has produced. 145pp. 5⅜ x 8½. 20487-1 Pa. $1.75

THE DEPRESSION YEARS AS PHOTOGRAPHED BY ARTHUR ROTHSTEIN, Arthur Rothstein. First collection devoted entirely to the work of outstanding 1930s photographer: famous dust storm photo, ragged children, unemployed, etc. 120 photographs. Captions. 119pp. 9¼ x 10¾.
23590-4 Pa. $5.00

CAMERA WORK: A PICTORIAL GUIDE, Alfred Stieglitz. All 559 illustrations and plates from the most important periodical in the history of art photography, *Camera Work* (1903-17). Presented four to a page, reduced in size but still clear, in strict chronological order, with complete captions. Three indexes. Glossary. Bibliography. 176pp. 8⅜ x 11¼.
23591-2 Pa. $6.95

ALVIN LANGDON COBURN, PHOTOGRAPHER, Alvin L. Coburn. Revealing autobiography by one of greatest photographers of 20th century gives insider's version of Photo-Secession, plus comments on his own work. 77 photographs by Coburn. Edited by Helmut and Alison Gernsheim. 160pp. 8⅛ x 11. 23685-4 Pa. $6.00

NEW YORK IN THE FORTIES, Andreas Feininger. 162 brilliant photographs by the well-known photographer, formerly with *Life* magazine, show commuters, shoppers, Times Square at night, Harlem nightclub, Lower East Side, etc. Introduction and full captions by John von Hartz. 181pp. 9¼ x 10¾. 23585-8 Pa. $6.00

GREAT NEWS PHOTOS AND THE STORIES BEHIND THEM, John Faber. Dramatic volume of 140 great news photos, 1855 through 1976, and revealing stories behind them, with both historical and technical information. Hindenburg disaster, shooting of Oswald, nomination of Jimmy Carter, etc. 160pp. 8¼ x 11. 23667-6 Pa. $5.00

THE ART OF THE CINEMATOGRAPHER, Leonard Maltin. Survey of American cinematography history and anecdotal interviews with 5 masters—Arthur Miller, Hal Mohr, Hal Rosson, Lucien Ballard, and Conrad Hall. Very large selection of behind-the-scenes production photos. 105 photographs. Filmographies. Index. Originally *Behind the Camera.* 144pp. 8¼ x 11. 23686-2 Pa. $5.00

DESIGNS FOR THE THREE-CORNERED HAT (LE TRICORNE), Pablo Picasso. 32 fabulously rare drawings—including 31 color illustrations of costumes and accessories—for 1919 production of famous ballet. Edited by Parmenia Migel, who has written new introduction. 48pp. 9⅜ x 12¼. (Available in U.S. only) 23709-5 Pa. $5.00

NOTES OF A FILM DIRECTOR, Sergei Eisenstein. Greatest Russian filmmaker explains montage, making of *Alexander Nevsky,* aesthetics; comments on self, associates, great rivals (Chaplin), similar material. 78 illustrations. 240pp. 5⅜ x 8½. 22392-2 Pa. $4.50

AMERICAN BIRD ENGRAVINGS, Alexander Wilson et al. All 76 plates. from Wilson's *American Ornithology* (1808-14), most important ornithological work before Audubon, plus 27 plates from the supplement (1825-33) by Charles Bonaparte. Over 250 birds portrayed. 8 plates also reproduced in full color. 111pp. 9⅜ x 12½. 23195-X Pa. $6.00

CRUICKSHANK'S PHOTOGRAPHS OF BIRDS OF AMERICA, Allan D. Cruickshank. Great ornithologist, photographer presents 177 closeups, groupings, panoramas, flightings, etc., of about 150 different birds. Expanded *Wings in the Wilderness*. Introduction by Helen G. Cruickshank. 191pp. 8¼ x 11. 23497-5 Pa. $6.00

AMERICAN WILDLIFE AND PLANTS, A. C. Martin, et al. Describes food habits of more than 1000 species of mammals, birds, fish. Special treatment of important food plants. Over 300 illustrations. 500pp. 5⅜ x 8½. 20793-5 Pa. $4.95

THE PEOPLE CALLED SHAKERS, Edward D. Andrews. Lifetime of research, definitive study of Shakers: origins, beliefs, practices, dances, social organization, furniture and crafts, impact on 19th-century USA, present heritage. Indispensable to student of American history, collector. 33 illustrations. 351pp. 5⅜ x 8½. 21081-2 Pa. $4.00

OLD NEW YORK IN EARLY PHOTOGRAPHS, Mary Black. New York City as it was in 1853-1901, through 196 wonderful photographs from N.-Y. Historical Society. Great Blizzard, Lincoln's funeral procession, great buildings. 228pp. 9 x 12. 22907-6 Pa. $7.95

MR. LINCOLN'S CAMERA MAN: MATHEW BRADY, Roy Meredith. Over 300 Brady photos reproduced directly from original negatives, photos. Jackson, Webster, Grant, Lee, Carnegie, Barnum; Lincoln; Battle Smoke, Death of Rebel Sniper, Atlanta Just After Capture. Lively commentary. 368pp. 8⅜ x 11¼. 23021-X Pa. $6.95

TRAVELS OF WILLIAM BARTRAM, William Bartram. From 1773-8, Bartram explored Northern Florida, Georgia, Carolinas, and reported on wild life, plants, Indians, early settlers. Basic account for period, entertaining reading. Edited by Mark Van Doren. 13 illustrations. 141pp. 5⅜ x 8½. 20013-2 Pa. $4.50

THE GENTLEMAN AND CABINET MAKER'S DIRECTOR, Thomas Chippendale. Full reprint, 1762 style book, most influential of all time; chairs, tables, sofas, mirrors, cabinets, etc. 200 plates, plus 24 photographs of surviving pieces. 249pp. 9⅞ x 12¾. 21601-2 Pa. $6.50

AMERICAN CARRIAGES, SLEIGHS, SULKIES AND CARTS, edited by Don H. Berkebile. 168 Victorian illustrations from catalogues, trade journals, fully captioned. Useful for artists. Author is Assoc. Curator, Div. of Transportation of Smithsonian Institution. 168pp. 8½ x 9½. 23328-6 Pa. $5.00

SECOND PIATIGORSKY CUP, edited by Isaac Kashdan. One of the greatest tournament books ever produced in the English language. All 90 games of the 1966 tournament, annotated by players, most annotated by both players. Features Petrosian, Spassky, Fischer, Larsen, six others. 228pp. 5⅜ x 8½. 23572-6 Pa. $3.50

ENCYCLOPEDIA OF CARD TRICKS, revised and edited by Jean Hugard. How to perform over 600 card tricks, devised by the world's greatest magicians: impromptus, spelling tricks, key cards, using special packs, much, much more. Additional chapter on card technique. 66 illustrations. 402pp. 5⅜ x 8½. (Available in U.S. only) 21252-1 Pa. $3.95

MAGIC: STAGE ILLUSIONS, SPECIAL EFFECTS AND TRICK PHOTOGRAPHY, Albert A. Hopkins, Henry R. Evans. One of the great classics; fullest, most authorative explanation of vanishing lady, levitations, scores of other great stage effects. Also small magic, automata, stunts. 446 illustrations. 556pp. 5⅜ x 8½. 23344-8 Pa. $5.00

THE SECRETS OF HOUDINI, J. C. Cannell. Classic study of Houdini's incredible magic, exposing closely-kept professional secrets and revealing, in general terms, the whole art of stage magic. 67 illustrations. 279pp. 5⅜ x 8½. 22913-0 Pa. $3.00

HOFFMANN'S MODERN MAGIC, Professor Hoffmann. One of the best, and best-known, magicians' manuals of the past century. Hundreds of tricks from card tricks and simple sleight of hand to elaborate illusions involving construction of complicated machinery. 332 illustrations. 563pp. 5⅜ x 8½. 23623-4 Pa. $6.00

MADAME PRUNIER'S FISH COOKERY BOOK, Mme. S. B. Prunier. More than 1000 recipes from world famous Prunier's of Paris and London, specially adapted here for American kitchen. Grilled tournedos with anchovy butter, Lobster a la Bordelaise, Prunier's prized desserts, more. Glossary. 340pp. 5⅜ x 8½. (Available in U.S. only) 22679-4 Pa. $3.00

FRENCH COUNTRY COOKING FOR AMERICANS, Louis Diat. 500 easy-to-make, authentic provincial recipes compiled by former head chef at New York's Fitz-Carlton Hotel: onion soup, lamb stew, potato pie, more. 309pp. 5⅜ x 8½. 23665-X Pa. $3.95

SAUCES, FRENCH AND FAMOUS, Louis Diat. Complete book gives over 200 specific recipes: bechamel, Bordelaise, hollandaise, Cumberland, apricot, etc. Author was one of this century's finest chefs, originator of vichyssoise and many other dishes. Index. 156pp. 5⅜ x 8. 23663-3 Pa. $2.50

TOLL HOUSE TRIED AND TRUE RECIPES, Ruth Graves Wakefield. Authentic recipes from the famous Mass. restaurant: popovers, veal and ham loaf, Toll House baked beans, chocolate cake crumb pudding, much more. Many helpful hints. Nearly 700 recipes. Index. 376pp. 5⅜ x 8½. 23560-2 Pa. $4.00

THE SENSE OF BEAUTY, George Santayana. Masterfully written discussion of nature of beauty, materials of beauty, form, expression; art, literature, social sciences all involved. 168pp. 5⅜ x 8½. 20238-0 Pa. $2.50

ON THE IMPROVEMENT OF THE UNDERSTANDING, Benedict Spinoza. Also contains *Ethics, Correspondence,* all in excellent R. Elwes translation. Basic works on entry to philosophy, pantheism, exchange of ideas with great contemporaries. 402pp. 5⅜ x 8½. 20250-X Pa. $3.75

THE TRAGIC SENSE OF LIFE, Miguel de Unamuno. Acknowledged masterpiece of existential literature, one of most important books of 20th century. Introduction by Madariaga. 367pp. 5⅜ x 8½.
20257-7 Pa. $3.50

THE GUIDE FOR THE PERPLEXED, Moses Maimonides. Great classic of medieval Judaism attempts to reconcile revealed religion (Pentateuch, commentaries) with Aristotelian philosophy. Important historically, still relevant in problems. Unabridged Friedlander translation. Total of 473pp. 5⅜ x 8½. 20351-4 Pa. $5.00

THE I CHING (THE BOOK OF CHANGES), translated by James Legge. Complete translation of basic text plus appendices by Confucius, and Chinese commentary of most penetrating divination manual ever prepared. Indispensable to study of early Oriental civilizations, to modern inquiring reader. 448pp. 5⅜ x 8½. 21062-6 Pa. $4.00

THE EGYPTIAN BOOK OF THE DEAD, E. A. Wallis Budge. Complete reproduction of Ani's papyrus, finest ever found. Full hieroglyphic text, interlinear transliteration, word for word translation, smooth translation. Basic work, for Egyptology, for modern study of psychic matters. Total of 533pp. 6½ x 9¼. (Available in U.S. only) 21866-X Pa. $4.95

THE GODS OF THE EGYPTIANS, E. A. Wallis Budge. Never excelled for richness, fullness: all gods, goddesses, demons, mythical figures of Ancient Egypt; their legends, rites, incarnations, variations, powers, etc. Many hieroglyphic texts cited. Over 225 illustrations, plus 6 color plates. Total of 988pp. 6⅛ x 9¼. (Available in U.S. only)
22055-9, 22056-7 Pa., Two-vol. set $12.00

THE ENGLISH AND SCOTTISH POPULAR BALLADS, Francis J. Child. Monumental, still unsuperseded; all known variants of Child ballads, commentary on origins, literary references, Continental parallels, other features. Added: papers by G. L. Kittredge, W. M. Hart. Total of 2761pp. 6½ x 9¼.
21409-5, 21410-9, 21411-7, 21412-5, 21413-3 Pa., Five-vol. set $37.50

CORAL GARDENS AND THEIR MAGIC, Bronsilaw Malinowski. Classic study of the methods of tilling the soil and of agricultural rites in the Trobriand Islands of Melanesia. Author is one of the most important figures in the field of modern social anthropology. 143 illustrations. Indexes. Total of 911pp. of text. 5⅝ x 8¼. (Available in U.S. only)
23597-1 Pa. $12.95

AN AUTOBIOGRAPHY, Margaret Sanger. Exciting personal account of hard-fought battle for woman's right to birth control, against prejudice, church, law. Foremost feminist document. 504pp. 5⅜ x 8½.
20470-7 Pa. $5.50

MY BONDAGE AND MY FREEDOM, Frederick Douglass. Born as a slave, Douglass became outspoken force in antislavery movement. The best of Douglass's autobiographies. Graphic description of slave life. Introduction by P. Foner. 464pp. 5⅜ x 8½. 22457-0 Pa. $5.00

LIVING MY LIFE, Emma Goldman. Candid, no holds barred account by foremost American anarchist: her own life, anarchist movement, famous contemporaries, ideas and their impact. Struggles and confrontations in America, plus deportation to U.S.S.R. Shocking inside account of persecution of anarchists under Lenin. 13 plates. Total of 944pp. 5⅜ x 8½.
22543-7, 22544-5 Pa., Two-vol. set $9.00

LETTERS AND NOTES ON THE MANNERS, CUSTOMS AND CONDITIONS OF THE NORTH AMERICAN INDIANS, George Catlin. Classic account of life among Plains Indians: ceremonies, hunt, warfare, etc. Dover edition reproduces for first time all original paintings. 312 plates. 572pp. of text. 6⅛ x 9¼. 22118-0, 22119-9 Pa.. Two-vol. set $10.00

THE MAYA AND THEIR NEIGHBORS, edited by Clarence L. Hay, others. Synoptic view of Maya civilization in broadest sense, together with Northern, Southern neighbors. Integrates much background, valuable detail not elsewhere. Prepared by greatest scholars: Kroeber, Morley, Thompson, Spinden, Vaillant, many others. Sometimes called Tozzer Memorial Volume. 60 illustrations, linguistic map. 634pp. 5⅜ x 8½.
23510-6 Pa. $7.50

HANDBOOK OF THE INDIANS OF CALIFORNIA, A. L. Kroeber. Foremost American anthropologist offers complete ethnographic study of each group. Monumental classic. 459 illustrations, maps. 995pp. 5⅜ x 8½.
23368-5 Pa. $10.00

SHAKTI AND SHAKTA, Arthur Avalon. First book to give clear, cohesive analysis of Shakta doctrine, Shakta ritual and Kundalini Shakti (yoga). Important work by one of world's foremost students of Shaktic and Tantric thought. 732pp. 5⅜ x 8½. (Available in U.S. only)
23645-5 Pa. $7.95

AN INTRODUCTION TO THE STUDY OF THE MAYA HIEROGLYPHS, Syvanus Griswold Morley. Classic study by one of the truly great figures in hieroglyph research. Still the best introduction for the student for reading Maya hieroglyphs. New introduction by J. Eric S. Thompson. 117 illustrations. 284pp. 5⅜ x 8½. 23108-9 Pa. $4.00

A STUDY OF MAYA ART, Herbert J. Spinden. Landmark classic interprets Maya symbolism, estimates styles, covers ceramics, architecture, murals, stone carvings as artforms. Still a basic book in area. New introduction by J. Eric Thompson. Over 750 illustrations. 341pp. 8⅜ x 11¼.
21235-1 Pa. $6.95

PRINCIPLES OF ORCHESTRATION, Nikolay Rimsky-Korsakov. Great classical orchestrator provides fundamentals of tonal resonance, progression of parts, voice and orchestra, tutti effects, much else in major document. 330pp. of musical excerpts. 489pp. 6½ x 9¼. 21266-1 Pa. $6.00

TRISTAN UND ISOLDE, Richard Wagner. Full orchestral score with complete instrumentation. Do not confuse with piano reduction. Commentary by Felix Mottl, great Wagnerian conductor and scholar. Study score. 655pp. 8⅛ x 11. 22915-7 Pa. $12.50

REQUIEM IN FULL SCORE, Giuseppe Verdi. Immensely popular with choral groups and music lovers. Republication of edition published by C. F. Peters, Leipzig, n. d. German frontmaker in English translation. Glossary. Text in Latin. Study score. 204pp. 9⅜ x 12¼.
23682-X Pa. $6.00

COMPLETE CHAMBER MUSIC FOR STRINGS, Felix Mendelssohn. All of Mendelssohn's chamber music: Octet, 2 Quintets, 6 Quartets, and Four Pieces for String Quartet. (Nothing with piano is included). Complete works edition (1874-7). Study score. 283 pp. 9⅜ x 12¼.
23679-X Pa. $6.95

POPULAR SONGS OF NINETEENTH-CENTURY AMERICA, edited by Richard Jackson. 64 most important songs: "Old Oaken Bucket," "Arkansas Traveler," "Yellow Rose of Texas," etc. Authentic original sheet music, full introduction and commentaries. 290pp. 9 x 12. 23270-0 Pa. $6.00

COLLECTED PIANO WORKS, Scott Joplin. Edited by Vera Brodsky Lawrence. Practically all of Joplin's piano works—rags, two-steps, marches, waltzes, etc., 51 works in all. Extensive introduction by Rudi Blesh. Total of 345pp. 9 x 12. 23106-2 Pa. $13.50

BASIC PRINCIPLES OF CLASSICAL BALLET, Agrippina Vaganova. Great Russian theoretician, teacher explains methods for teaching classical ballet; incorporates best from French, Italian, Russian schools. 118 illustrations. 175pp. 5⅜ x 8½. 22036-2 Pa. $2.00

CHINESE CHARACTERS, L. Wieger. Rich analysis of 2300 characters according to traditional systems into primitives. Historical-semantic analysis to phonetics (Classical Mandarin) and radicals. 820pp. 6⅛ x 9¼.
21321-8 Pa. $8.95

EGYPTIAN LANGUAGE: EASY LESSONS IN EGYPTIAN HIEROGLYPHICS, E. A. Wallis Budge. Foremost Egyptologist offers Egyptian grammar, explanation of hieroglyphics, many reading texts, dictionary of symbols. 246pp. 5 x 7½. (Available in U.S. only)
21394-3 Clothbd. $7.50

AN ETYMOLOGICAL DICTIONARY OF MODERN ENGLISH, Ernest Weekley. Richest, fullest work, by foremost British lexicographer. Detailed word histories. Inexhaustible. Do not confuse this with *Concise Etymological Dictionary*, which is abridged. Total of 856pp. 6½ x 9¼.
21873-2, 21874-0 Pa., Two-vol. set $10.00

TONE POEMS, SERIES II: TILL EULENSPIEGELS LUSTIGE STREICHE, ALSO SPRACH ZARATHUSTRA, AND EIN HELDENLEBEN, Richard Strauss. Three important orchestral works, including very popular *Till Eulenspiegel's Marry Pranks,* reproduced in full score from original editions. Study score. 315pp. 9⅜ x 12¼. (Available in U.S. only)
23755-9 Pa. $7.50

TONE POEMS, SERIES I: DON JUAN, TOD UND VERKLARUNG AND DON QUIXOTE, Richard Strauss. Three of the most often performed and recorded works in entire orchestral repertoire, reproduced in full score from original editions. Study score. 286pp. 9⅜ x 12¼. (Available in U.S. only)
23754-0 Pa. $7.50

11 LATE STRING QUARTETS, Franz Joseph Haydn. The form which Haydn defined and "brought to perfection." *(Grove's).* 11 string quartets in complete score, his last and his best. The first in a projected series of the complete Haydn string quartets. Reliable modern Eulenberg edition, otherwise difficult to obtain. 320pp. 8⅜ x 11¼. (Available in U.S. only)
23753-2 Pa. $6.95

FOURTH, FIFTH AND SIXTH SYMPHONIES IN FULL SCORE, Peter Ilyitch Tchaikovsky. Complete orchestral scores of Symphony No. 4 in F Minor, Op. 36; Symphony No. 5 in E Minor, Op. 64; Symphony No. 6 in B Minor, "Pathetique," Op. 74. Bretikopf & Hartel eds. Study score. 480pp. 9⅜ x 12¼.
23861-X Pa. $10.95

THE MARRIAGE OF FIGARO: COMPLETE SCORE, Wolfgang A. Mozart. Finest comic opera ever written. Full score, not to be confused with piano renderings. Peters edition. Study score. 448pp. 9⅜ x 12¼. (Available in U.S. only)
23751-6 Pa. $11.95

"IMAGE" ON THE ART AND EVOLUTION OF THE FILM, edited by Marshall Deutelbaum. Pioneering book brings together for first time 38 groundbreaking articles on early silent films from *Image* and 263 illustrations newly shot from rare prints in the collection of the International Museum of Photography. A landmark work. Index. 256pp. 8¼ x 11.
23777-X Pa. $8.95

AROUND-THE-WORLD COOKY BOOK, Lois Lintner Sumption and Marguerite Lintner Ashbrook. 373 cooky and frosting recipes from 28 countries (America, Austria, China, Russia, Italy, etc.) include Viennese kisses, rice wafers, London strips, lady fingers, hony, sugar spice, maple cookies, etc. Clear instructions. All tested. 38 drawings. 182pp. 5⅜ x 8.
23802-4 Pa. $2.50

THE ART NOUVEAU STYLE, edited by Roberta Waddell. 579 rare photographs, not available elsewhere, of works in jewelry, metalwork, glass, ceramics, textiles, architecture and furniture by 175 artists—Mucha, Seguy, Lalique, Tiffany, Gaudin, Hohlwein, Saarinen, and many others. 288pp. 8⅜ x 11¼.
23515-7 Pa. $6.95

THE EARLY WORK OF AUBREY BEARDSLEY, Aubrey Beardsley. 157 plates, 2 in color: *Manon Lescaut, Madame Bovary, Morte Darthur, Salome,* other. Introduction by H. Marillier. 182pp. 8⅛ x 11. 21816-3 Pa. $4.50

THE LATER WORK OF AUBREY BEARDSLEY, Aubrey Beardsley. Exotic masterpieces of full maturity: *Venus and Tannhauser, Lysistrata, Rape of the Lock, Volpone,* Savoy material, etc. 174 plates, 2 in color. 186pp. 8⅛ x 11. 21817-1 Pa. $4.50

THOMAS NAST'S CHRISTMAS DRAWINGS, Thomas Nast. Almost all Christmas drawings by creator of image of Santa Claus as we know it, and one of America's foremost illustrators and political cartoonists. 66 illustrations. 3 illustrations in color on covers. 96pp. 8⅜ x 11¼. 23660-9 Pa. $3.50

THE DORÉ ILLUSTRATIONS FOR DANTE'S DIVINE COMEDY, Gustave Doré. All 135 plates from Inferno, Purgatory, Paradise; fantastic tortures, infernal landscapes, celestial wonders. Each plate with appropriate (translated) verses. 141pp. 9 x 12. 23231-X Pa. $4.50

DORÉ'S ILLUSTRATIONS FOR RABELAIS, Gustave Doré. 252 striking illustrations of *Gargantua and Pantagruel* books by foremost 19th-century illustrator. Including 60 plates, 192 delightful smaller illustrations. 153pp. 9 x 12. 23656-0 Pa. $5.00

LONDON: A PILGRIMAGE, Gustave Doré, Blanchard Jerrold. Squalor, riches, misery, beauty of mid-Victorian metropolis; 55 wonderful plates, 125 other illustrations, full social, cultural text by Jerrold. 191pp. of text. 9⅜ x 12¼. 22306-X Pa. $6.00

THE RIME OF THE ANCIENT MARINER, Gustave Doré, S. T. Coleridge. Doré's finest work, 34 plates capture moods, subtleties of poem. Full text. Introduction by Millicent Rose. 77pp. 9¼ x 12. 22305-1 Pa. $3.00

THE DORÉ BIBLE ILLUSTRATIONS, Gustave Doré. All wonderful, detailed plates: Adam and Eve, Flood, Babylon, Life of Jesus, etc. Brief King James text with each plate. Introduction by Millicent Rose. 241 plates. 241pp. 9 x 12. 23004-X Pa. $5.00

THE COMPLETE ENGRAVINGS, ETCHINGS AND DRYPOINTS OF ALBRECHT DURER. "Knight, Death and Devil"; "Melencolia," and more—all Dürer's known works in all three media, including 6 works formerly attributed to him. 120 plates. 235pp. 8⅜ x 11¼. 22851-7 Pa. $6.50

MAXIMILIAN'S TRIUMPHAL ARCH, Albrecht Dürer and others. Incredible monument of woodcut art: 8 foot high elaborate arch—heraldic figures, humans, battle scenes, fantastic elements—that you can assemble yourself. Printed on one side, layout for assembly. 143pp. 11 x 16. 21451-6 Pa. $5.00

DRAWINGS OF WILLIAM BLAKE, William Blake. 92 plates from Book of Job, *Divine Comedy, Paradise Lost,* visionary heads, mythological figures, Laocoon, etc. Selection, introduction, commentary by Sir Geoffrey Keynes. 178pp. 8⅛ x 11. 22303-5 Pa. $4.00

ENGRAVINGS OF HOGARTH, William Hogarth. 101 of Hogarth's greatest works: *Rake's Progress, Harlot's Progress, Illustrations for Hudibras, Before and After, Beer Street and Gin Lane,* many more. Full commentary. 256pp. 11 x 13¾. 22479-1 Pa. $7.95

DAUMIER: 120 GREAT LITHOGRAPHS, Honore Daumier. Wide-ranging collection of lithographs by the greatest caricaturist of the 19th century. Concentrates on eternally popular series on lawyers, on married life, on liberated women, etc. Selection, introduction, and notes on plates by Charles F. Ramus. Total of 158pp. 9⅜ x 12¼. 23512-2 Pa. $5.50

DRAWINGS OF MUCHA, Alphonse Maria Mucha. Work reveals draftsman of highest caliber: studies for famous posters and paintings, renderings for book illustrations and ads, etc. 70 works, 9 in color; including 6 items not drawings. Introduction. List of illustrations. 72pp. 9⅜ x 12¼. (Available in U.S. only) 23672-2 Pa. $4.00

GIOVANNI BATTISTA PIRANESI: DRAWINGS IN THE PIERPONT MORGAN LIBRARY, Giovanni Battista Piranesi. For first time ever all of Morgan Library's collection, world's largest. 167 illustrations of rare Piranesi drawings—archeological, architectural, decorative and visionary. Essay, detailed list of drawings, chronology, captions. Edited by Felice Stampfle. 144pp. 9⅜ x 12¼. 23714-1 Pa. $7.50

NEW YORK ETCHINGS (1905-1949), John Sloan. All of important American artist's N.Y. life etchings. 67 works include some of his best art; also lively historical record—Greenwich Village, tenement scenes. Edited by Sloan's widow. Introduction and captions. 79pp. 8⅜ x 11¼. 23651-X Pa. $4.00

CHINESE PAINTING AND CALLIGRAPHY: A PICTORIAL SURVEY, Wan-go Weng. 69 fine examples from John M. Crawford's matchless private collection: landscapes, birds, flowers, human figures, etc., plus calligraphy. Every basic form included: hanging scrolls, handscrolls, album leaves, fans, etc. 109 illustrations. Introduction. Captions. 192pp. 8⅞ x 11¾. 23707-9 Pa. $7.95

DRAWINGS OF REMBRANDT, edited by Seymour Slive. Updated Lippmann, Hofstede de Groot edition, with definitive scholarly apparatus. All portraits, biblical sketches, landscapes, nudes, Oriental figures, classical studies, together with selection of work by followers. 550 illustrations. Total of 630pp. 9⅛ x 12¼. 21485-0, 21486-9 Pa., Two-vol. set $14.00

THE DISASTERS OF WAR, Francisco Goya. 83 etchings record horrors of Napoleonic wars in Spain and war in general. Reprint of 1st edition, plus 3 additional plates. Introduction by Philip Hofer. 97pp. 9⅜ x 8¼. 21872-4 Pa. $3.75

THE COMPLETE WOODCUTS OF ALBRECHT DURER, edited by Dr. W. Kurth. 346 in all: "Old Testament," "St. Jerome," "Passion," "Life of Virgin," Apocalypse," many others. Introduction by Campbell Dodgson. 285pp. 8½ x 12¼. 21097-9 Pa. $6.95

DRAWINGS OF ALBRECHT DURER, edited by Heinrich Wolfflin. 81 plates show development from youth to full style. Many favorites; many new. Introduction by Alfred Werner. 96pp. 8⅛ x 11. 22352-3 Pa. $4.00

THE HUMAN FIGURE, Albrecht Dürer. Experiments in various techniques—stereometric, progressive proportional, and others. Also life studies that rank among finest ever done. Complete reprinting of *Dresden Sketchbook*. 170 plates. 355pp. 8⅜ x 11¼. 21042-1 Pa. $6.95

OF THE JUST SHAPING OF LETTERS, Albrecht Dürer. Renaissance artist explains design of Roman majuscules by geometry, also Gothic lower and capitals. Grolier Club edition. 43pp. 7⅞ x 10¾ 21306-4 Pa. $2.50

TEN BOOKS ON ARCHITECTURE, Vitruvius. The most important book ever written on architecture. Early Roman aesthetics, technology, classical orders, site selection, all other aspects. Stands behind everything since. Morgan translation. 331pp. 5⅜ x 8½. 20645-9 Pa. $3.75

THE FOUR BOOKS OF ARCHITECTURE, Andrea Palladio. 16th-century classic responsible for Palladian movement and style. Covers classical architectural remains, Renaissance revivals, classical orders, etc. 1738 Ware English edition. Introduction by A. Placzek. 216 plates. 110pp. of text. 9½ x 12¾. 21308-0 Pa. $7.50

HORIZONS, Norman Bel Geddes. Great industrialist stage designer, "father of streamlining," on application of aesthetics to transportation, amusement, architecture, etc. 1932 prophetic account; function, theory, specific projects. 222 illustrations. 312pp. 7⅞ x 10¾. 23514-9 Pa. $6.95

FRANK LLOYD WRIGHT'S FALLINGWATER, Donald Hoffmann. Full, illustrated story of conception and building of Wright's masterwork at Bear Run, Pa. 100 photographs of site, construction, and details of completed structure. 112pp. 9¼ x 10. 23671-4 Pa. $5.00

THE ELEMENTS OF DRAWING, John Ruskin. Timeless classic by great Viltorian; starts with basic ideas, works through more difficult. Many practical exercises. 48 illustrations. Introduction by Lawrence Campbell. 228pp. 5⅜ x 8½. 22730-8 Pa. $2.75

GIST OF ART, John Sloan. Greatest modern American teacher, Art Students League, offers innumerable hints, instructions, guided comments to help you in painting. Not a formal course. 46 illustrations. Introduction by Helen Sloan. 200pp. 5⅜ x 8½. 23435-5 Pa. $3.50

A MAYA GRAMMAR, Alfred M. Tozzer. Practical, useful English-language grammar by the Harvard anthropologist who was one of the three greatest American scholars in the area of Maya culture. Phonetics, grammatical processes, syntax, more. 301pp. 5⅜ x 8½. 23465-7 Pa. $4.00

THE JOURNAL OF HENRY D. THOREAU, edited by Bradford Torrey, F. H. Allen. Complete reprinting of 14 volumes, 1837-61, over two million words; the sourcebooks for *Walden*, etc. Definitive. All original sketches, plus 75 photographs. Introduction by Walter Harding. Total of 1804pp. 8½ x 12¼. 20312-3, 20313-1 Clothbd., Two-vol. set $50.00

CLASSIC GHOST STORIES, Charles Dickens and others. 18 wonderful stories you've wanted to reread: "The Monkey's Paw," "The House and the Brain," "The Upper Berth," "The Signalman," "Dracula's Guest," "The Tapestried Chamber," etc. Dickens, Scott, Mary Shelley, Stoker, etc. 330pp. 5⅜ x 8½. 20735-8 Pa. $3.50

SEVEN SCIENCE FICTION NOVELS, H. G. Wells. Full novels. *First Men in the Moon, Island of Dr. Moreau, War of the Worlds, Food of the Gods, Invisible Man, Time Machine, In the Days of the Comet.* A basic science-fiction library. 1015pp. 5⅜ x 8½. (Available in U.S. only) 20264-X Clothbd. $8.95

ARMADALE, Wilkie Collins. Third great mystery novel by the author of *The Woman in White* and *The Moonstone.* Ingeniously plotted narrative shows an exceptional command of character, incident and mood. Original magazine version with 40 illustrations. 597pp. 5⅜ x 8½. 23429-0 Pa. $5.00

MASTERS OF MYSTERY, H. Douglas Thomson. The first book in English (1931) devoted to history and aesthetics of detective story. Poe, Doyle, LeFanu, Dickens, many others, up to 1930. New introduction and notes by E. F. Bleiler. 288pp. 5⅜ x 8½. (Available in U.S. only) 23606-4 Pa. $4.00

FLATLAND, E. A. Abbott. Science-fiction classic explores life of 2-D being in 3-D world. Read also as introduction to thought about hyperspace. Introduction by Banesh Hoffmann. 16 illustrations. 103pp. 5⅜ x 8½. 20001-9 Pa. $1.50

THREE SUPERNATURAL NOVELS OF THE VICTORIAN PERIOD, edited, with an introduction, by E. F. Bleiler. Reprinted complete and unabridged, three great classics of the supernatural: *The Haunted Hotel* by Wilkie Collins, *The Haunted House at Latchford* by Mrs. J. H. Riddell, and *The Lost Stradivarious* by J. Meade Falkner. 325pp. 5⅜ x 8½. 22571-2 Pa. $4.00

AYESHA: THE RETURN OF "SHE," H. Rider Haggard. Virtuoso sequel featuring the great mythic creation, Ayesha, in an adventure that is fully as good as the first book, *She*. Original magazine version, with 47 original illustrations by Maurice Greiffenhagen. 189pp. 6½ x 9¼. 23649-8 Pa. $3.00